Previously published Worldwide Suspense titles by
SLOANE STEELE

IT TAKES A THIEF
BETWEEN TWO THIEVES

TO CATCH A THIEF

SLOANE STEELE

W🌐RLDWIDE™

TORONTO • NEW YORK • LONDON
AMSTERDAM • PARIS • SYDNEY • HAMBURG
STOCKHOLM • ATHENS • TOKYO • MILAN
MADRID • WARSAW • BUDAPEST • AUCKLAND

W⦿RLDWIDE™

Recycling programs
for this product may
not exist in your area.

ISBN-13: 978-1-335-52308-2

To Catch a Thief

First published in 2021 by Carina Press,
an imprint of Harlequin Enterprises ULC.
This edition published in 2022 with revised text.

Copyright © 2021 by Shannyn Schroeder
Copyright © 2022 by Shannyn Schroeder, revised text edition

Harlequin Enterprises ULC
22 Adelaide St. West, 41st Floor
Toronto, Ontario M5H 4E3, Canada
www.ReaderService.com

Printed in U.S.A.

TO CATCH A THIEF

To everyone who's willing to do
what it takes to make things right

ONE

LOGAN FORD WALKED around the cubicles in the FBI field office and knocked on his boss's door. SSA Taggert had sent him undercover, and while Logan had jumped at the chance, he felt like he was spinning in circles, and he hated nothing more than wasting his time. There was something about this case—cases— that poked and prodded at him. Like a slightly out-of-focus photograph. Or a jigsaw puzzle missing a few key pieces. And he was the kind of guy that couldn't let a puzzle go unsolved.

"What's going on?" Taggert asked.

Logan entered and sat in one of the old chairs, even though Taggert hadn't invited him to. He did it mostly because he liked to irritate Taggert, which probably wasn't the wisest move. This was the man who could approve his permanent transfer back to Chicago. "This op is stuck in neutral."

Taggert couldn't get warrants for anything like financials on these guys. All Logan could do was talk to them and he was an outsider.

"Look, there are a lot of eyes on this," Taggert said. "We've had two separate people pop up with forgeries of paintings that are worth a whole hell of a lot of money."

Logan held up a hand. "I'm not saying that there isn't something there. These people are shady. But I don't have an in. They're telling Logan Freemont, insurance agent, that they bought authentic pieces."

"Atlas Insurance agrees that when the items were purchased, they were authenticated."

"That's the first piece of questionable stuff. Both pieces were insured by Atlas."

"How many companies insure artwork like this?" Taggert slid his chair back and laced his fingers behind his head.

"More than Atlas. But Max Ingram and Randall Scott are friends. They probably share information along the lines of 'I gotta guy for that.' It's not enough in and of itself to be suspicious."

"You said the Atlas connection was the first piece. What else do you have?"

Logan propped an ankle across his knee. He had nothing substantial, but his gut told him these guys were pulling something. He just couldn't figure out what. "Both artifacts were purchased within two weeks of each other about five years ago, and now they're both attempting to sell at the same time."

"Ingram's was stolen." Taggert squinted. "I mean it was stolen from him. He wasn't selling it."

"But he planned to. Same auction house had an appointment for next week."

"You think they're buying authentic, sitting on them, and then trying to sell forgeries?"

Logan took a breath and tried to explain his hunch. "I saw Scott's face when I told him I agreed with the first assessment that the Mathis was a forgery. He looked so sure that the first appraiser was wrong. I'm not saying he's innocent, but…it feels like there's something else at play. I think someone's out to get these guys."

"What makes you think that's what's happening?"

"I trust my gut."

"It's a bit of a stretch with no evidence."

Knowing who forged the paintings would be evidence. That would be enough to connect the two cases. "Why aren't we bringing in the art fraud division on this? They're the experts."

"Because right now we don't know what the crime is."

"We've seen the forgeries. We know there's some kind of fraud happening."

"Counterfeit art is all over. They're particular about where they spend their resources. But we have sent them the forgeries to inspect."

"I only have a minor in art history." And he'd taken those classes because he figured it'd be a good place to pick up girls. "I don't know how long I can pull this off. At some point, someone with more knowledge is going to pick up on my lack of expertise."

Mia Benson came to mind as one such person. As a museum curator, she knew art. Her family connections put her in the same social circles as these men. He'd been trying to get her alone to pick her brain. He had little doubt that she might be able to shed some light on these men and their purchasing habits. She might be able to help him flesh out his hunch.

But she'd shut him down cold. He wasn't used to a woman not giving him a chance at all. He'd been rejected before, but never summarily dismissed, and that's what Mia had made it feel like. He couldn't help but take it personally since she knew nothing about him other than the insurance cover story. Maybe she didn't like insurance agents. "I'm going to do some background on Mia Benson. I think she could be useful."

Taggert narrowed his eyes. "Do I know that name?"

"Probably. Her father was half of the Benson and Towers pyramid scheme. They're in the wind."

Taggert scooted forward with more force than necessary and leaned his forearms on the desk. "What does she have to do with this?"

Logan shook his head. "Nothing directly as far as I can see. But she knows the men, and she's a curator at the Art Institute. When the appraiser told Scott he had a forgery, he asked Mia to be a second opinion."

"Did she agree that it was a forgery?"

"Yeah."

"Then she's not her father. He would've lied and taken a cut of the profit when Scott sold." He offered a dry chuckle. "All jokes aside, though, if she's around this situation, even as a minor player, you need to keep an eye on her. You should touch base with the agents on her father's case. They might have some insight."

Logan agreed and added that to his ever-growing to-do list. He didn't get a bad vibe from Mia. Regardless of who her father was, Logan didn't think she had anything to do with this.

"We can give it a little time," Taggert continued. "If nothing else pops, we'll set it aside. But right now, people much higher on the ladder are looking at the forgeries. Rich, powerful men are loud."

Logan stood. "You don't have to tell me. I'll find something, though. I just need the right thread to pull." Because if he didn't, he'd probably get shuffled to another city. He'd been trying to transfer back to Chicago for years. He'd missed home, and solving this case would give him the collateral to stay.

"Poke around some more. Atlas is giving us access to whatever we need. They don't want to insure worthless crap, so if it turns out to be an in-house issue, they'll deal with it."

Logan nodded and left the office. Having access to Atlas's files might show him which string to unravel. In the meantime, next on his agenda was a visit to a local field agent who'd brought in the original Devereaux painting after it had been stolen from Ingram. Hopefully, Agent Eden Stokes might be able to shed some light on the forgeries.

As much as he hated wasting his time, he hated letting criminals get away with fraud even more. Someone had a plan to make money off the art. If it wasn't the current owners, it was a thief who planted the forgeries. Either way, he'd bring them down.

WHEN MIA ENTERED THE River North apartment she and her team used as a base of operations, she found Nikki in her usual place, lying halfway upside down on the couch, shoveling potato chips in her mouth. After the last job, she'd decided to move out to live with Wade, her former partner in crime.

"What are you doing here?" Nikki asked, swinging her legs around to sit upright.

"We have a job to plan." She looked over to the desk. "No Audrey?"

"She ran out to get some more energy drinks. She and your cousin have been staying up late."

Mia closed her eyes and shook her head. She didn't

need to think about Jared and their hacker. "Do we have anything yet?"

Nikki pointed at the TV. "I'm studying the auction house. Once the pieces are delivered, they must go into storage, right? They don't unpack and rush to authenticate, do they?"

"They will absolutely have them authenticated, but I have no idea what the process is at this particular auction house. I can find out."

"Good. If they have them in storage, it'll be like the Devereaux."

"No. Not like the Devereaux. The auction house will certainly have better security. Especially since there will be a Picasso for sale. I wouldn't be surprised to find they had around-the-clock monitored security." She pulled out her phone and made notes about who to contact to get information about the auction. She briefly considered adding Logan Freemont to that list. As an insurance agent for Atlas, he would probably know the ins and outs of McNamara's. But then she brushed the thought away. She didn't need to encourage the man. Or tip her hand by bringing his attention to these particular pieces.

"As long as I don't have to run another con. That takes too much out of me. Give me a good old-fashioned break-in any day."

"If you can't break in, what other options do we have?" Mia wondered. Even after the heists they'd completed, this was still far from her area of expertise.

Nikki inhaled deeply and blew out the breath, puffing her cheeks. "Steal them before they get picked up, or hit the delivery truck. But that one is assuming they both get picked up by the same truck on the same day.

Lot of assumptions. Plus, hitting the truck would mean they would know they were stolen. The counterfeit would be pointless."

The front door opened and Audrey came bopping in wearing baggy clothes that did nothing for her figure. "Hey, they were all out of cupcakes, but—" She froze when she saw Mia. "What are you doing here?"

"I came to see where we are on the next plan."

"Oh." Audrey handed Nikki a small box of donuts. Her light brown hair was falling out of her loose ponytail, as usual, and she tucked it behind her ears.

"Oh, what?"

Audrey shrugged. "I don't know. It's just that you were mostly hands-off on the last job. I figured we were just gonna do our thing." She waved a hand between herself and Nikki.

"Being hands-off didn't serve me too well. If you recall, I was roped into playing a paranoid freak."

"Yeah, you were pretty good there." Audrey chuckled, popped open an energy drink, and sat behind the desk. She immediately began typing at the computer without telling anyone what she was doing.

"Nikki was running down options other than breaking into the auction house," Mia explained.

Audrey nodded. "The obvious move would be to make the switch at their homes before they ship. We're pretty good at that."

"Unless we have to alter the frames like we did for Scott's house," Nikki said. "They would probably take note of them being cut—especially after what happened to their buddy."

Mia looked at the TV. "Can you pull up the paintings? I don't think we'll need to do any alterations."

Audrey tapped away and a moment later they were staring at the Moreau that belonged to Keaton Bishop. It was a nightmarish painting created in the early twentieth century. Moreau had been known for sampling styles of other artists, and this one was part of his surrealism period. Mia had always preferred a Degas to a Dali, but over the past few years, the twisted reality of surrealism had begun to pique her interest.

"The canvas itself is small. It's only a foot and a half square," she said as she focused on the painting, a garish image of a man groping a woman who was obviously uninterested.

"I'd kick some dude in the family jewels if he grabbed me like that," Audrey said.

Nikki huffed. "I'd cut him."

Mia wasn't sure what she would do. She'd led a fairly sheltered life, and while in her teens plenty of boys had gotten handsy, it hadn't been this level of harassment, but she had heard of girls who ran into problems. In their circles, however, things were handled quietly and discreetly. Nothing about Nikki or Audrey was quiet or discreet. Part of her wanted more of that. "Anyway…the Spenser might pose a slightly bigger problem, in that it is a slightly bigger painting."

Audrey switched the image on the screen. This one favored cubism, and Mia definitely found it more soothing than the Moreau. The painting showed another couple, holding hands but each looking in a different direction, away from each other. It was how she often pictured her parents.

"This painting is two by three. Not unwieldy, but not quite compact. The good thing is that for both of these, there is no exterior frame. The canvas, the stretcher bars, and the hanger. That's it."

"Does London already have them done?"

Mia nodded. She'd checked in with their forger earlier in the day to verify.

"When's the auction?" Audrey asked.

"Not for about three weeks. They're still accepting new pieces for the auction."

Nikki swung an arm over the back of the couch. "This seems riskier than you usually like. What's up with that?"

"Since when do you care about risk?" Mia retorted. Then she waved a hand. "It's what makes the most sense. Both of these paintings are going to auction. When I devised this plan, I hadn't considered how fast any of our marks would move."

Plus, her father had called. He'd reached out because he was getting desperate. Her plan was working. One way or another, she was going to get justice for her father's victims. First, she was paying restitution through sales of this artwork. Then, she was going to make him come out into the open so he would have to face the consequences of his actions.

"Mia?" Audrey's voice startled her.

"Yes?"

"We lost you for a minute there. Anything else we need to know?"

"No." She put her phone back in her purse. "Do you have the other list ready? The one with the recipients?"

Audrey smiled and clapped her hands. "You know I do." She pointed to the TV again, where images of McNamara's were replaced with family photos. "This is the Bhatt family. They lost their family-owned convenience store. This week they got the store back, including the deed to the building."

"What is this?" Nikki asked.

"I asked Audrey to put together the information about the families we're helping. You can see the good we're doing." Mia needed the reminders because so much of what they were doing made her feel not much better than her father.

"I wouldn't care if you were just lining everyone's pockets. This is fun."

Mia shot a look at the thief. "If I'm not mistaken, Wade cares."

Nikki's eyes narrowed at the reminder that Wade wanted her to go straight.

Audrey clicked through to another picture. "This is the Jackson family who will be able to afford to give their daughter the wedding of her dreams. Sorry no wedding photos as it won't happen for another six months. And this is Marianne Jenkins, who lost everything because of your father. Literally everything. She's sixty years old and fell apart when she found she had nothing. She was living on the streets."

Mia spun to look at Audrey. "How did you find her?"

"I have my ways. She is now set up in a beautiful senior living community." Audrey became a little misty-eyed looking at the happy old woman. "The money from the Devereaux is going to reach so many more people."

"Good. Because while getting to my father is my ultimate goal, doing this is the more important piece." She picked up her purse. "I'll do some checking and see what I can find out about the upcoming auction. There's a charity function tomorrow night and most of our favorite players will be in attendance, so we should be able to get some information."

Audrey flopped back in her chair and rolled her eyes. "God. Not another party. Don't you people have anything better to do?"

Mia couldn't help but smile. Since Audrey and Jared made their relationship public, Audrey had attended exactly two functions as his date, and at one of them she'd been there to help Nikki steal a sculpture. "You don't need to attend this one. I think I can handle information gathering."

Audrey executed a fist pump.

"I'll stop by tomorrow to pick up surveillance equipment, so the two of you can see and hear what I do. It'll save a step for debriefing." Mia picked up her purse and left to go to the museum, where she was now in charge of building an amazing new exhibit.

When she had pitched the idea of a special exhibit on crime and punishment in art, she hadn't expected it to be so well-received. She'd hoped to be able to gather a small collection, something with meaning to feed her restlessness while plotting against her father.

Instead, everyone at the Art Institute was on board for her vision and it had grown into a major undertaking. And as excited as she was to head up such a project, her side hustle of stealing from her father and his cronies was taking its toll.

But she knew they were on the right track. They just needed to forge ahead and keep the pressure up. Unfortunately, added pressure on her father also meant more possible attention on their operation. She just hoped they could complete all the thefts before things blew up.

TWO

THE FOLLOWING EVENING, Mia fidgeted again with the necklace Audrey had given her. It was a little too much for her liking, but seeing as it had a camera in it, she was stuck wearing it.

"Stop touching the damn thing," Audrey muttered into the comm in Mia's ear.

Even though she wanted to respond, Mia held her tongue so her driver wouldn't think she was in the back seat talking to herself. When the car stopped in front of the gallery, Mia thanked the driver and got out. Cars in front of hers and behind had couples stepping out in their black tie attire. In moments like these, Mia despised not having a date. It was painfully obvious to everyone how alone she was.

For the most part she wasn't lonely. She rather enjoyed her own company. While her cousin Jared often attended as her plus-one, she did miss the physical aspects of having a boyfriend. Someone to hold her hand as she stepped from a car. Someone to share snarky insights with during a boring function. Someone to dance with when the alcohol made her feel loose and limber.

Mia walked through the doors of the Montague Gallery. She was fashionably late to the function. Doing so enabled her to miss the press and publicity, and allowed her to blend in with no notice. So very differently than her expectations on arrival ten years ago. Even six years

ago. She'd enjoyed the spotlight of being rich and successful. Now she preferred to keep her head down and
her success to herself.

After scanning the area, she picked up a flute of
champagne from the first waiter she saw.

In her ear, Nikki said, "Starting so soon, Mia? Tsk-tsk."

Sipping the golden liquid, Mia nodded to a few
guests, most of the usual players she saw at these functions. High-top tables were artfully scattered about the
room. Some were already occupied by accommodating
husbands who had been dragged to the event by their
wives. A bar was in one corner and a string quartet was
set up in the opposite corner with a small dance floor
in front of the musicians. No one was dancing yet, but
they would start once the warmth of alcohol lured them
to the dance floor.

Mia inhaled deeply through her nose. With a smile
locked on her face, she spoke with a tight jaw. "That's
enough, Nikki."

Claire Winthrop chose that moment to walk by. "Excuse me?" she asked. "Mia! Were you speaking to me?"

"No. I'm sorry. It was nothing." Mia put her hand
on the woman's arm. "Claire, it's so good to see you."

"It's been far too long. I've been in Greece enjoying
some rest and relaxation. What have you been up to?"

"Work has been keeping me busy."

"You work at a place like this, right? Selling pictures and whatnot?"

"Actually, I'm a curator at the Art Institute."

Cue the false laugh. "I'm sorry. I've never really
paid attention to art. It's all just pretty things to me."
Claire looked over Mia's head and waved. Turning her
attention back to Mia, she said, "We really must get
together soon."

Mia nodded and drank her champagne.

"Prime example of why I hate these events," Audrey said.

Mia smiled in response, even though Audrey couldn't see. In a few short months, her revenge plot and meeting Nikki and Audrey had altered her outlook on much of her life. She used to feel comfortable—even at home— at a party like this. Ever since her father fled the country, she'd questioned everything about her life.

She scoped out the space, making sure to shift her entire body as she did, so that Nikki and Audrey would have full view of the room. The gallery had cleared its first floor for the fundraiser. The second floor held the art collection being sold to raise money for the children's charity of the week. Caleb Small, owner of the Spenser painting they were after, stood at a high-top table near the dance floor, cradling a glass of brandy, as Randall Scott, their first mark, droned on, entertaining himself.

Mia made her way over to the table to see what information Caleb would give up. Between the next two men on their list to steal from, Caleb Small and Keaton Bishop, she'd take a conversation with Caleb any day. He was like a stodgy old uncle who would give you a dollar from his pocket to make you smile before shooing you off. Keaton, on the other hand, always made her feel slightly uncomfortable. Like he was undressing her with his eyes. He also constantly tried to set her up with his son. It was tiresome because Chad was a creep. And a boring one at that.

"Caleb, Randall, how are you doing?"

"Mia, it's good to see you. You're in your element here, aren't you?" Randall Scott said.

She smiled and nodded. "I'm really sorry, again, that

I couldn't be more help with your Mathis painting. Any word on what happened?"

The corners of Scott's mouth drew down. "Unfortunately, no." He lowered his voice and brought his face closer. "And the insurance company is backpedaling. As if I didn't have it appraised by their people."

"I can't believe it." She feigned her surprise again, as she hid her enjoyment of rubbing salt in his wounded reputation. "You bought the real painting. What could have happened to it?"

Randall shook his head. "It must've been switched at some point. Unfortunately, we've had the painting for so long that we can't go back and look at security footage. Everyone involved in the sale agreed that we had an authentic Mathis. It makes no sense."

"That's quite the mystery." She turned and looked at Caleb. "Speaking of paintings, did I hear correctly that you're planning to sell the Spenser you have in your collection?"

"You heard right."

"Why are you selling? It's a beautiful painting."

"I think the market is right. The auction house has hinted there might be a Picasso on the auction block at the same time. How could I turn down a live auction with other masterpieces?"

"I've been swamped at work, but I heard there was a Picasso. Do you happen to know which one?"

"I didn't think to ask," Caleb said. "It's Picasso. Does it matter which one? Whoever shows up to the auction hoping to get a Picasso might settle for a Spenser when they realize only one person wins the auction."

"Pump him for info," Nikki said. As if Mia was unaware of her goal tonight.

"That's quite the boon for you and everyone else

planning to sell. How do you like working with Mc-Namara's?"

"I like how they run things over there. They're really hands-on."

"Have you sold with them before?"

"Jennifer had a hideous sculpture given to her by a cousin or someone. We couldn't get rid of it fast enough."

She sipped her champagne and considered how to get more information. Caleb might not even know much, but it was worth a try. So she put on her wide-eyed look asking her "uncle" for a favor without really asking. "I really wish my studies covered more about auctions. It seems like it's one of those things that doesn't sink in until you get on-the-job training. I know so little about how they work."

"Laying it on a little thick there, don't you think?" Nikki sneered.

"Shoot me an email and I'll get you in touch with my girl Gwen over at McNamara's. I'm sure she'll be happy to talk to you about it. Thinking about switching careers?"

She shook her head. "Oh, not at all. I love the museum. But if I want to continue taking on bigger roles to advance my career, understanding the process of auctions, and of course, networking with local auction houses can only help."

He winked at her. "Always good to have the inside track."

Her thought exactly. She drained her glass. "Thanks for the chat, gentleman, but since my glass is empty, it's time for me to move on and find another. Enjoy your evening."

They said their farewells and told her she should go find a young man to dance with. Meanwhile, Nikki and

Audrey both chatted in her ear, which was enough to give anyone a headache. While they argued the merits of Mia contacting the auction house to get more information, Mia skirted the dance floor and wandered to the back of the gallery to go upstairs where actual art could be viewed.

Before she even got to the stairs, a beefy hand landed on her arm.

"Mia Benson!"

Oh, Lord. Chad Bishop was here. Even if he did have information about the Moreau painting his father was selling, Mia had no desire to talk to the man. She heard her father's voice in her head: *Appearances mean everything, Mia.* So she pasted on a smile and turned. "Chad. It's been a while."

"It's good to see you out and about." He leaned in to kiss her cheek.

It took everything she had not to recoil.

"Let's get you a drink."

Based on the smell emanating from him, he'd already had plenty.

"Actually, I was just headed upstairs to look at the artwork."

He was already waving a waiter over with a tray full of champagne. "Come on. You can stay for one drink. The crap up there is no better than the stuff my parents are always buying." He handed her a glass of champagne.

"*Another* glass, Mia?" Nikki filled her voice with scandal.

Chad leaned against the railing at the bottom of the stairs. "I've been meaning to reach out. I've missed seeing you at these things."

"I've been to plenty of functions. I see your parents regularly."

"You know what I mean." He stroked a finger down her arm. "We should go out sometime."

"Thanks, but I'm not interested. I have a lot going on in my life right now."

He scoffed. "Please. Your little museum job is cute, but where's it going to get you? Being seen with someone like me would go far to repairing the Benson name."

Her face heated and she pressed her lips together.

"Mia. There you are. I've been looking all over for you."

Mia blinked and turned to see Logan standing next to her. She took in the sight of him, wearing a tuxedo that was neither as expensive nor as well-fitted as the ones worn by everyone around them. But he still managed to wear it well.

His smile was bright as he took the glass of champagne from her and set it on a nearby table. "They're playing our song. I know how much you love to dance."

Chad raised a brow.

She held up a single finger to tell Logan to wait. "The last thing I need to repair my name is to be seen with the likes of you. Every single woman in our circle knows better than to be alone with you. I did not choose my father, but you do choose your behavior." She started to turn, but paused and looked back. "And as far as your parents' taste in art, I would think that you'd rather like the Moreau they're selling. It definitely suits your personality."

Chad's mouth dropped open and Mia turned to Logan, immediately regretting mentioning the painting. She allowed him to lead her to the still-empty dance floor. Once he spun her into his arms, she said, "That was quite the move."

"You looked like you were suffering being in a conversation with that guy."

"And you thought I needed to be rescued?"

He tilted his head and offered a grin. "I stand corrected." He took her in his arms and they began to dance.

"What if I had a boyfriend and now you made me look like a cheater?"

The hand on her back pressed her closer, but not indecently so. Surprisingly, the man could actually dance. And lead at that. Her heels brought her nearly to his chin, allowing her to see little more than the strong line of his shoulders, the close beard was more than a five o'clock shadow, and the laugh lines that bracketed his mouth. None of which singularly was a turn-on, but all at once? She was just a woman.

"When I ran into you at the gallery and asked you out, you would've said if you were involved with someone. Instead you turned me down because of your last name." As he spoke, his breath feathered softly across her hair.

She chuckled. "That was my feeble attempt at saving your reputation, which you have now ruined by dancing with me again. Once at Max Ingram's house and again now? People will definitely start talking."

"Let them talk."

He had no idea how utterly painful that could be.

A throat cleared over the comms. "You're supposed to be doing recon on Small and Bishop, not dancing and actually…socializing," Nikki said, the final words engulfed in laughter.

Shuffling occurred on the other end of the comms and Mia closed her eyes to put it out of her mind and enjoy being held by a good-looking man who didn't care about her last name.

A few seconds later, Audrey said, "Ignore Nikki. Have a little fun."

"But make sure to turn off the camera before gettin' naked," Nikki snarked. "We don't need photographic evidence of your fun."

With her lids still shut, Mia rolled her eyes. Listening to Audrey and Nikki was like having the worst baby-sitting job on the planet. "So tell me, Logan, what are you doing at this event? It seems like an odd choice."

"Why? Because you don't think I could afford it?"

The thought had crossed her mind. Tickets were twelve hundred apiece. "I've been attending events such as these for years, and I've never seen you."

"Atlas is footing the bill. We insure some of the pieces here, and in light of what's happened recently, they want to have as many of their people involved in the art scene as possible to try to figure out what's going on."

"Wait. You think the Mathis and the Devereaux aren't the only problems?" She stepped back to look up into his eyes.

His smile wavered. "They have no idea, so we're keeping our eyes open."

LOGAN HAD NO IDEA what had possessed him to inter-fere with Mia's conversation, much less pull her onto the dance floor, but he began to feel it was a mistake in more ways than one. The scent of her hair wafted up and had him inhaling deeper. When she stepped back and stared up at him with those bright hazel eyes, he knew he was in trouble.

She wasn't the vapid, poor little rich girl he'd thought she might be. He definitely had met his fill of vacuous personalities over the past few weeks. But Mia was fas-cinating. She held her head high even though she knew people talked about her. Even though people like Chad thought he could manipulate her because of her family problems. Even though he had underestimated her twice within a half hour.

The song ended and she stepped out of his arms completely.

"Can I get you a fresh drink?" he asked, suddenly wanting to extend their time together.

"Thank you, but I'm headed upstairs to look at the art. That's where I was going before Chad caught me."

"I'll leave you to it then, unless you'd like some company?"

She studied him with her mouth barely curved. "I suppose if you were to decide to view the art at the same time, it wouldn't do any harm."

They walked up the stairs in silence. At the top, he placed a hand on her back as they stepped around a couple heading down to the party. His fingers skated over the silky material of the dress that clung to her form. It was cool and smooth and he had the urge to stroke her all over. But he was supposed to be working.

"Can I ask you a question?"

"Feel free to ask. I reserve the right to not answer," she said with a small smile.

"Of course." He tucked his hands into his pants pockets as they walked. "As we were walking away from Chad, you mentioned a Moreau painting his father is selling. What does it look like?"

She bit down on her lip to mask the smirk. "It's called 'My Way.' The image is surrealist and it depicts a man groping a woman who is clearly horrified by the experience."

That explained quite a bit about her relationship with Chad. He filed the information away to look into later.

He'd been poring over Atlas's records and he knew Bishop was a client, but he hadn't paid attention to the artwork insured. Given what he knew, though, it was too much of a coincidence that the man was selling.

Logan wondered if he'd be able to get in to see it before it shipped. If the painting in Bishop's house was authentic, then he could follow it to the auction house, like chain of custody. Somewhere in the chain, the link was broken and the forgeries were being slipped in to replace the originals. Cybercrimes had been scouring the internet to find sales of the original painting, but they'd come up empty-handed for Scott's. Ingram's was a whole different situation. The rightful owner's heir suddenly popped up with the painting and donated it per his father's wishes.

With any luck, his meeting with Agent Stokes tomorrow would prove fruitful.

Mia stopped in front of a painting of a mother and child. Logan read the tag beside the painting. *Note to self: do more homework and know this stuff before arriving at an event.*

"The brushstrokes on this are amazing."

Brushstrokes? He'd assumed the art was a print. He didn't see brushstrokes. He leaned closer and the faintest of lines could be seen where the colors blended.

"It is beautiful." It was a safe comment seeing as the sunset depicted in the background was objectively pretty.

"Do you have a favorite? In college, I was all about pointillism, but in recent years, glazing has caught my eye."

He searched his memory for any information relating to the words she spoke. Pointillism. The park painting. Lots of dots. "Pointillism was okay. I prefer the Impressionists, though."

See? He'd paid attention in class. When he wasn't flirting with his female classmates.

Mia sighed as she moved on to the next painting. "I understand love for the masters, but it sometimes feels like people choose them as their favorites because everyone knows them. Although I will always make an exception for Degas."

"Why is that?"

"I was a dancer when I was younger."

She said nothing more. Gave no further hints. Maybe he should've paid closer attention in class.

They walked past three more paintings in silence. Logan didn't know what else to talk about. "So you like Degas. What are your feelings about Van Gogh?"

"He was prolific. He played with light and movement. But I don't feel passion when I look at his work."

"Really? He's known as one of the most passionate artists."

Mia glanced up at him with a raised brow.

"Come on. The man cut off his ear for love. Sick and twisted, but passionate."

She shook her head. "That's legend. Most historians agree that wasn't what actually happened."

Crap! This was why he shouldn't be discussing art. "But the story originated somewhere. Its basis is rooted in his passion."

"I guess I'll give you that point."

Nice save.

"Mia!" a pretty blonde called from the opposite corner of the studio.

"Carolyn. It's so good to see you," Mia said as she crossed the small room.

Logan hesitated and decided to follow.

Carolyn looked around. "No Jared tonight?"

"No, he had plans." Mia leaned forward and lowered her voice. "And he really only attends art functions because of me."

Carolyn eyed him. "So you didn't need Jared because you had a date. Introduce us?"

Mia's gaze swung to him, as if just realizing he was still there.

Logan extended his hand past Mia. "Hi, I'm Logan Freemont, and although I would be more than happy to be Mia's date, we actually just happened to run into each other here."

Carolyn took his hand in a barely there grasp. Really kind of limp. "Oh, that's too bad."

"It was nice to meet you, Carolyn, but I'll let the two of you catch up." He turned to Mia. "Thank you for the dance. I'll be around if you'd like to go for another spin. Or if you decide you'd like to go out for coffee. Or dinner. Or anything."

She smiled and shook her head. "I'll see you around, I'm sure."

He backed away, watching her until he reached the stairs. Then he winked, turned his back, and went to gather more information. And probably Google Degas and Van Gogh.

THREE

"Giiirl. How did you say no to that?" Carolyn said as soon as Logan descended the stairs.

"Rather easily."

"But why? Did you not see the smile? And the wink?"

"Oh, I saw them all right." She took a deep breath. "I don't have time for a relationship right now." She waved in the general direction Logan had gone. "Feel free."

"As nice as it is for you to offer, I know when a man is smitten, and it wasn't me he winked at."

"Whatever. What's going on with you?" Mia genuinely liked Carolyn. Her father and Carolyn's had been friends, so they had spent a lot of time together as teenagers at family get-togethers and society functions. However, Carolyn's mother had held out hope that Carolyn and Jared would end up together.

"More of the same."

"She's not on the list of people we need intel from," Audrey said in her ear.

Was that a hint of jealousy Mia heard?

"Can I ask you a personal question?" Mia asked.

"Absolutely." Carolyn pointed toward the railing, away from the art, that overlooked the first floor. Not really private, but better than the middle of the room.

They walked over and Mia peered over the edge. She immediately saw Logan, who stood near the back looking at the crowd.

"Shoot," Carolyn prompted.

"Do you know what's going on with our fathers' friends?"

Carolyn's face grew serious. "What do you mean?"

"It seems like so many of them are selling artwork. It feels rushed, like there's something going on."

Carolyn touched her arm. "Did you talk to Jared about my dad?"

"No. Why?"

"When Jared and I went out to dinner a while ago, I mentioned that my dad was looking to sell some property. I overheard the bunch of them talking about liquidating art and jewelry and hiding the profits. I've been worried."

"Why all of a sudden are they making these moves?"

"I have no idea."

"Any guesses?"

"I really don't know."

Mia was pretty good at reading people, and Carolyn was genuinely worried. Part of her sincerely hoped Steven Draper wasn't involved in this latest mess. For Carolyn's sake.

They continued to look out over the crowd below them while Carolyn moved on to more mundane conversation. When Mia figured she'd shown her face enough at the event, she excused herself to leave. She wouldn't get more information from these people tonight.

While waiting for the car, she talked into the comm but pulled out her phone as if to make a call. "I'm done. I'll see you both tomorrow."

"No. You need to come here. We need to talk."

That sounded ominous, which was the last thing Mia

needed, so instead of being irritated that she was being summoned—yet again—a hint of worry crept in.

At the apartment, Audrey and Nikki were deep in conversation about the possibilities for the next heist.

"All right. I'm here. What is so pressing that you needed to talk to me tonight?" Mia set her purse on the table and unclasped the camera necklace. Then she set her earpiece beside it.

"Who is that Logan guy again?" Nikki asked.

"Seriously? You had me come back here to give me a hard time about a man flirting with me?" She huffed.

"His name, Mia. What is his name?"

"Logan Freemont. Why?"

Nikki strode over to the TV where Audrey had images from the event already cued up. "While you were talking to what's-her-face—"

"Carolyn," Audrey provided.

"You were facing the crowd. Look at Logan."

Mia stared at the screen where Logan was looking at guests. "What am I looking for?"

"That dude's a cop."

"What? No, he's not." Mia's heart pumped wildly. What was Nikki accusing her of?

"He's watching the crowd the way a cop does. I know those eyes. I've seen them hundreds of times. They're all the same."

"He works for Atlas Insurance. I told you. His company is worried about the thefts and forgeries. Wouldn't that give him the same *type* of look?"

"Audrey?" Nikki said.

"Already on it," she called from behind her computer screen.

"On what?"

Audrey typed and scrolled, staring at her screen. "There is no Logan Freemont listed as an employee of Atlas Insurance."

"He's probably from a different office. New York, maybe."

Audrey scoffed. "I hacked their internal system. No Logan."

Mia sank to the back edge of the couch. What was going on?

"Okay," Nikki said. "We treat him like he's an undercover cop, which he probably is." She took a deep breath. "You need to call him."

Mia heard Nikki talking, but the words didn't register.

"Mia."

Her head snapped up and she schooled her features. "What?" she asked sharply.

"The guy has a thing for you. You need to call him."

"I will not."

"Mia." Nikki paused and fisted her hands. "We can use this to our advantage."

"What if he suspects what we're doing?" All of her planning. Five years' work. Gone.

Nikki laughed.

"This isn't funny."

"Sure it is." Nikki pointed at the TV screen to a picture of Mia and Logan. "That is not the face of a suspicious man. That look says, 'I want you.'"

Mia huffed again. Her brain was full of static. She couldn't think about anything. It felt like the moment she found out her dad had fled the country. Which didn't truly make sense seeing as she had zero relationship with Logan.

But there was the possibility.

So many things suddenly added up. The suit that

wasn't quite expensive enough, insurance agent or not. His lack of opinion when discussing art. The way he looked confused when she mentioned glazing. And then there had been calling Van Gogh an Impressionist. Any one of those things could have been excused due to distraction, but all of them together now made sense. He probably didn't know anything about art.

Mia closed her eyes and took a deep breath. When she reopened her eyes, she looked at Nikki, her composure back in place. "How, exactly, do you think we can use this?"

"I'm so glad you asked," Nikki said with a saucy grin as she plopped on the couch. "Of course, it would be nice to know what branch of law enforcement he's with, but even without that knowledge, you just need to con him into giving you information about the case he's working on. That way, we know how close he's getting and we can continue to operate undetected."

Mia stared at Nikki. "How am I to *con* him into anything?"

"Really? Your dad is a notorious con artist. He got people to fork over millions, and you learned nothing from him?"

She'd definitely learned from her father. His lessons were burned into her memory and she'd held on to them as she worked to whittle away everything he'd done:

1. Spending money to get the best is worth it 99% of the time.

2. Endearing yourself to others makes it easier to manipulate them.

3. Loyalty to the right people is vital to success.

The first, she had no problem with. It was the reason her inheritance had taken a hit; she wanted the best thief, forger, and hacker money could buy. And that ended up flowing directly into number three because these women, along with her cousin, were loyal, which had led to their collective success.

Conning Logan Freemont was going to require number two, and there, she was out of her depth. He was not like her father's friends, where she could bat her lashes and pretend to be stupid. He would never buy it.

"In theory, I know what you're looking for. You want me to pretend to be enamored with Logan, lead him on, and get him talking." She licked her lips. She didn't like to admit inadequacies. "But I'm not very good at faking it, so to speak."

"I beg to differ. We've watched you at numerous society functions and you fake it with all those people. Every time you talk to Randall Scott or Max Ingram or any of the others."

Audrey nodded. "Not to mention the fact that most of the interactions we witness with all of these snooty rich bastards are pretty damn phony."

They had a point, but faking pleasantries with them was something she had been trained for.

"All right. Where do we start?"

LOGAN STILL FELT LIKE he was spinning his wheels attending all of these art events. It wasn't like thieves were stealing during a party. Not to mention that they still had no proof that this was a theft ring. As far as the Bureau was concerned, they had forgeries circulating.

But in his gut, Logan knew.

He just couldn't find the missing pieces to connect

everything. And his continued running into Mia Benson wasn't helping.

The file the Bureau had on her was less than helpful. Reams of paper were devoted to her father, but they had almost nothing on her. She'd lived an unremarkable life, especially once her father fled. Prior to his indictment, she'd been a society princess with solid footing in the world of old money as well as in the world of self-made millionaires. Her mother's family was legacy. The Washington name carried weight.

Benson had built his financial consulting firm using the Washington name and reputation, but created his company with his brother-in-law from the ground up. No Washington money had been used in the venture.

The Washington women were shrewd. They protected what was theirs. That included their children once the men had been indicted.

Mia had dropped from the society pages. Her fiancé broke off the engagement. She lost a museum job in New York.

She rebuilt her life and from the outside looking in, it appeared as though nothing affected her. But Logan had seen the pain when she mentioned her last name as she warned him off. She was a law-abiding citizen who spoke quietly to those close to her about how much her father's deeds bothered her. She'd spent her own money hiring a private detective to track him down.

She'd even shared his last-known location with the FBI. She wanted her father to face the consequences of his actions.

All of that added up to her having nothing to do with the forgeries.

But something continued to niggle at him. He didn't

know if it had to do with Mia or the job or both. So, he went to the one place where he was just one of the kids looking for comfort in a home-cooked meal and the ability to forget his problems for a while: Mama Mae's house.

Cruising down the block, he took in his surroundings. The houses looked a little more run-down than he remembered, but families still sat on stoops to talk while kids ran through sprinklers. He squeezed his SUV into a spot at the end of the block. The one thing he hated about driving in the city—finding parking.

He hadn't lived here in over a decade, but he still viewed it as home. He'd landed here as a foster kid when he was twelve, full of piss and bitterness. Mama Mae and Joe had taken him in and let him be an asshole until he realized there wasn't anything he could do to make them give him the boot.

That realization changed his life.

He grabbed the tray of cookies and pie from the passenger side and walked down the block and around to the back of the house. Only strangers used the front door. The skinny three-story house was unique in the neighborhood full of bungalows. It was old and always needed work. The blue-gray asbestos siding was still intact, which completely boggled Logan's mind when he considered how many baseball, football, and hockey puck hits it had taken over the years.

He slid up the handle on the chain-link gate and tested the wooden steps to see if they were good. Then he swung the door open and called, "Who's home?"

Mama Mae rounded the corner with her hands on her hips. "All these years and you still haven't figured out how to enter the house without yelling?"

"How else would you know it's me?" He bent over and kissed her cheek.

"If you came around more often, we'd get used to it."

"I like to keep you on your toes." He set the pie and cookies on the island in the middle of the kitchen.

"Why do you insist on bringing that junk every time you visit?"

"Because the kids get excited over this crap and that means I get more of your cooking."

"Oh, you." She pushed a hand at him.

"Where are all the kids?"

Mama Mae had been taking in foster kids for about as long as Logan had been alive. She sought out the kids no one else wanted—the troublemakers, the teenagers. She gave them a place and loved them until they were ready to leave.

"Katie is at softball practice and Paris is doing homework at the library. Anton is probably running the streets as usual." She took it all in stride, but she was getting too old for running a teenager down like she had when Logan was young.

"He's not adjusting yet?"

Mae took the cookies from the bag and opened the tray. "It takes time. He's only been here a little more than a month. It took you three times as long to settle in. He's testing the waters. Wanting to make sure we won't stop him from seeing his friends. They're all he has."

"He has you and Joe."

"Anton hasn't figured that out yet. So what's the reason for the visit?" She bustled around the kitchen making a fresh pot of coffee and opening up a dish that contained homemade banana bread.

"Why does there have to be a reason? Maybe I just missed your beautiful face."

"Yeah, I almost believe that." She sat at the kitchen table. "Pull up a chair. Tell me about work." Her dark blue eyes assessed him.

Every time he came for a visit he was struck by the fact that Mae looked older. Her hair had always had gray in it, but now it was more gray than brown. He took a slice of banana bread and a napkin and sat across from her. "I'm working an undercover operation."

"Is it dangerous?" From the outside, Mae looked all soft, but she was built of steel.

"Not at all. Some paintings that people tried to sell have been found to be counterfeit. They have me posing as an agent with the company that insures them."

"Art? That is..."

"What?"

"Unusual."

"Why do you say that?"

"You were never much of an artist."

"Ouch." He put a hand to his chest. "The things you find out about your parents when you become an adult."

"I can see you're devastated."

"I leveraged the art history classes I took in college, so my boss thought I would be best suited for the job."

She squinted her eyes and smiled. "Did he actually look at your grades from those classes?"

"You're a riot today. I enjoyed learning about art."

"I thought the FBI had specialists for that kind of thing."

He chewed the moist bread before responding. "They do. The experts are focused on the counterfeits. I'm trying to see if there's a connection."

"What else?"

"What do you mean?" He popped another piece of bread into his mouth.

"You've had plenty of difficult jobs without needing to come home. You typically land on my doorstep when it's girl trouble."

Paris took that moment to walk through the door. "Who's having girl trouble?" She looked at them and said, "Oh, hey, Logan. What kind of trouble? Did your charm finally fail you?" Paris asked.

He had no idea why he'd thought coming to a house full of mouthy teenagers would make him feel better. "My charm is just fine. In fact, I didn't even hit her with a full blast yet. She's a little skittish."

"What's her name?" Paris already had her phone out.

"Mia Benson."

A few taps on the screen and Paris had photos of Mia pulled up. "Whaaat? She is so not your type. Where'd you meet a rich lady like her anyway?"

"On this undercover job I'm working. She knows about art and I think she can help me."

"Oh, so it's not like relationship stuff. It's work."

"Yes." The girl sounded completely disappointed, so Logan was not going to fuel any ideas about how much he liked Mia.

"Figures. She's too hot for you anyway." Then she rose, took two more cookies, and left the room.

Coming home was always a nice reality check anytime he started to forget who he was.

FOUR

MIA PACED HER living room with her phone in hand. She'd agreed to call Logan and make plans but she was still trying to figure how that would play out. She'd told him she wasn't interested in dating, but now she suddenly changed her mind? That was attractive. No, she needed a plausible reason to call him. To actually seek him out to make the call.

"Just do it, already," she said aloud to herself and dialed the number she'd gotten from Randall Scott.

"Hello?" Even over the phone she could tell he was smiling. The man was always smiling.

"Hi, Logan? It's Mia Benson."

"Mia? It's nice to hear from you. What can I do for you?"

"I wanted to apologize for leaving the gallery the other night without saying goodbye. I wasn't feeling well."

"That's okay. But I have to admit that I thought you might've been dodging me."

"I don't make a habit of dodging people. I prefer to face things head-on."

"I can definitely appreciate that."

"Anyway, I'd like to make it up to you. You were very kind in getting me away from Chad."

"Even though you didn't need to be rescued."

"It was still a lovely dance."

"But nowhere near as much fun as witnessing you hand that slimeball his ass."

She swallowed the chuckle that his comment caused. People in her circles didn't speak that way in general, much less about one of their own. Yet another reminder that he was there to do a job. And so was she.

"I wondered if you'd like a tour of the Art Institute? I know it's last minute, but I have some time in my schedule this afternoon if you're free."

"Isn't that where you work?"

"Yes, which gives me unique access."

"So I would be getting a VIP private tour."

"Only the best for the man who swooped in to save me from a slimeball."

"What time does this tour start?"

"Any time after two. Let me know what works for you."

He was silent for a moment and then said, "I'll be there around three thirty if that's okay. I have some work things to wrap up."

"Lots of policies and underwriting, I bet."

"Uh, yeah. I'll see you this afternoon."

Gotcha again. The man hesitated when thinking about the fact that he was supposed to be an insurance agent. Hopefully getting him to open up and give her information would be easy. "See you then."

As soon as they disconnected, she pulled out her burner phone and texted Nikki and Audrey. We have a date for this afternoon. I will stop by the apartment shortly to get whatever tech you want to stick to me.

Nikki texted back, What are you wearing?

The same clothes I'll be working in.

Boring!

She did not have time for Nikki's antics. She put the phone in her purse and headed out. When she arrived at the apartment a short while later, she let herself in and saw the usual display of Nikki sprawled on the couch, and Audrey typing away at the computer.

"Ew! You've got to be kidding," Nikki called as she spun around to face Mia.

"What?"

"You need to keep the man interested." Nikki pointed at her up and down. "That outfit screams, 'Don't look at me!'"

Mia glanced down at her favorite Chanel skirt. Her green silk blouse brought out her eyes. And her heels always made her rear end and legs look phenomenal. "I'm going to work. I need to look professional."

"But you're also going on a date. So you need to look sexy."

"We're meeting at the museum."

Nikki huffed a sigh, rolled her eyes, and then looked at Audrey. "And I thought you needed help."

Mia clenched her jaw. "I do just fine on my own. I might not be a con artist extraordinaire like some people, but I do understand the basic tenets. Your lie or persona or what have you needs to have hints of truth. I work at a museum. I love art. He insures art. That common interest should be enough to make him comfortable."

"But he's only pretending to like art," Audrey said. "That'll probably keep his guard up because he'll be afraid of making a mistake."

Great. Even the hacker felt the need to critique her plan.

Nikki jumped up and walked over to Mia. "We can still work with this." She circled Mia, making her feel like she was on display. "After work, lose the blazer and undo a few buttons. Offer a bit of skin. Just enough to tease the imagination." She snapped her fingers. "Can you drop the camera onto a different piece of jewelry?"

Audrey wheeled her chair around the desk. "Already done. Try this." She handed Mia a new necklace. It looked like a small locket. "Don't try to open it."

Mia reached up and clasped it around her neck.

Nikki grinned. "Perfect. When you open the top two buttons, the point of the heart will naturally draw his eyes down."

"Keeping a man's interest has rarely been an issue for me. The problem I face is getting him to give me information without letting him know that I know who he is."

"Steer the conversation to the forgeries you already know he's looking into. Look at him all doe-eyed and he'll practically open his files for you."

"I'm not good at any of those things. I don't steer the conversation, I ask pointed questions. I've never looked doe-eyed at anyone." At least no one she was attracted to. Her father's cronies? Sure. Maybe she needed to think of Logan that way. But his smile kind of prevented that.

"We get it, Mia. You're a badass who rules everything. Think of this as playtime. Pretend to be someone you're not." She pointed behind Mia. "Channel Audrey."

"Hey," Audrey protested. "I'm not doe-eyed and I'm every bit as competent at my job as she is at hers."

"But you do the lost, innocent look so well. I haven't been able to pull off innocent since I was about ten."

Nikki smirked. "If you don't think you can pull off in-génue, you can always go for tramp."

Mia held up a hand. "I've heard enough. I'll figure something out." She turned and looked at Audrey. "Is there anything else I need?"

"If you could get a look at his ID, that would help. A real name, anything to help me figure out who he is."

"No problem. Why don't I pick his pocket while I'm at it?"

Nikki's eyes popped wide. "Oh. That's actually a good idea."

"I was joking."

"No. I mean, I don't expect you to do it, but if I know where you guys are going to be, I can lift his wallet. You distract him and I can snag his ID."

"Since I offered him a private tour of the museum, we'll be in areas you won't be able to access. Let me see how this goes. After today, he might never want to see me again. After all, I brushed him off a couple of times, so I don't think naïve schoolgirl interests him." She picked up her purse to go to work. "Where are we on figuring out the next job?"

"We're working on it now. We'll have something ready later today," Audrey said.

Mia didn't believe a word of that. Nikki was covered in potato chip crumbs, and a video game was frozen on the TV screen. But she didn't comment because she was trying to let them complete their process for planning in the ways that worked for them. They'd been successful so far, even more so as Mia had given them more leeway.

Mia focused on her actual job and shoved thoughts of grifting from her mind. This had not been part of her plan. She was the mastermind who decided who they would steal from and what they would steal. Gathering information to keep them all from being discovered had never crossed her mind.

LOGAN SMILED AS HE disconnected from his call with Mia. A tall woman with her blond hair pulled into a tight knot at the back of her head entered the conference room.

"Whew, looks like somebody got some good news."

"Yes, it was a nice surprise." He extended his hand. "Logan Ford. Nice to finally meet you in person, Agent Stokes."

She shook his hand. "I'm sorry about shuffling things and putting you off. This whole Devereaux thing created a huge mess."

Logan turned and spread his arm. "Take a seat. The Devereaux is what I need to talk to you about."

Stokes pulled out a chair and sat, twisting to remain facing him. "Do you think my Devereaux has something to do with your forged Mathis?"

"I'm not sure. But I'm not a believer in coincidences, and it seems like a lot for two paintings owned by two different men who happen to be friends and being insured by the same insurance company end up being forged."

"Well, when you lay it out like that, it does seem fishy. But this whole thing has been beyond weird."

"Can you run it down for me?"

"A few weeks ago, on a Saturday night, Sunday morning, Max Ingram reported the Devereaux missing from his house. His son Brad had had a pool party the night before, so there were a number of guests coming and going and Brad didn't bother to get extra security. On Tuesday, the Devereaux was delivered by courier to the Carlisle Museum with provenance paperwork. There's a whole other case being sorted about where and when Ingram bought the Devereaux because he has phony papers."

"Where does the forgery come into play?"

"The Carlisle had the Devereaux they received locked up waiting for authentication. In the meantime, a week later, I get a call from a friend of mine saying he has a way for me to get Marco Wolf."

"Just out of the blue like that?"

"He runs a security consulting business, so he knows a lot of people. Anyway, he gave his guy my number and we got the time and place for Wolf to receive the stolen Devereaux. The one at the museum was a forgery."

Logan scribbled information in his notebook. This was beyond coincidence; this was a setup. To what end, though? Experts had authenticated the Devereaux that was brought in by the FBI. Where had the forgery come from?

"The guy who gave you Wolf. Who's he?"

Stokes leaned forward and propped her elbow on the table. "He's an old-time con man and thief. He's been picked up a bunch of times over the years, but stealing a masterpiece is way out of his league."

"How'd he get tied up with Wolf?"

"Gambling debt. He owed Wolf's bookie. This was payment."

"What's this guy's name? The one with the debt?"

"Jack Russo. Goes by the name Dodger." She paused and then scooted closer. "Here's another tidbit for you that you won't find in the official report. It wasn't Dodger that made the call to me."

Logan leaned back in his chair and flipped his pen over in his hand. "Who did?"

"I'm not really sure, and my friend who passed along my contact info isn't saying. But Dodger's old. I talked to a much younger man."

"And why did you leave this out?"

She squinched her face and gave him a look like he was stupid. "This case doesn't need any more complications. We scooped Dodger up, and he asked for his deal. So he at least knew what the score was."

"Can you send me your file on him?"

"No problem. But I'm telling you, he's no more a forger than a thief of masterpieces."

"Someone's gotta know something about why a forgery was sent to the Carlisle. Let's say Dodger did steal the Devereaux, and his plan all along was to use it to pay off his gambling debt. Where's the handoff to the museum?" His pen twirled faster around his fingers, the rhythm attempting to keep up with his thoughts.

"I don't know anything about what happened at the Carlisle. Not my area, not my call." She stood. "If there's nothing else?"

He tossed his pen on the table and shook her hand. "Thanks for your help. This has been quite enlightening."

"Really? Sounds to me like it just created a ton more questions."

He raised a finger. "But as I pick apart the questions, they reveal answers. Each answer takes me a little closer to the truth."

"What truth?"

"These art collectors are shady. I don't know what they're doing, but it's off."

"Good luck. I'll get those files to you today."

"Hey, one more thing. Can you give me the name and number of your friend? The security consultant?"

"Why? He was just playing middleman."

"I'd just like to ask him a few questions."

"Devon James. I'll send his contact info with the rest."

After Stokes left, Logan went through his notes again. He needed to talk to the original owner of the Devereaux. And talk to Max Ingram again to find out where he got the painting and why he thought it was the real deal.

Maybe the guys in art fraud would have some information now that they had two forgeries in their possession. If they could determine who the forger was, that would be another piece to the puzzle.

MIA STARED AT THE clock above Anya's head as the intern continued talking—into the second hour now—about the need to add a social justice section to Mia's planned *Crime and Punishment* exhibit. The slide show was hopefully nearing the end. Anya was a fellow for exhibition design this semester.

Anya spoke, waving her arms. "Just think. If we could get a few Vincent Valdez or Jacob Lawrence pieces, they would be an even bigger draw."

"What do you think?" Robert Schetzer, her direct superior, asked.

"It's an interesting idea, but I'm not sure that either of those artists fit the theme of crime and punishment."

"But…" Anya stretched the word out. "If we tweaked the theme to be justice, it could be all-encompassing."

Mia had known Anya would try to usurp her control of this exhibit; she just hadn't thought it would happen so early. "That changes the entire feel of the program. The board approved the exhibit—actually one much bigger than I originally proposed—because they liked my take on looking at real crime and how criminals are punished. While social justice warriors are often punished for their supposed crimes, it's a stretch. Most people do not then look at them and call them criminals. Certainly not in the same way a murderer or rapist is."

"Excellent point," Robert said.

At least he was on her side.

"But what makes a criminal? Someone who breaks the law. It's not about whether the law is just," Anya argued.

"Martin Luther King Junior was arrested for protesting. Has anyone considered him a criminal? Did his time in jail act as punishment?"

"Well, not exactly. But the racists who wanted him there would agree that he was a criminal." Anya stacked her pages of notes and tapped their edges together on the table as she spoke. Her nerves were obvious.

"Over the course of history, we can see the injustice in that. Will we ever say the same of someone like Charles Manson? Jeffrey Dahmer? No. This exhibit is meant to highlight how different cultures throughout history have dealt with their criminals. Adding in beautiful, heart-wrenching art that portrays people's fight for independence or equality would send a mixed message."

As Mia spoke, Anya's paper tapping slowed and her face fell. Mia hadn't wanted to hurt her feelings, but this was Mia's first exhibit. One she had created, proposed, and pitched. She wasn't going to stand by while that vision was altered. The room grew quiet and Anya packed up.

Then Mia had another thought. "However," she started, and Anya's gaze shot up to meet hers. "If you can find art that depicts crime against those social justice warriors, or hate crimes in general, we can take some space to explore that."

"Really?" Anya's eyes widened. She was younger than Mia by about five years. She was enthusiastic and wanted to prove her worth. Such networking was the best way to secure employment after completing her doctorate. Mia should know. She'd had to lean heavily on the relationships built during her internship after she lost the job in New York because of her father's indictment.

Mia truly didn't want to tear Anya down. "Yes. Take the week, put together a proposal of artifacts and how you think they can fit into the exhibit, and we'll discuss it."

Robert stood. "It looks as though you have this handled. Let me know if you need anything from me."

He left and Anya continued to put away her presentation.

"Your ideas are good, Anya. I don't want you to think that because they don't fit this exhibit, they're not worthy. I'll be happy to have you on my team for this project."

For the first time since the meeting started, Anya stopped fidgeting and she sent Mia a smile. "Thank you, Dr. Benson. That means a lot to me."

Mia nodded and walked briskly back to her office.

She let her assistant know that she was expecting a guest and that she should be paged when he arrived. She sent a flurry of emails to the other people on her team for the exhibit. They had two months to finish planning and then a month for construction. She'd played a role in all of the stages preparing for an exhibit of this size, but she'd never been the lead. There was far more paperwork and emails than she imagined.

Before she realized how much time had lapsed, her assistant knocked on her door and peeked in.

"Logan Freemont is downstairs for you."

"Thank you, Jasmine." She stood, tucked her phone in her blazer pocket, and grabbed her keys and ID. "I'm not sure how long I'll be, so if I don't see you, have a good evening."

Jasmine gave her a knowing smile and Mia left it at that.

In the elevator, she put in her earpiece and pressed the button so Audrey and Nikki could hear her. She touched the locket. "I assume you can see and hear me now?"

"Roger that," Audrey said and then laughed.

The elevator doors opened and Mia headed to the concierge desk, her heels clicking on the marble floor. Logan was leaning against the counter, phone in hand. Whether he heard her coming or it was something else that caught his attention, he looked up and their eyes met. A jolt of awareness surged through her.

And then he made it worse by smiling. His laugh lines deepened, still not hidden by the beard.

Seriously. How could the man have the perfect amount of scruff day in and day out?

She returned his smile. "I'm glad you could make it."

"And miss out on a personal VIP tour? Not a chance."

She handed him a visitor's sticker and he peeled away the backing and affixed it to the lapel of his suit coat.

She tilted her head and turned. "This way."

He walked a few steps behind her, head back, looking at the atrium.

She chuckled. It was an awe-inspiring view. The museum was beautiful. "You can see all this another day. I'm going to show you some things up close."

Two strides and he was practically brushing her arm. He lowered his voice. "There are a number of things I'd like to see up close and personal, but most would not be appropriate with the museum's patrons as the audience."

Mia's skin flushed.

"Oh, this dude is good," Nikki said. "He's throwing out some worthy lines. And unpracticed. That's on-the-spot thinking right there. So he's quick."

"I think he just really wants to sleep with her," Audrey added.

Mia's cheeks flamed.

"The two ideas are not mutually exclusive," Nikki retorted.

"What I have planned is most definitely suitable for an audience, but it is up close and personal." She swiped her ID to unlock the elevator to take them to the basement.

"Okay. Not gonna lie. I've always wondered what it would be like to be taken to a section of the museum that's off-limits. It's like being taken to a CIA black site."

So many bizarre things just came out of his mouth. "As an insurer, you've never been to the restoration rooms?"

"Nope."

"Well, we definitely won't lock you up and torture you."

"Good to know."

The elevator dinged and Mia held out her arm to guide him. "We've recently brought most of our Van Gogh works to be cleaned before going out on loan to a museum in California. Since you mentioned your love of Van Gogh, I thought you would enjoy the chance to see them like this."

"Talking about a guy who cut his ear off isn't exactly sexy," Nikki said.

"Shh…she's making him comfortable so he'll talk," Audrey countered.

Mia wondered if this was what she and Jared sounded like when Nikki and Audrey were on a job.

"That's very thoughtful. Thank you," Logan said.

Mia swiped her ID to unlock the conservation department. Inside the door, she handed him a pair of gloves.

"I get to touch them?"

"No. But protocol requires we wear gloves."

He tugged the gloves into place. His hands were big and the gloves didn't quite fit, leaving the bottom of his palm exposed.

"Hi, Erin. This is my friend Logan."

"The Van Gogh fan." Erin flipped her magnifying glasses up and extended a hand to Logan.

"We'll just wander, if you don't mind," Mia said.

"Go ahead. Let me know if you have any questions." Erin slipped her glasses back down and turned her attention to inspecting the painting on the table in front of her.

Mia stopped at the next table, where three Van Goghs were waiting to be inspected and cleaned. Logan stepped closer and studied the first one. She waited for a sign, the look of awe or excitement she routinely saw in the eyes of someone faced with a masterpiece.

She stood back and gave him space. When he did look up at her, there was interest but not love. Would she have seen it if Nikki had not pointed out that he was law enforcement?

"What do you love most about Van Gogh?" she asked.

"He's weird," Logan responded without hesitation.

Far from art criticism.

"He's brilliant in his use of color, but compared to the other Impressionists, he's out there. Take *The Starry Night*. Beautiful painting, but I've never seen a swirly sky."

"Do you know art at all?" The question was sharper and more accusatory than she'd intended, but there was no pulling it back now. Something about this man made her impulsive and reckless. Her mouth rarely got away from her.

"No," Nikki muttered. "You're not supposed to let him know you know."

Logan pressed his lips together and stepped back from the table. Would he come clean now and tell her who he really was? He came closer to her and spoke in a hushed tone. "What gave me away?"

"Both the other day and just now, you referred to Van Gogh as an Impressionist. He was Postimpressionist. That's Art History 101." Now maybe they could get somewhere.

"And there goes that opportunity," Nikki groused.

FIVE

LOGAN SMILED AND cursed himself. Now he had to figure out how to spin this. "I did, in fact, take art history in college. It just wasn't my major."

Mia laughed. It was sudden and so obviously uncharacteristic, she looked surprised it happened. She put her hand over her mouth.

For a brief moment, her tough exterior slipped. He wondered what it would take to make that happen again. "Why is that funny?"

"I didn't think you'd be honest." She pointed at the paintings. "Then how did you end up at a job where you're expected to insure items you know nothing about?"

"I know some things. I'm just not an expert. We have appraisers whose sole job is authenticating." He took another step closer and lowered his voice a little more. "But if I'm being totally honest here, I leveraged that meager art education for the promotion that got me this position. I figured on-the-job experience would be more meaningful anyway."

She pursed her lips as if unsure what to do with the information. He took the moment to really look at her. Her bright hazel eyes, sharp cheekbones, and full lips where the corners had a natural tilt to them that hinted at a sneer. Beautiful.

She blinked and he stepped back. Holding out his

hand, he said, "Show me what you've got. I have a feeling you could give me quite the education."

"Tell me, Logan, do those lines actually work on women?"

"Sometimes." He waited until she walked past him to the next painting. "Does that mean they aren't working on you?"

"Maybe." She pointed at a painting of a bedroom. "Van Gogh did this same painting three times. When he moved into what is referred to as 'the yellow house,' he was excited about doing something new. He started with this."

"How do you know he was excited?"

"He wrote to both his brother, Theo, and his friend Gaugin about it. He sketched the room for them to see and he talked about the colors he wanted to use."

"So this is one of those rare times people aren't just putting meaning where they think it should be? The artist actually said it."

"Very much so. The three paintings are nearly identical, but small changes were made, such as the paintings on his wall."

"Do you have all three?"

She shook her head. "No. We just have this one. One is in Amsterdam and the other in Paris. They were together for a while for an exhibit, but they're all back to their homes now."

"It looks like a kid painted it. It's all crooked." He pointed to the angled lines.

"Some say he did that intentionally; others think the house itself was angled. But for him, it was about color and the importance of the emotions color could convey."

"And what do you think?" he asked as they moved down the line to another painting.

"About what?"

"Does color convey meaning and emotion?"

She paused and tilted her head while she thought. Her dark hair swayed over her shoulder, revealing her neck. "I suppose. There are colors that humans associate with certain feelings. Black for fear or mourning." She angled her face to look at him. "Red for lust."

Tempting. He cleared his throat, and then directed his attention to the paintings again. "What's the process with these? I'd hate to be the person tasked with cleaning priceless art. What if you scratch it? Or paint flakes off?"

Mia smiled. "It's some science, some artistic talent." She flicked a thumb over her shoulder to Erin. "People like Erin pore over these inch by inch, inspecting each minute detail with precision."

She called Erin over, who walked them through the process of cleaning and restoring a painting. Erin showed him various pieces all being worked on in different ways. When Erin shifted back to the job she was attending to, Mia showed him some before and after photos. It was amazing.

"I still can't imagine handling priceless works of art every day."

"When something matters to you, you treat it with respect and care for it. That's why we're all here."

"Would you like to go to dinner?"

She blinked rapidly. "Now?"

"It's a little early, but that means we'll get a table easily."

"All right. I have a few things to wrap up here, so why don't you choose a place and I'll meet you there?"

"Or I could just wait for you here." He looked around. "Not here, here. I can wander the museum until you're ready."

She stared at him. Had she been planning to blow him off? Send him on his way and not show up?

"If you don't want to go to dinner with me, that's fine. You can just say so."

Her features softened. "No, it's not that. I didn't expect you to want to wait."

He shrugged. "Like you so aptly pointed out, I have a lot to learn."

She smiled brightly. "I'll walk you upstairs."

They walked in silence to the elevator. When they got to the main floor, he said, "Text me when you're ready. You still have my number?"

"Yes." She turned to go back to her office.

"Did you drive to work? Or can we take my car?"

"You drove?"

"I drive everywhere."

"That makes very little sense in Chicago."

"I like being in control of when I leave."

"Until you're stuck in traffic and you're late and can't find parking."

"I do just fine." He held her gaze and tried to read her face, but she rarely revealed anything.

"I'll be down soon."

He flashed her a smile and watched as she walked away. Halfway down the hall, she glanced over her shoulder. The corner of her mouth tilted up a bit more. He didn't know what it was about Mia Benson, but he liked her.

He really hoped that when he got a full file on her, he didn't discover that she was involved in this mess.

THE NONSTOP CHATTER IN her ear made Mia want to strangle someone. She held it together until she got back in her office. She closed the door behind her and then said, "Shut up."

She was finally met with blissful silence. She inhaled deeply and closed her eyes. "The two of you rambling in my ear most certainly made me look like an idiot."

"We were trying to be helpful," Nikki said.

"Believe it or not, I am totally capable of having a conversation without help." She rubbed her forehead between her eyebrows and sighed. "I'm going to have dinner with the man, but you will not be joining us. I will see what information I can get, but given his ability to spin lies, I'm not very hopeful."

"But I wanna watch," Nikki whined. "He's pretty to look at."

"You have your own pretty boy to look at," Audrey said. "I want to see Mia's face when he smiles at her like that.'"

Yes, Mia knew exactly what smile Audrey referred to, and just the mention warmed her blood again. She was torn. Part of her wanted to believe he was flirting with her because he was genuinely attracted to her. But there was a niggling fear that he was only testing her the same way she was testing him: to get information.

Certainly, if he were on a fishing expedition, he'd back off if she showed real interest. "All right, ladies, I'm going to dinner. Anything specific I should watch for?"

"Pay attention to where he leads the conversation. If

he starts asking about specific things, he's onto you. If he allows you to direct the conversation, he's looking to take you home."

"Ever helpful, as always, Nikki. I'm taking out the earpiece now."

"Stay out of trouble," Nikki warned.

Mia rolled her eyes and removed the comm. Those words were normally spoken to Nikki. Mia put the earpiece in her purse and gathered her things. After touching up her makeup, she opened another button on her blouse. An image flashed in her mind of Logan's large hands fumbling with the remaining buttons. She blew out a cool, calming breath.

She didn't have time for silly fantasies. For all she knew, Logan had somehow connected her and her team to the forgeries. And if that was the case, what would their next move be? Should they shut everything down, even though they were making a difference? The idea of letting her father get away again pushed all lustful thoughts from her mind.

She'd have time for fun and men once she brought her father to justice.

After slicking on a little gloss and spritzing on a hint of perfume, she removed her blazer and left it hanging on the back of her door. She was ready for her date.

Date. Ha! How pitiful that the only date she'd had in almost a year was with a man who might be looking to arrest her.

She locked up her office and sent Logan a text to let him know she was on her way back down. When she arrived downstairs, she glanced around but didn't see him. She began to feel silly hovering near guest services, waiting for a man. Then she looked up and saw him walking down the grand staircase. As he moved, he observed all over and tucked a small notebook in his pocket. He walked as if he owned the space, yet he still didn't quite fit.

"Doing some sketching?" she asked when he reached the bottom.

"Taking notes on the Impressionists so the next time I speak with another professional, I won't sound like an idiot." He smiled. "Where to?"

"I thought you were going to choose while you wandered."

"I could always do Gino's East. It's not too far."

Pizza? The man asked her out to dinner and wanted pizza?

She wasn't sure exactly what her face said, but he suddenly added, "But I'm open to anything if you don't like pizza."

"Who doesn't like pizza?" She'd been accused of being a snob plenty of times in her life, but Chicago was a pizza city. "Pizza would be fine." Whether he was a cop or an insurance agent, it was unlikely that he could easily afford some of the restaurants on Michigan Avenue.

He pushed the door open that led to Michigan Avenue. "Wait a minute. You're not one of those weird pizza people, are you?"

"Weird how?"

"Someone who wants fruit and kale slapped on some cauliflower crust."

A laugh bubbled up again. This man was dangerous for her resting bitch face. "I'm not averse to vegetables on my pizza but I prefer a regular crust and lots of cheese."

He nodded in approval of her answer. "And how do you feel about meat?"

"I suppose it depends. I'm not a *meat lover* where I want a pile of various meats on a crust, but I wouldn't say no to sausage or pepperoni."

"Whew. Dodged a bullet there. Thin crust or deep dish?"

"Thin crust, of course. Unless I'm looking to drown my sorrows in a pile of melted cheese that is stuffed pizza."

"Excellent answers all around."

"Really?"

"Yeah, why?" They walked around the building and to the parking garage.

"You said you lived in New York. While I never lived there, I've been a number of times and New Yorkers have very definite opinions about Chicago pizza."

"I'm a native Chicagoan. Born and raised. I've only been in New York for a few years."

Long enough to not have recognized her last name when she mentioned it. Or was that part of his persona?

Inside the garage, he led her to a black SUV. His car even looked like it belonged in a TV show about cops.

He opened the passenger door and she considered how to climb into the seat without her skirt becoming indecent. Behind her, Logan chuckled.

"Need a hand?"

She glared at him over her shoulder. "I have it. Thanks."

She braced a hand on the open door, hiked her pencil skirt up, and stepped in. Once seated, she adjusted her clothes again. When Logan got in behind the steering wheel, she said, "It's not nice to laugh at short people."

"I don't think your height had anything to do with it. It was the impractical skirt."

"My skirt is completely practical for the work I do. If I were four or five inches taller, I could step up without issue. So my height is exactly the problem."

He chuckled as he started the engine.

"How long have you been working for Atlas?" Asking about someone's work history was a normal date thing to do, right?

"About six years. I started in their corporate insurance department, but wanted a switch. Like I said, the promotion was in the art department."

"Why the switch?"

"More money. And it would afford me the opportunity to be back in Chicago. I missed home." He turned onto Michigan Avenue. "Gino's East really okay with you?"

"I wouldn't have agreed if it wasn't."

"I should've guessed that."

"What is that supposed to mean?" She angled her body to look at him.

"You strike me as a woman who says and does exactly what she wants."

"Is that a problem?"

"For me? Not at all." He drove in silence behind a city bus, inching along until he could change lanes to go around. "How long have you been at the Art Institute?"

"About five years. More if you count the time I interned. I got a job there right out of college. It was convenient because I did my PhD work at Northwestern."

He let out a low whistle. "Beautiful and brilliant. Should I call you Doctor Benson?"

"No need to be formal. I only use the title at work."

"Are you the resident Van Gogh expert for the museum?"

"No," she said a little too sharply. "My field is European medieval art."

"You seemed to know a lot about Van Gogh."

"I've spent a lot of time studying various periods and artists."

He turned into the parking garage next to Gino's East. After sliding out the passenger side, Mia adjusted her skirt again, swearing to herself that if she had to do this again, she would be driving. Since they were early for the dinner crowd, they were seated immediately.

And now Mia had no idea how to steer the conversation to the thefts. After the waitress took their drink order—white wine for her and beer for him—Logan took a drink of water.

"I'm glad you finally agreed to go on a date with me."

She popped her eyes wide. "This is a date?"

The shocked look on his face was priceless.

"I'm kidding. I'm not dense. You did ask me out numerous times. You're quite persistent."

"Only when I really want something."

His words caused another warm flush. She drank water to cool her now dry throat. "And why did you *really want* a date with me?"

"I'm attracted to you."

"There are plenty of attractive women in Chicago."

"Not too many who know the art world like you do."

"So this is work for you?" She narrowed her eyes and tried to decide if she should be offended.

"Definitely not. But I was hoping to pick your brain about the Devereaux and the Mathis."

Mia took another sip of water, this time to hide the stab of disappointment. He had only been interested in her because of the forgeries. Even though she knew that had been a possibility going into this date, it didn't hurt any less. Part of her had wanted him to want her, not her name, not her knowledge. Just her.

The waitress returned with their drinks and a basket of bread and took their pizza order. Mia sipped on her wine. "What do you want to know about those paintings?"

"You're friends with both Randall Scott and Max Ingram, right?"

"I wouldn't say we're friends. They're family friends, through my parents."

"But you know them well enough that you saw the paintings in their homes, right? Before they were discovered to be forgeries?"

"Randall's, yes. He used to have it at the landing of the stairs in the front hall. You could see it from the foyer. I'm not sure if I even saw the Devereaux in person. I've been to the Ingrams' house, and I don't recall seeing it there. To be completely honest, I'm not sure I even knew they owned a Devereaux."

"Really? That seems like something a man would brag about. To be the owner of the last known Devereaux."

"Maybe he did brag to his friends."

Logan leaned his forearms on the table. "Where do you think these forgeries came from?"

"I have no idea. I'm sure you'll find out at your job that forgeries are quite common in the art world. Many people don't worry about provenance. They want the wow factor of beautiful art in their home. If I'm not mistaken, the FBI has a whole division devoted to art crimes."

"You're right, but if it's that prevalent, how do people like Ingram and Scott make sure they're getting the real thing?"

"I suppose they count on experts, like your appraisers, to confirm. But even that isn't an exact science. You can get multiple appraisers who disagree about a painting and its authenticity."

"It sounds like it could be quite the racket for someone who was ambitious enough."

"How so? A forger would have no way of knowing if the appraiser would notice inconsistencies."

Their waitress arrived with their pizza. She set it on a stand in the middle of the table and served each of them a slice. "Can I get you anything else?"

Mia pointed to her glass. "I'll have another."

With romance off the table, this was her chance to play along and find out exactly what Logan knew and if he had any clue who she really was.

SIX

MIA ORDERING ANOTHER drink was a good sign. She wanted to stay and she was relaxed enough to enjoy a drink. "I'll have another, too," he said.

She cut into her pizza with a knife and fork. Logan looked at his own plate to hide his smile. She would never fit in with his family. She was so prim and proper. But he couldn't help but like when she got a little flustered.

After he swallowed his first bite, he continued the conversation. "If you had an inside guy at the insurance company, you could guarantee the appraiser would approve a forgery. If he was taking a payoff, he would look the other way on janky provenance and he'd give it the stamp of approval."

Mia set her silverware down. "Is that what you think is happening? Someone from your company is intentionally insuring forgeries?" Her voice was low as if she was worried that someone might actually be interested in their conversation.

"It's a possibility that we're looking into." He paused. "I hope I can count on your discretion."

"Absolutely."

"What are your thoughts on the possibility?" He dug into his pizza, hoping that she'd talk about these men.

"If you're asking me if I think these men are capable of such a devious act, probably. They were good friends with my father after all. I believe they were all aware of what my father and uncle were doing. They did nothing to stop them. So if given the chance to run their own scam, I think they'd do it." She took a sip of wine. "And if they could stand back with their arms up and plead naivete, pointing the finger at others? Even better." She delicately put another nibble of pizza in her mouth.

Her accusation held no emotion, just an objective observation. It was a little eerie, but he appreciated her honesty.

"How do you think they'd go about doing it? It seems risky that right after Scott's painting was deemed a forgery, Ingram's was found to have false provenance, and another forgery popped up." He finished his slice of pizza and went for another.

"While these men aren't stupid, they are used to doing whatever they want without worrying about the consequences. I think there's something to the concept that many successful CEOs are narcissists and sociopaths. They don't care about others—even those they consider friends. Maybe because Randall was caught with a forgery, Max decided to make a move. The spotlight was on Randall."

"There's so much that doesn't add up. Without title insurance, you're stuck with a forgery. Insurance won't pay out if the appraisal was wrong."

"Randall didn't have title insurance?"

"I can't discuss those specifics." Besides, he had a feeling she already knew that. Scott had called her to his defense. "And if Ingram wanted to pass off a forgery, why report it stolen?"

Mia smirked. "You have me there. I don't have the mind of a criminal. Regardless of where I got my DNA."

"That's good to know." He'd hate to have to arrest her. "Can I ask you another question?"

"It seems as though you're full of them today." But she raised her brows and waited.

"If I hadn't attempted to rescue you from Chad Bishop at the gallery, would you have gone out with me?"

She blinked rapidly. His question clearly caught her off guard. "I don't know. As I said, you are quite persistent. And you have some charm. But the fact that you don't care what my last name is, or who my father is, is by far the most attractive thing about you."

"Note to self: don't go to Mia Benson when you need an ego boost."

She laughed again. The surprised kind where she didn't see it coming. "I'm sometimes honest to a fault."

"Not a bad way to be." He spent far too much time surrounded by people who were liars and cheats. He'd take her blunt honesty. And maybe he'd up his charm. "I'll just have to work a little harder to impress you. I'm up for the challenge."

The look she gave him showed interest, assuming he was reading her correctly. She was tough, all right, but intriguing.

They enjoyed the pizza and another drink while chatting about their favorite places to visit in the city as native Chicagoans.

"I work at a museum, so I typically don't visit others unless it's work related. I'm also not very outdoorsy. I love the Joffrey. I see most of the performances."

"I remember you saying you were a dancer. Did you ever think about doing it professionally?"

The corners of her mouth dipped. "Maybe when I

was a child. By the time I was a teen, I knew I didn't have the natural talent. I danced because I loved it."

"Do you still dance?"

"Occasionally. Never for an audience. I no longer practice routinely. How about you? What is your Chicago thing?"

"I love to try the hole-in-the-wall neighborhood restaurants. The ones that never make 'best of' lists because only the locals know about them. I'm not much of a museum-goer either, but I do like the Field Museum."

"Boys and their dinosaurs."

"Sue is great, but when I was about thirteen, I had visions of being Indiana Jones. Finding lost artifacts. My grandfather showed me the movies." Grandpa Stan, Joe's father, had connected with him in a way no one else had. He hadn't treated Logan like a reject. He had been just another kid.

Mia leaned back in her seat. "So you do have an interest in art."

"By college, it was pretty much just about the girls. Indy always got the girl." He drank his beer. "But my grandfather had told me a story about a painting his family had that had been stolen. His father had bought it right before the Depression. Even when things got rough, his father held on to the painting, saying that one day it would provide for them, their children, and their children's children." It was weird telling her about this. He didn't talk about it often, but Mia could appreciate the story. "Then it was gone. I thought I could be like Indy and find it."

"I'm sorry to hear that. Did your grandfather ever find out what happened to it?"

"I don't think so. He died a couple years later." They

dropped into silence. *Way to go, Logan. What was that about upping your charm game? This sucked.* "I'm sorry. We were having a nice time—at least I think you were enjoying yourself—and I just pulled the whole mood down. I don't even know how that happened. I don't talk about Grandpa Stan often. You're easy to talk to."

"I'm glad you shared the story with me. I hate the pretense and games that usually go along with first dates."

"What about you? Since you didn't plan on being a dancer, have you always wanted to be a curator?"

She smiled. "What child says, 'When I grow up I want to be a curator'?"

He grinned. "I actually can picture a little Mia saying exactly that."

Her smile fell. He hadn't meant to insult her. In his head, Mia was an adorable, tiny thing with a vocabulary bigger than she was.

"I considered law—my mother is a lawyer. I started college thinking I'd go into business like my father. But, like you, I had been close to a grandparent. My grandmother was an artist." She finished her wine. "She was actually a seamstress, and her clothing was amazing. Even when she wasn't doing something for work, she was crafting and creating. From a young age I loved being with her and helping her organize and present her crafts."

"Is she still alive?"

"No, thank God. I think she would've literally killed my father for the grief he's caused my mother. Grandmother had no tolerance for anything improper. Illegal would push her over the edge."

"Can I ask you about your father? I understand if the topic is off-limits."

"What do you want to know?"

"After you told me who your father was, I read the news. You and your mom really had no idea?"

Her chuckle was dry. "No, we didn't. And even if we did, to admit it now would still be admitting guilt."

"Obviously he looks guilty because he ran, but is he?"

"Absolutely."

Logan didn't know what to do with that. Most people would've at least extended the possibility of innocence for their parent.

"I'm sure you figured I would be the dutiful daughter defending my father. That ended the moment he left. He lied to everyone and only worried about himself. I paid a private investigator to find him. His last known location was Montenegro, which I informed the FBI of, but there's no extradition. The man doesn't deserve my loyalty."

"You are a fascinating woman, Mia Benson. Would you like another glass of wine?"

"No, thank you. I should be going."

He waved the waitress over to get the bill. "Can I drive you home?"

"I'm going to visit a friend, so I'll just call a car."

"Are you sure? It's no bother."

"I'm sure. Thank you for the offer."

While she called a car, he settled the bill and took the leftover pizza. "You're welcome to the leftovers," he said.

"You enjoy them." She glanced at her phone. "The car is ten minutes away, so I should go wait outside."

"I'll wait with you." They walked out of the restaurant and stood to the left of the door, between the entrance and the parking garage. "Can I see you again?"

"That would be nice. This was by far the least painful first date I've had in years."

"Okay. That's just not going to do. 'Least painful' isn't even a compliment. I can do better."

"How do you propose to do that? The date is over in…five minutes when my car arrives."

"Challenge accepted." He stepped closer and she backed up until she was against the brick wall behind her. Her eyes widened and she sucked in a gasp. "I'm going to kiss you, unless you say you don't want me to."

HOLY HELL. WHAT had she gotten herself into? Logan had literally backed her into a corner. She could tell him no and he would pull back, but she suddenly realized that she didn't want him to. He lowered his frame so his mouth was mere inches from hers.

"Mia?"

"Yes," she whispered, her lungs frozen.

"Is that a yes I should kiss you?"

She slowly nodded, her hair sticking to the brick behind her.

Logan's right hand came up and cradled her jaw. He closed the distance between them without breaking eye contact. He stared into her as his lips brushed hers. His thumb caressed her cheek and he tilted his head to interlock lips, soft but sure. His eyes closed and his tongue tipped out, gentle but seeking.

Mia fisted her hands at her sides to keep from grabbing him. But she allowed her eyes to flutter closed and pretended that this was a normal first date and

Logan was a regular man who just wanted to be with her. Once she did that, she also began true participation in the kiss, meeting his tongue and pressing her body slightly closer, just enough to feel the heat from him.

Her phone buzzed and she tore away. "My car is here," she said breathlessly.

He stepped back and she edged around him to get to the car. As she opened the door, he asked, "Well?"

She looked back at him. He was so good looking.

"Did I at least get bumped up from 'not painful'?"

She pressed her lips together to stop the smile, but the movement conjured the feel of his lips on hers. "I'd say you got up to adequately pleasant."

She slid into the car.

"You're killing me here, Mia," he yelled. "But there's always next time."

She closed the door and waved goodbye to him. As soon as the driver pulled from the curb, she texted Nikki and Audrey to let them know she was on her way back to the apartment. At the moment she was grateful she'd had the sense to remove the comm in her office. If Logan had seen it in her ear, she'd have had no explanation. She wasn't about to put the comm back in now; she wasn't prepared to hear Nikki and Audrey's questions.

The trip to the apartment was only a few miles, but even with sticking to streets, the car hit rush-hour traffic. The slower pace allowed Mia to replay her date with Logan. Nikki had told her to steer the conversation to figure out what he knew, but he chose to talk about the forgeries. She hadn't needed to prompt anything. Did that mean she wasn't suspected of anything? His asking her out was a coincidence? Or was he suspicious and was gauging her reactions?

But the forgeries weren't all they'd discussed. It had very much felt like an actual date. If he thought she was behind the thefts, would he have acted that way? Would he have kissed her?

Mia's head spun and she didn't like it. Her life was well-ordered and controlled. She did more than steer a conversation—she drove the whole plan. Logan should be nothing more than a pothole to be filled. She was a problem-solver and as long as she continued to view him as a problem, she'd be fine.

All of that was predicated on her forgetting that kiss ever happened.

That was by far the more difficult issue for her to tackle. She closed her eyes and considered the conversation she'd had with Logan. It felt personal, but if he were undercover, he would take on a new persona, have a backstory.

His great-grandfather's painting. If she asked about it and he couldn't give her the details, that would certainly be a red flag. Of course, that would require another date.

No, not date. It would require her to talk to him, maybe see him again. It wouldn't have to be a date.

But you want it to be.

She shut that thought down along with the memory of their kiss. As the car neared the apartment, Mia braced herself for Nikki. Audrey she could handle. The hacker was more reserved, but Nikki was in-your-face, loud, and open, ignoring most acceptable boundaries. She left the car and let herself into the apartment.

Both Nikki and Audrey were hunched over the table looking at prints and plans. When she closed the door, they both became quiet and stared at her.

"Heck of a date, huh?" Nikki said.

"It was interesting," Mia replied.

Audrey snickered. "We might have lost comms to hear what was going on, but the silent movie we watched from the camera in the locket was pretty hot." She waved her hand as if fanning herself.

"Oh, yeah." Nikki propped her chin on her hand. "How was the kiss? Please tell me it was good. I might cry if a hot man like that kisses like a dog."

Mia swallowed the laugh that the image conjured. "How do you know he kissed me?"

"For a good two minutes we saw nothing but the knot of his tie."

She should have removed the necklace when she took the comm out. "The kiss was fine. I figured turning him down might be detrimental to the plan. If I turn him away, it would be hard to get information from him."

Liar. You wanted that kiss.

Nikki narrowed her eyes as if she could hear that quiet voice that whispered in the recesses of Mia's long-neglected libido.

"Good job. Let's talk about what you learned." Nikki kicked out a chair between the two of them.

Mia looked at the chair. Instead of sitting, she set her purse down and leaned against the back of the couch. "I'm afraid I didn't learn much. I didn't have to do much steering of the conversation. He wanted to talk about the forgeries."

"Oh…that's bad," Nikki said. "He wants to trip you up."

"Or," Audrey interrupted, "he wants to talk to her as an expert."

Over the weeks, Mia had learned that Audrey usually looked for the good in people and situations. But it didn't mean she was wrong. "If I had to guess, I'd say it's the latter. He doesn't know art as well as he should for the position he has."

"Which would make sense if he's a cop," Nikki pointed out. "Lull you into a sense of security."

"If he's law enforcement, why interact with me and risk tipping his hand? This is real life, not purposefully placed drama for the screen."

"Because you're not a criminal, and he knows it. Only stupid, greedy, or inexperienced criminals get caught. While you're not stupid or greedy, you are inexperienced. If he can crack you without a warrant, it makes his life easier."

Mia rubbed her forehead. "So what do I do?"

Nikki smiled and rubbed her hands together. "We teach you the art of the con."

SEVEN

NIKKI HAD TRIED to explain to Mia the nuances of being a con artist, and after two long hours of frustration, they'd called it a night. But Mia had agreed to come back to the apartment tonight after work for another session. Nikki was sure this would be the only way to figure out what Logan knew without giving away anything. To Mia's mind, a con artist was just an excellent liar.

Like her father.

She'd usually made sure she did nothing to imitate him, but in this moment, she needed to channel his energy. She understood it, but she had no idea how.

She let herself into the apartment and found Nikki on the couch making out with her boyfriend, Wade. When Mia closed the door, they slowly separated and turned their attention to her. "This is not an hourly motel, so please keep your extracurriculars at home."

Nikki snorted and rolled her eyes. "Wade, you remember Mia."

He stood and extended a hand. His blond hair was mussed from Nikki's hands, but his clothes were still in place. His blue eyes sparkled with mischief. "Nice to see you again, Mia."

Although she shook his hand—she wasn't rude—she said, "Why exactly are you here?"

Nikki popped to her knees on the couch. "I hate running a con, so I brought in reinforcements. Not only is

Wade an excellent con man, but he has the ability to teach."

Mia shot her a look.

"I know I'm not a good teacher," Nikki said with her hands raised.

That was an understatement. By the time Mia had huffed out last night, the two of them had been ready to come to blows. Sometimes Mia thought they were more alike than she wanted to admit.

"Okay, Wade, teach away." Mia placed her purse on the table and crossed her arms, waiting for instruction.

"When I say 'con artist,' what do you think?"

"Liar, cheat, thief."

"She ain't wrong," Nikki said as she sank back down on the couch.

"You're not wrong, but there is a whole lot more to it. First lesson, a con artist's best—most important—tool is her brain. A good con artist is smart, so we have that going for us. Other things in our favor are that you already have authority and social proof because of your degrees and job. You're respected in your field."

Nikki twisted and let her arms dangle off the back of the couch as she faced them. "You know what you're talking about, so he's going to listen to you."

"As Wade pointed out, I am intelligent; therefore, I don't need your running commentary."

"So sorry for trying to be helpful." Nikki rolled away and lay on the couch.

"I'm good at what I do," Mia said to Wade. "How does that help me be a con artist?"

Wade pulled out two chairs at the table and gestured for her to sit. "Let me explain how cons work."

Mia sat, feeling stiff and out of place, even though

she had chosen this apartment as their base of operations. Only a few weeks ago Wade had been their rival in stealing the famed Devereaux. His arrival had caused chaos. Not that he was at fault for the second forgery being found out—they'd planned all along for the forgeries to be discovered. They just hadn't planned on it happening in such a quick succession.

"The number one thing to remember about running a con is that you need to play to the mark's emotions, not his intelligence."

Nikki's arm shot up in the air. "You might need to teach her how to do emotion. There are rumors she's a robot."

"Shut up, Nikki," both Mia and Wade said.

Nikki simply devolved into laughter.

"Nikki filled me in a bit about this guy—Logan?— and she said you went out with him last night. Tell me about your date." Wade leaned forward, all his focus on her every word.

Mia recounted as much of the conversation as she could. It wasn't quite verbatim, but it was close.

When she finished, Wade leaned back. "For a novice, you accomplished a lot. You might be a natural."

"How does anything I told you help us?"

"It doesn't help your case—yet. Part of the reason, actually most of the reason, Nikki doesn't like running a con is because it takes time and patience. You're in the beginning stages, laying the groundwork and the trust. Your date put you in a good position."

"I don't understand. It just felt like a date."

"Good. That means you pulled it off."

"He directed the conversation and asked most of the questions. I didn't realize it at the time, but looking back now, I can see that. Nikki said I should steer the conversation."

Wade tilted his head to the side. "In a perfect world, yes, but since you didn't have a direction, you did pretty good. You were an excellent listener, which is something else a good artist needs to be. It felt like a date because you were swapping personal stories. He could connect to you because from the beginning, you allowed yourself to be vulnerable with him."

Mia stiffened. She didn't show vulnerability; she couldn't afford to.

"I don't mean to imply that you fell apart and needed him to take care of you. Women like you and Nikki, you'd rather die than allow that." Wade smiled as he spoke Nikki's name. "But by bringing up the realities of your life with your struggles because of your father, it was enough for him to empathize."

"Still don't see how that helps."

"And I'm seeing that you are about as patient as Nikki. So let's keep it simple. Rule one: be confident. It's the name of the game. If you're confident, you're more believable."

"No problem there," Nikki called.

"No comments needed from the peanut gallery." Mia couldn't believe she was getting another list of rules. "Go on."

"Rule two: use the mark's name when you talk to him. It helps forge a connection, makes it personal. Rule three: mimic his body language. If he leans in, so do you. If he tilts his head to the side, you mirror it. We like to see ourselves reflected in others."

"That's it? Imitation?"

"That's the beginning. It's about building trust and

rapport. Then you can exert your influence. It gets a little harder there. Rule four: let the mark win. In your case, you'll have to give him something—an idea, a tip, something useful, so he's successful. Then he'll be more likely to come back for more. Rule five: start small and build up. Ask for a small favor, nothing of consequence. Next time something a little more, but still not needy. You're building a pattern of him giving and getting used to giving."

"I think I can do that. I also think I have a way to trip him up. That painting he mentioned of his grandfather's. If I ask about that, it would be in character for me. But if he can't tell me the artist or what it looks like or anything, that chips away at his character, doesn't it?"

Wade crossed his arms. "Possibly. It depends on how well his persona was put together by the cops and whether there's any truth to the story."

"Don't forget to tell him about the kiss," Nikki blurted.

Wade stared at Mia.

"Logan kissed me at the end of our 'date.' I quipped about the date being the least painful one I'd been on recently. He felt the need to bring it up a notch."

"And did he?"

Oh my Lord, yes. "Yes."

"Okay, let me add an addendum to the rules. If you fall for the mark, you're sunk."

"You have no worries there. But I find it amusing that the two of you are going to caution me about falling for the enemy." She looked back and forth between Wade and where Nikki still lay hidden by the back of the couch.

Nikki shot up. "Yes, my dear, learn from our mistakes," she said sweetly and batted her lashes.

"I can handle a bit of attraction. I have excellent self-control."

"So you admit there's attraction."

"Well, I'm not blind."

Nikki burst out laughing. "Yeah, I guess you'd have to be to not want him."

"Hey," Wade said.

"Pheromones and physical attraction do not necessarily lead to falling for anyone." Mia stood. "I'm going home to develop a list of questions and favors to ask Logan. Tomorrow I have a meeting to gather that other information you and Audrey need." She didn't know how much Nikki revealed to Wade about their ongoing jobs, so Mia wasn't about to spill that she was going to the auction house.

Nikki saluted her.

Mia turned back to Wade. "Thank you for the lessons. Much more helpful than the so-called advice Nikki spouted yesterday."

"You're welcome," he said and stood. Turning to Nikki he said, "Ready to go home?"

"I thought you'd never ask."

To Mia, he said, "Good luck."

I'll need it.

LOGAN SPENT THE ENTIRE day trying to keep images of Mia Benson flushed from his kiss out of his mind. The task was monumental because he'd been surrounded by files from Atlas Insurance. The company had finally forwarded the policies related to all local art. Logan enlisted the help of Agent Stokes to go through the files to look for connections.

The forged paintings had been authenticated by different men, so that was another dead end. It didn't appear to be an inside job.

"What if we bring a forgery to them and have each of their guys authenticate it? If one's crooked, we can bribe him," Stokes said.

Logan leaned back in his chair. "In theory, maybe, but art appraisal isn't an exact science. At least not without running expensive tests. Most people rely on the appraisal, but you can easily have people disagree—especially if it's not in their area of expertise."

"Are you sure there's a connection? Other than these guys being friends."

"I'm sure. I just have to figure out what it is. I already know Scott and Ingram purchased within a couple weeks of each other and both planned to sell soon."

"Maybe they're riding the market. I assume the market for art fluctuates like the stock market. I'm way out of my depth here."

"What if the timing has something to do with it?"

Stokes shrugged. "Let's dig in and see how many new artifacts Atlas insured that month."

They printed reports and spread them out on a conference table. They created a timeline of art purchased five years ago. Thirty pieces consisting of paintings, sculptures, jewelry, and books.

"I think we can dump the books from the list," Logan said.

"What about the jewelry?"

"It might not quite fit the category of artwork, but I think it's easily enough forged for a quick profit."

"That only knocks down the list to twenty-eight."

There was some overlap in the agents who wrote the policies and those who did the authentication, but that would be expected. The Chicago office of Atlas Insurance wasn't that big. "Let's start looking for connections between the owners. Ingram and Scott are friends. How many others are friends with them?"

They divvied up the list and sat back with their computers. Day turned to evening and they ordered some crappy Chinese food from down the block so they could keep working. Stokes was as dogged as he was. Even though the Devereaux case was as good as closed because the original painting was with the rightful owner, she also felt it was all too fishy.

Stokes poured more rice and chicken onto her paper plate and began eating with her chopsticks. Logan had had a girlfriend try to teach him to eat with chopsticks once. He never got the hang of it, so he ate with a cheap little plastic fork. He swore the restaurant intentionally bought toddler-sized utensils to make you feel incompetent. Adults used chopsticks.

He scrolled on his computer and shoved in a mouthful of food. Scrolled and scooped. "The society pages are filled with these guys. I've already loosely connected all fourteen on my list."

"Me, too. We have to look for some deeper connections."

"Try their personal social media. Look for the parties that are personal—birthday, anniversary, vacations. Who do they hang out with because they want to? Instead of just people they know because they travel in the same circles." He couldn't believe all twenty-eight people were involved. It had to be a smaller group or someone would've noticed in the last five years.

A sudden thought struck him. "Have any of these

been sold? Did we take out the pieces where the policy is no longer in force?"

"Atlas just marks if a policy is closed. Not the reason."

"We need the reason. If they canceled the policy because they sold, we need to find out where they sold and if an authentication was done. Real artifacts can be taken off the list."

They did another deep dive into the twenty-eight pieces of art and found eight that had been sold prior to this year. "No red flags on any of these sales?"

Stokes shook her head. "They've all been picked up by other companies, so I think they would've authenticated."

"Eight more down. Now let's start with who's friends with Ingram and Scott." Logan printed a picture of each man and their forged paintings. He stuck them in the center of their board.

Then he went back to his cold dinner and social media. "I dread going on Facebook." He used it to keep up with some college buddies, but other than that, he tried not to visit too often.

"It's the only way I have to keep up with family in Florida."

"Is that where you're from?"

"Nah. I'm a Chicagoan, but my parents moved to Florida when they retired to be close to the grandbabies. How about you? I heard you just transferred from New York?"

"I've been bouncing around since finishing Quantico. New York was my longest stint at eighteen months. I've been wanting in on this office for years. This is home."

She smiled. "And if you crack this, you can write your own ticket."

"Assuming it's as big as I think it is." He clicked on another Facebook page. He just kept clicking to see who friended who and how many posts they responded to. There were a lot. "Who has time to comment on and like all these posts?"

"People who don't have real jobs." Stokes sighed. "I'm beat and these lines are starting to blur. Pick it up tomorrow?"

"I'm gonna stick it out a bit more. See you tomorrow."

She gathered her trash and tossed it in the already full can in the corner. He shoved his plate away, a small fire kindling in his gut. They'd made headway. He still couldn't see the connections, but he knew they were there.

He took a break from the looking at the art collectors and switched over to a search for Mia. She didn't have an active Facebook page. While the profile existed, she hadn't posted anything there since her father's arrest. He found an Instagram page that looked like it was hers. Lots of art pictures. He scrolled. Yeah, it was hers. She posted a picture of the lions outside the museum. She, however, appeared in very few. No candid shots of her and friends. No parties or random selfies.

Logan Freemont had a sparse social media presence. Logan Ford had less. He'd used social media to keep up with Mama Mae and when one of the kids introduced her to the latest thing, she always asked him to check it out to make sure it was safe. It was how he'd been lured into Snapchat and had even tried out Tik-Tok—only for viewing because he didn't have time to actually create videos. He preferred personal communications like texts.

A well-placed meme or gif could make someone's day and he excelled at finding just the right one to make a friend laugh. He wondered if he could get Mia to smile by sending her a gif. It might be worth a try, especially since he wanted another date. While he thoroughly enjoyed talking to her, the kiss was beyond memorable.

And if the kiss was that good, things would only get better. He opened his phone's texting app and found the message from her from when they were at the museum. Then he thought about what kind of gif to send. Something sexy but funny. Nothing too over-the-top because although he was still learning about Mia, he was sure that over-the-top wouldn't appeal to her.

He sent her Joey from *Friends* saying, "How you doin'?"

Her response? Logan?

He answered yes and then, Would you like to go to dinner tomorrow? And added a gif of Lady and the Tramp sharing a spaghetti plate.

The bubbles popped up and disappeared. She probably thought he was childish for sending gifs.

Then a gif of Moira Rose from *Schitt's Creek* appeared on his screen saying she'd like to RSVP as pending.

Looked like Mia Benson had a sense of humor. And understood pop culture better than he expected her to. He wanted to keep her playful side engaged, so he sent Alexis Rose from the same show saying, "Harsh." And then he immediately followed with Judd Nelson from *The Breakfast Club* saying, "I'm crushed."

She came back with a sexy woman. "It is what it is," and followed with Shania Twain saying, "That don't impress me much."

This time, rather than a gif, he just responded with a simple text: Let the wooing begin.

EIGHT

MIA SAT IN the outer office of McNamara's Auction House, waiting for Gwen Schafer, Caleb Small's "girl" who would give her an insider's view of the auction procedure. While she waited, she couldn't help but look back over her conversation with Logan last night. She'd felt silly at first, answering him with a gif, but it seemed to fit. And based on his reaction, it had been the right move.

She'd be lying if she said she hadn't been intrigued by his declaration of his intent to woo her. Ten years ago, men might've made the attempt, but that was simply because of her last name. Now that name was reason enough for no man to consider wooing her. She should be grateful to have their attention. As if.

No man was worth all that.

But if Logan's kiss was used to gauge his ability to woo, she was in trouble.

"Dr. Benson?" a woman called from the door.

Mia stood and met her. "Yes."

"I'm Gwen. So sorry to keep you waiting."

"No problem at all. Thank you for taking time out of your schedule for this. I've never been behind the scenes of an auction, and when Caleb told me he was planning to sell his Spenser, I became curious."

"Things are a little busy around here. Our next auction is shaping up to be one of the biggest we've had in years." She opened the door behind her and ushered Mia through. "What would you like to know?"

"I'm really interested in the process from acquisition to sale. I know what it looks like from the buyer's perspective, but now that I've been working as a curator and I know everything we have to do behind the scenes… Well, you know."

Gwen laughed lightly. "I do. Let's start where the art does. This way." She led Mia down a hall toward the back of the building.

If she were given to fanciful ideas, Mia would consider the location perfect for a serial killer scene on a crime show.

Gwen pushed open doors to a warehouse that was dim but clean. "Of course, as you're aware, the actual work starts in my office, talking to prospective sellers, arranging for pickup, delivery, and authentication. I doubt you need to witness the amount of paper shuffling I do any given day." Another light laugh.

"Our systems sound similar in that way. You arrange for the delivery of the art? I thought that was the owner's responsibility."

"It is, technically, but we offer it as an additional service. We have a number of licensed, insured contractors we work with, and it makes things easier for the owner."

They walked through the space filled with crates and shelves of items, just lying out.

As she walked by, Mia couldn't tell if any were priceless artifacts, but it still appeared very irresponsible. "You bring in the art and it just sits in this warehouse?"

Gwen turned and walked backward while she talked. "This is the receiving area. The truck comes in, we accept the delivery and uncrate it to make sure nothing was damaged." She swirled her hand around above her head. "It might not like look like much, but we have top-of-the-line security with guards monitoring the cameras twenty-four-seven."

"I'm assuming the authentication doesn't take place here. No offense, but the lighting is dreadful."

"We bring each piece to the rooms we're heading to now. I imagine they look similar to the conservation rooms at the Art Institute." They entered a hallway and Gwen opened one door and flicked on the light. It did, in fact, resemble the conservation rooms. Various types of lighting and magnifying glasses, as well as gloves and brushes. "I can't show you all of the rooms because they're being used, but they're similar to this one. As you know, authentication often lasts days."

"Sometimes longer. What happens if the authentication does require more time or an additional opinion?"

"We don't take second opinions. If our staff deems an artifact...unsuitable, we return it to the owner."

Mia smiled at the way Gwen stumbled over *unsuitable*. "Is there greater concern about forgeries as of late?"

"I assume you're referring to the Mathis and the Devereaux?"

Mia nodded.

"We have faith in our staff. We have excellent security. And we've never miscalculated the authenticity of an artifact." It wasn't boastful; Gwen simply stated fact.

Which, of course, caused huge issues for Mia and her team.

"Once a piece is authenticated?" Mia prompted.

"Then it goes to our showroom. We place every piece on display in a manner to highlight its best qualities. We photograph them and create the auction brochure." They pushed through another set of doors to a large room that was clearly divided into a staging area and a prop area.

Mia carefully looked around, as she had in each room on this journey, making sure her camera necklace captured images for Nikki. Security cameras were posted in the corners, but she didn't see any motion sensors as she had in the warehouse.

"And then the items sit here until auction day when people can view them?"

"Yes."

Mia stepped closer to a painting on the wall. It didn't look famous or terribly expensive. Even so, nothing was roped off to keep viewers at a distance. She supposed the assumption would be that wealthy people had the manners to know not to touch the art. She ran a finger over the edge of the frame. "This is beautiful."

"Please don't touch," Gwen said, the slight edge of panic in her voice.

"Sorry. I would never touch the painting. I was looking at the frame."

"I understand. But that is already set for an auction we have going tomorrow, so the security is live. If you move the painting, it will set off the alarm."

"Oh." Mia placed a hand on her chest. "I'm so sorry. Of course, I should know better. I was just thinking about how when I'm in the back, such as the conservation rooms, there are no alarms directly on the paintings."

Gwen leaned forward. "We're trying a new method with these." She pointed to a placard on the wall.

It cautioned people to not attempt to touch or move artifacts because doing so would trigger the magnetic alarm. Mia stood directly in front of the sign so Audrey would be able to get enough details to investigate, but based on the information in front of her, it seemed like stealing from the auction house was not the way to go.

Gwen led her back through the maze of rooms and halls to the front of the building.

"Thank you so much for indulging me," Mia said. "It was definitely enlightening."

"No problem. I love to talk shop with people who understand. Those outside of the art world simply don't get it."

"I know what you mean," Mia commiserated. "Let me know if there's a way for me to repay the favor. A VIP tour of the museum maybe."

All the talk of the conservation rooms and VIP tours had her thinking of Logan again.

"That would be fabulous," Gwen said.

"I'll be in touch and we can set something up." She shook Gwen's hand and stepped out into the bright late-morning sun.

Then, using her burner phone, she called Nikki. "I just finished at the auction house."

"And?"

"We're well and truly screwed."

LOGAN SAT IN THE conference room again, this time waiting for Agents Halloran and Lewis who were heading up the investigation on Benson and Towers. His search into Mia had netted very little, and as his attraction grew, he needed to make sure he could pursue her without conflict. He played on his phone while he waited, looking over their conversation from the previous night.

He'd created a challenge, and wooing Mia would require finesse and consideration. She came from money, so he didn't think gifts would win her over. No, Mia needed experiences different than what she was used to. Other than their first date over pizza, the only times he'd seen her so far was at fancy parties and fundraisers and at work. He wondered what she liked to do for fun.

The door beside him opened and two agents walked in. Logan stood and tucked his phone in his pants pocket.

The first man, who was about as tall as Logan but built like a linebacker, reached out and said, "Ron Lewis."

"Logan Ford." Then Logan turned toward the shorter man, who was barely five foot five, and shook his hand.

"Tim Halloran." He gestured for Logan to sit back down. "What can we do for you?"

"I'm working an art theft and forgery case and SSA Taggert suggested I reach out to you about some possible overlap with your Benson and Towers case."

Lewis perked up at the mention of Benson and Towers. "What do you got?"

"I don't know if it's anything, but I've met Mia Benson and I wanted to get your take on her."

"Ice princess," Halloran said. "You think she's stealing and forging art?"

"Personally, no. But seeing as the two cases we have involve men who are friends with her family...due diligence and all that."

"Oh." Lewis deflated a little.

"What do you think about Mia? Does she fit into your case at all?"

Halloran sat back and steepled his fingers in front of his mouth. He looked a little like a villain in an action movie. "She claims she knew nothing about what her father was doing."

"Do you believe her?"

"It doesn't matter what I believe. You know that. I've got no proof."

"But," Lewis said, "once he fled, she was pissed. She came at us like we hadn't been doing our job. Even paid for a PI to track him."

"Really?" Although he already knew this part, Logan didn't want them to know he'd been seeing Mia socially.

"She shared the findings with us. Looks like he and Towers are still in Montenegro, which does nothing for us, but why go to those lengths if she's in on it?"

Logan agreed.

Halloran, on the other hand, had a different take. "Maybe she's all about making sure he takes the fall. That would explain why she wouldn't authorize us to tap her phone."

"Why would you ask?"

"She came to us about week or so ago and said Dad called her looking for money. I asked if we could tap her line to get a bead on him, and she refused."

Logan couldn't blame her. That would be giving up all privacy in the hopes they could trace. And if the men were still in a non-extradition country, a trace would be pointless.

"My point is that she didn't have to tell us," Lewis said.

Logan sided with Lewis. And it had nothing to do with wanting to date her. "This case I'm on has me a little out of my depth. I was thinking about chatting her up, see if she could offer some insight into the forgeries. It's her world, you know?"

"I don't know about what she can do to help you, but I'd keep an eye on her. She's smart. I'll give her that. Maybe too smart."

Halloran definitely had it in for the Benson family.

"You think she's into something?" Logan listened to his gut all the time, but maybe Halloran's gut was attuned to something Logan was missing.

Lewis waved his hand. "Nah. He just hates 'em all. Those rich, think-we're-better-than-you types."

"*Hate* is a strong word. I dislike them because they think they can do whatever they want without having to face the consequences. Decades—hell, centuries—have taught them that they're above the law."

Logan nodded. He'd seen his share of rich assholes, but Mia hadn't looked down on him, and he was obviously not in the same social bracket. He stood. "Thanks for your time. I appreciate it."

"Before we head out, can you tell me what family friends are involved in your case?" Halloran whipped out a small notebook.

"Randall Scott had a painting that was discovered to be a forgery when he went to sell. He swears it was legit when he got it. A painting was stolen from Max Ingram's house. Within a couple days, it was delivered to the Carlisle Museum, which as it turns out is the rightful owner. Ingram had bogus papers. But then in a weird twist, the one in the museum was a forgery and the original was confiscated in an FBI bust after a tip."

"Sounds like the soap operas my mom used to watch," Lewis said.

Logan lifted his arms as if to say, "What can I say?"

Halloran scribbled his notes. "I'll check my files and let you know, but those names sound vaguely familiar."

"And I'll let you know if I find any crossover with your case."

They said goodbye and Logan went back to the other conference room, where he'd left Eden Stokes still researching the art bought and sold over the last five years.

Logan walked the length of the table and looked at the photos she had spread out. It appeared as though she'd made some headway, but he couldn't make sense of her system.

"Dude. You were totally onto something with the dates." She jumped up from her chair, forcing him to step back. She shoved the chair away and pointed at the pictures. "Of the twenty purchases we narrowed down that haven't been sold, fourteen are friends with Ingram and Scott."

"Not too surprising. They run in the same circles."

"Yes, well, the fact that they all bought around the same time five years ago got me to thinking that maybe it wasn't a coincidence. There was some impetus behind the purchases."

Logan waited, as it seemed like she was running up to a big reveal.

"Guess who else was friends with these fourteen men?"

Logan's stomach sank. He suddenly had a feeling about where this was headed.

"Dwayne Benson and Cesar Towers. They fled five years ago. I wasn't anywhere near the case, but the whole city was watching. It was the financial world's equivalent to watching one of Illinois's governors— Blagojevich or Ryan—getting hauled in."

"Okay. So Benson and Towers hit the road and their

friends drop a ton of money on art. And?" He had ideas, but he wanted to see if she came to similar conclusions.

"I think they might be funneling money to them."

That's where Logan arrived, too. He nodded. "I just came from talking to the agents on that case. Benson called his daughter, Mia, a couple weeks ago looking for money."

Stokes clapped. "Oh. That's it then." A moment later, she narrowed her eyes. "How do the forgeries fit?"

"Maybe they're keeping the original and trying to sell the forgery. Get their friends money without actually losing anything."

"Makes sense. We should go back to the ones that have sold and have them authenticated again, you think? Maybe they've already gotten away with it."

Logan circled the table again, studying the photos. Most of these men he'd seen at the functions he'd attended over the past couple of weeks. The tightness in his chest loosened a little with the knowledge that Mia had not done any purchasing. She most likely wasn't part of the scam. "Unless she's the one making the sales. Or the forgeries," he said under his breath.

"What was that?" Stokes asked.

"Nothing. Just thinking." Halloran's attitude had definitely burrowed into his head. He tapped Keaton Bishop's picture. "I overheard that he's selling soon." He closed his eyes and replayed the conversation between Mia and Chad. "A Moreau. Hideous from what I understand."

Stokes scattered pages and snatched a picture from the table. "This is it! If we follow this painting, we might be able to catch them."

He looked at the photograph of the painting. It was

hideous. "Atlas believes Bishop has the original. I'll call them and see if they can arrange an inspection before he sells."

"What if it turns out to be a forgery already? Then we tip our hand."

"And if they know Atlas is looking, they'll either sit and wait, lulling Atlas back into security, or they'll dump them faster. Atlas can't be everywhere at once." Logan pulled out a chair and sat. "We need an undercover inspection. Someone to look at it and determine if it's authentic without Bishop knowing."

"You got the chops for that?"

"I'm faking this job all over the place. But I have an idea." Randall Scott had called Mia. She probably had the knowledge to be able to assess the painting. He just couldn't decide if asking for her help would be advantageous or risky.

NINE

MIA PACED THE living room in the apartment while Nikki and Audrey studied the video she made of the auction house.

"The warehouse is covered in security. If we wait until it's in the showroom, it's already been authenticated, and replacing it there won't matter. It would just make McNamara's appear fraudulent." Which would mean that insurance would pay out and her father would still have access to the money.

"What if I get them in the room? Between the warehouse and showroom when they're doing their tests?"

"How are you going to get in?" Mia asked.

"I'll figure it out."

Audrey ran the footage again. "Maybe Mia has a point. How fast can we create a plan to snag them from their houses?"

"I don't know when they're being picked up. It could be mere days." Mia didn't like feeling this stressed. She planned and accounted for a myriad of possibilities so she was not caught off guard.

"That's okay. We got this." Nikki stood in front of the TV, looking more alert than Mia had ever seen her. "How are things coming with Logan?"

Mia blinked rapidly at the sudden change of topic. "I don't know. He asked to see me again and did some flirting via gifs last night. He plans to woo me."

"That sounds promising," Audrey said.

It sounded horrendous to Mia. She couldn't afford to have her attention split in so many directions. The museum exhibit, the heists and all that went with those, and now fake dating Logan Freemont. She didn't see the point. "I think we should just avoid contact with him and go about our business."

"That's walking away from free information. If we know where he's coming from, then we can avoid him or misdirect him. We won't be taken by surprise," Nikki said, her eyes never leaving the TV screen. "You did a really good job of capturing all the security here. I'm impressed. We might make a thief out of you yet."

Mia waved her hand. "I've no desire to be a thief."

Nikki snickered. "A little late for that, babe."

"I'm sure you know what I mean." The easy way with which Nikki spoke with her was another chink in Mia's armor. She was beginning to really like these women. They were becoming a part of her life in ways she never expected. In less than two months, her entire life had changed. What would it look like two months from now?

The heists should be over. With a little luck, her father would be back in the States facing charges. Audrey and Nikki would move on—quite possibly to legitimate employment. Where would she be?

Maybe when this was all over, she could enjoy time with Logan—or someone like him. She could find what Jared and Audrey had found: someone who understood and accepted them for who they were. The problem was, right now, she wasn't sure she knew who she was anymore.

She refocused on the video Nikki was studying.

"I don't think they have the hallway monitored, and I didn't see any security in the authentication rooms. But all of the spaces on either side are covered from every angle. Have you looked at Caleb's and Keaton's houses?"

"We don't have much to go on. Satellite photos as an overview, and the random sketches you offered," Audrey pointed out. "And like you said, we don't know when they're moving. We could devote all of our time to planning on going into their houses, only to miss our opportunity."

"I bet Logan would know," Mia said. "He works for Atlas—or at least he's pretending to—so he would know when something he's insuring would be moved. Not alerting Atlas about a move could void the insurance."

Nikki crossed her arms. "Do you think you could get the information from him without tipping him off?"

"Let's hope so." Mia gathered her things and went to work. She had a full day of meetings and calls about her exhibit, and tonight was her weekly dinner with her mother. She needed time to plan her date with Logan. She wanted to appear willing but not eager to spend time with him.

Although she was tempted to play his gif game, she opted for a direct approach. She sent a simple text asking about his great-grandfather's missing painting. If it was real, she would probably be able to find some information, unless of course, it was imaginary or had always been off the grid.

She sat in her office attempting to read emails and staring at her phone, waiting for his response. Which just irritated her more. She no longer waited on men.

About twenty minutes later, he responded. Sorry. I was in a meeting and didn't want to explain to my boss that I was texting my girlfriend.

I am far from being your girlfriend.

That's only because I haven't kicked my wooing into full gear. You won't be able to resist.

She responded with a laughing-crying emoji.

Laugh it up now. I can be very persuasive. You'll see.

The promise in his words caused a flutter in her belly. *Stop it. This is a job.* She couldn't afford to be persuaded by the likes of Logan Freemont. *Focus.* Information about the painting?

You were serious? I thought that was a ploy to have a reason to text me. Are you free for dinner tonight?

Mia should say no because of her standing date with her mother. But ferreting out where Logan was in his investigation to see if she and her team were at risk was more important. It didn't escape her, though, that he didn't answer her question about the painting. I might be able to shuffle some things. I'll let you know.

His response? A toddler doing a happy dance.

She called her mother—Beverly Washington didn't text—to cancel their dinner plans.

"What other plans do you have?" Mama asked.

"A date."

Her mother's sharp intake of breath irked her. It wasn't as if she never dated.

"Is it serious?"

"We just met." If she told her mother it wasn't serious, Beverly would question why he was worthy of canceling their dinner. If Mia said it was serious, Beverly would want to meet him. Life as the child of a lawyer taught her to be cautious with her words.

"Do I know him?"

Mia smiled. "No. He's new to town."

"Where did you meet?"

"At a party at Max Ingram's house."

"Then who does he know?"

Mia wished she could see her mother's face for this part. "He doesn't. Not in the way you mean. He's a business acquaintance. He works for the company that insures Max's art." She was met with silence. "He's very funny and charming."

"I would like to meet him."

"If we last more than a few dates, I'll consider it. I see no need to scare a man off because my shark of a lawyer mother wants to interrogate him."

"I don't want to interrogate him. He's the first man you've mentioned in years. I want to meet the man who had the ability to finally turn your head."

Mia shuffled papers on her desk. Lying to her mother had never come easily, but after her father's deception, she and her mother agreed to be honest with each other even when it was uncomfortable. "Are you sure you aren't just making sure the Washington fortune is safe? As an insurance agent, he doesn't have family money. That's what makes him different."

"You know I don't care about that. That's what pre-nups are for."

Mia *did* know. Her mother had married her father even though he had nothing. She'd just assumed her mother would expect more from her.

"We are absolutely nowhere near the nuptials phase, so you can put your legalese away. Give me a chance to see if this goes anywhere."

"Fine, but I expect a full report at dinner next week."

"Yes, Mama. Have a good night." She clicked off and texted Logan to ask when and where she should meet him.

"READY FOR A TRIP?" Logan asked Stokes.

"Where to?"

"We need to talk to Max Ingram again. And Troy Evans, the man who donated the Devereaux to the Carlisle. There's a thread we're missing and I need to find it." He tossed her keys. "You drive. I have to do some research while we're on the move."

He didn't mention that the research involved planning his date with Mia. If he wanted to woo her, it had to be something better than a fancy candlelit dinner and a bottle of wine. He did some looking online and about ten minutes into his search, he decided he needed help. He glanced at Stokes. She was a woman, but he didn't want anyone at the Bureau to know he was going on a date with Mia Benson. He texted four of his foster sisters who had all grown up at Mama Mae's with him. It was a move he might regret, but he needed ideas fast.

Suddenly, he was in a rapid-fire text chain.

Sam: Cooking class—you need all the help you can get.

Carmen: Salsa night

Sam: Ohhh… I don't know if dancing is a good idea. Have we seen him dance?

Logan shook his head. I dance just fine. Carmen taught me to salsa, so if I suck, it's her fault.

Hana: Scrabble at The Darling. But salsa is cute.

Logan: She would definitely kick my butt at Scrabble. He imagined Mia was one of those girls who memorized every word that might've appeared on the SAT.

Jill: Brewery tour.

Logan: I would enjoy that. I don't think she's much of a beer drinker.

Jill: They have distillery tours too. Like a pub crawl but with whiskey.

Sam: How many dates in are you? Untitled has an awesome burlesque show. But that's for sure not first date material.

Logan: We're definitely not burlesque level yet.

Yet? Did he think this was going to go further? Definitely. As long as she wasn't involved with the forgeries.

Jill: A simple date at a nice restaurant isn't enough?

He wasn't sure how to explain that Mia's idea of nice and his were far apart. Plus, that was the kind of thing the men in her circle would do. Sure, they might fly her to Paris for that nice dinner, but it was still dinner. I want to do something different and fun. Thanks for all the suggestions. You've given me plenty to think about.

Sam: So when do we get to meet her?

Logan: You don't. He followed it with a gif of Taylor Swift saying that will never ever, ever happen.

Carmen: But we need to vet her like you do to our dates.

Logan sent another *Schitt's Creek* gif of David saying, "Absolutely not."

Then he put his phone away.

"That was a lot of texting," Stokes said, still zooming down the highway.

"My sisters."

"How many do you have?"

He hated that question because it always led to a lengthy discussion of why he had so many. "A lot. I grew up in foster care and my mom took in a lot of kids over the years."

"And you all keep in touch?"

"Yep. Mom wouldn't have it any other way."

"Cool." Then she dropped it.

Logan was really enjoying working with Eden Stokes. She was smart and quick and didn't mind the grunt work.

"Did you talk to Troy Evans after you got the Devereaux back?" Logan asked.

"I didn't personally. There's a statement in the file from him. He had the provenance papers to prove his father had been the rightful owner. Other than that, I don't think anyone thought it was important."

"Let me question Ingram. We've already been in touch."

"What do you hope to learn?"

"I want to know where he got the painting. I couldn't find a purchase record, but he obviously thought he had the real thing. And if it was real, who took it? Was it Troy Evans or are there other players involved?"

"You sure he'll talk without a lawyer?"

"I'm just from Atlas Insurance, trying to figure out what happened. I think he has more answers than he's let the cops in on."

"Why would he talk to you, though?"

"I'll try to convince him that we can get him money for his troubles. Money talks to these men, right? Unless you have a better plan?"

"Go for it." She took the off-ramp at Townline Road and wound through the lush, North Shore suburbs.

When he was a kid, he'd only gone as far north as Evanston, and he'd thought that was like entering a new world. But this, this was a different galaxy compared to the bustling concrete city. Trees so big that the boughs from each side of the street nearly touched in the middle of the avenue. Bright green lawns with no patches of brown. Houses that were as big as some of the apartment complexes he'd lived in before moving in with Mae. Even as an adult, he was a little awestruck at the size and beauty of everything.

Stokes pulled into Max Ingram's driveway and they walked to the front door. Dogs barked and growled inside. Then a woman shushed them.

The door opened a crack and Mrs. Ingram's face appeared in the small space. "Yes?"

"Hi, Mrs. Ingram. Logan Freemont from Atlas Insurance. We met a couple of weeks ago at a party here. We're here to talk with Max? We had a few more questions."

"Oh, of course. Give me a minute to put the dogs outside." The door closed and a few minutes later, she was back sans dogs. "Sorry, Zeus and Apollo are very protective. Max is in his office upstairs."

She turned and led them up the winding staircase to the second floor. As they moved through the house, Logan took note of the security.

"The night your son had the pool party and the Devereaux was stolen, was security engaged?"

The woman shook her head. "Brad rarely remembers to set the alarm and since it was an impromptu gathering, he didn't hire our usual security staff to keep guests away from private rooms."

She knocked on a door and opened it without waiting for a response. "Max, the insurance agent is here with more questions." She swung the door wide and turned back to them. "Can I get you anything to eat or drink?"

"No, we're good. Thank you." Logan crossed the room to where Max rose behind his desk. "Mr. Ingram, sorry to bother you again. This is Eden, my partner."

"Since when do insurance agents need a partner? Gabe always came alone."

"Gabe?"

"The agent who sold me the policy for the Devereaux."

He flicked a thumb behind him to where a hinged frame remained empty. "Please have a seat."

Logan and Stokes sat in the cool leather chairs in front of the desk and Ingram sat in his chair opposite them.

Logan pointed up at the empty frame and the safe behind it. "Was anything taken from the safe that night?"

"No. Just the painting."

"That's good. Not about the painting, but you know." Logan let out a breath. "I've been going over the file, and while I see the information provided when we wrote the policy, I don't see a receipt. You provided provenance that proved to be bogus—that Gabe unfortunately missed—but I can't find where you purchased the painting."

"That's because I didn't."

Stokes shifted forward in her seat. Logan waited for an explanation.

"I won it in a poker game. My friend had a crappy hand, but he was sure he could bluff. I've got the better poker face."

At the mention of a friend, Logan's Spidey sense tingled. "Can I ask the name of your friend? It might help us figure things out if we can trace where the painting came from."

Ingram chuckled. "Good luck with that. The bastard skipped town. Dwayne Benson traded me that painting in a poker game more than eight years ago."

Fuck me. Logan kept his expression neutral, regardless of his rapid heartbeat. "Do you have any reason to believe that Mr. Benson intentionally gave you a forgery?"

"Do you know who Dwayne Benson is?"

"I've heard the name."

"He was indicted for fraud. We were friends for decades and we made a lot of money together. That said, he had shady business dealings that caught up to him. He's probably sunning on some island right now, enjoying the money he absconded with."

Logan only believed about a third of what the man said. Ingram had probably known about Benson's scam the whole time. He profited from his friend's business. "So you think he was aware it was fake and passed it off as real? Any idea where he got it?"

"None. Have you found any connections between my son's party guests and whoever sold the painting?"

"Not that the police have shared with us."

"I'm just out all the money I paid your company for years to insure that painting." Irritation filled the man's face.

"It would be a different story if we can prove you were the rightful owner and had it stolen from you. Then you'd get a payout. Right now, there are still too many unanswered questions."

"Figures."

Logan took that as a sign that they were dismissed. "Thank you for your time. We'll let you know if we find anything out."

At the door, Logan turned back. "One more thing. Your wife said the dogs are very protective. Where were they the night of the theft?"

"My son said someone locked them in the pantry."

"That wasn't in the police report."

"We found out after the fact. Once Brad sobered the following day and I had him recall the entire evening.

He didn't think it was important. He figured it had been an accident."

Accident, my ass. That was how someone was able to go upstairs and steal the painting. No alarm, no dogs.

Once they were back in the car, Stokes started the engine. "Benson keeps popping up. You think the story is true?"

Logan shrugged. "He could be a convenient scapegoat. Or it could be true. All these men are shady."

Midday traffic wasn't too bad as they traveled back into the city to meet with Troy Evans at his office in Lincoln Park. They parked at a meter a half block from Evans's office. As they walked in the hot summer sun, Logan asked, "You want to take the lead on this one?"

"You sure?"

"You know this end of the case far better than I do."

"Okay."

Logan opened the door and let Stokes walk through first. At the reception desk, she flashed her badge at the receptionist and let her know that Mr. Evans was expecting them. The secretary made a quick call and directed us to his office. Evans was an accountant and his office was nice, but not able-to-afford-a-Devereaux nice.

The office door was open, but Stokes knocked before entering. Troy Evans stood as Stokes entered.

"Hi, Mr. Evans. Thank you for seeing us on such short notice. Agent Eden Stokes, and this is Agent Logan Ford."

Logan blinked because it had been a while since someone had introduced him using his real name. He'd been Logan Freemont for weeks.

"Please take a seat." He resumed his position behind

his desk. "Honestly, I don't know what else I can tell you. I gave the police a statement."

"You donated the Devereaux to the Carlisle Museum."

"Yes. It had been my father's wishes."

"How did the Devereaux happen to come into your possession?"

Evans leaned back in his chair and pressed his lips together. "I need to speak to my lawyer before I answer that question."

Stokes held up her hands. "We're not here to put you in a bind, Mr. Evans. We're just trying to get to the truth. We know Max Ingram had what he believed to be the original Devereaux and it was stolen from his house two nights before you delivered it to the Carlisle."

"I did not steal it from Mr. Ingram."

Stokes paused, on the verge of saying more, measuring her words. "Hypothetically, maybe you had a friend find it for you."

"Something like that. I hired a retrieval specialist."

"Do you currently have a way to contact this specialist?"

"No. The transactions only occurred online. The painting was couriered to me."

As they suspected, this had been a dark web transaction. They wouldn't find a trace.

"Do you know the name of the courier company?" Logan asked.

"No."

"When you received the painting, did you have any reason to think your specialist had given you a forgery?"

"Absolutely not. In fact, I'm one hundred percent sure that the painting I handed to the Carlisle was authentic."

"Then how do you explain the real painting being picked up in an FBI raid?" Logan asked.

"I have no answer for that. But I will say that my father had the Devereaux in his private den my entire childhood. I'm no expert, but I believe it was real."

Stokes shot Logan a look that said she didn't know what else to ask. They were still running in circles. They rose. Stokes slid her card on the man's desk. "Thank you for your time. If you think of anything else, please give me a call."

"I have no idea what happened after I handed the painting over to the Carlisle. While my methods might not have been totally legal, the painting didn't belong to Max Ingram."

Logan held up a hand. "Do you know when it went missing from your father's estate?"

"No. That's what made it so difficult to file a report. My father died suddenly and my mother had been so distraught that she never stepped foot in his den. When lawyers and financial advisers came to her with questions, she just pointed them in the direction of the den." He stood and extended a hand. "Sorry I couldn't be more help."

Logan mulled over the man's words. Financial advisers had gone to Evans's house. He'd be willing to place money that one of those advisers had been Dwayne Benson. It would explain how Benson came to have the painting in his possession.

Logan and Eden drove back to the office in silence. He felt like they finally had the frame of this puzzle assembled, but they still had no idea what the picture was.

After parking, Stokes turned to him. "What now?"

"I think we need to look at the piece that doesn't belong—the Carlisle."

TEN

STOKES STARED AT Logan for a beat. "Are you implying my investigation into the forgery at the Carlisle wasn't good enough?"

"No. We have a different angle now. When you investigated, you had your collar. It wasn't about the painting as much as it was about getting Wolf behind bars. This guy Dodger that you made a deal with. How did he get his hands on the Devereaux?"

"He didn't say. Just told me that the real one was in his possession and the one at the museum was fake." She paused. "And you're right. I didn't care about how or even why. I was after Wolf."

He checked the time. It was getting late in the day and he had a date. "Let's divide and conquer. I'll reinterview Dodger. You go to the museum and see what you can gather there. Tomorrow we'll reconvene and see if we can connect more dots."

"What about getting a look at the Moreau?"

"I'm going to work on that tonight. Dodger still in custody?"

"Nah. We cut him loose. He'll go to trial but probably not serve more than a couple months in county. I promised him a deal to get Wolf."

"That's fine. Can you text me his address?" Logan gathered his things and by the time he reached his car, Stokes had sent the address. Damn. He should've taken the museum. Dodger lived on the South Side, which would make it hard for him to get home and change. He didn't want to flake on Mia, so he was just going to have to drive fast.

When he drove through Dodger's neighborhood, Logan's first thought was that this was not where a high-end art thief lived. On the other hand, no one here would blink twice at criminal activity. He squeezed into a spot with his back bumper just over the yellow line for the fire hydrant. Hopefully, he'd be out of here before he had to talk a cop into not giving him a ticket.

A few people were hanging out on porches and at the corner. They all inched away or flat-out scattered as he made his way up the front walk. Guess he looked like a cop.

He climbed the steps to 2B and when he got in front of the door, he raised his hand to knock, but it swung open. A man about his age, a few inches shorter than him with light brown hair, jolted at his presence.

"Can I help you?"

"I'm looking for Jack Russo." He held up his badge.

The man's blue eyes flashed, surprised before becoming a mask, and he looked over his shoulder. "What'd you do now, Dodger? FBI is here."

"I haven't done a thing." A much older man crossed the room and met them at the door. He lifted a pant leg. "Monitor's still intact, so whatever it is, I didn't do it."

Logan smiled. "I just have a few more questions about the Devereaux."

The other man said, "I'll let you get to that. I was just on my way out."

Then he skirted around Logan and left.

"May I come in? This shouldn't take long."

Dodger moved away from the door. "Does it matter if I say no? Close the door behind you."

Logan crossed the threshold and was assaulted by the smells of Italian food and stale beer. It was like a frat house gone wrong.

Dodger shuffled over to a battered couch and sank down. Once seated, he grabbed a to-go container off the table and began eating.

Logan glanced at the other furniture and opted to stand. "I've spoken with Agent Stokes, who handled the arrest and your deal. I know you called her and explained that the Devereaux at the Carlisle was fake. How did you know that?"

"Because I had the real one?" The old man looked at him like he was stupid, as he shoved another forkful of pasta in his mouth.

"And how did you come into possession of the real one?"

"How do you think? I stole it."

"From where?"

The old man's brows furrowed and his mouth hung open. After a brief moment, he said, "The guy's house."

"Max Ingram?"

"If you say so. The owner of the house doesn't mean anything to me, just the contents."

Logan wasn't buying it. If it required breaking and entering, maybe. But this crotchety old man would've stuck out. Someone would've seen him and remembered him. He was too suspicious looking. "How did you take it?"

"What's with the twenty questions? I just admitted to stealing. Isn't that enough?"

"No." Logan lowered himself to sit on the arm of the

chair across from Dodger. "I don't think you have it in you to steal something that valuable in the middle of a party full of young people."

"Drunk people don't pay attention. I should know— it's my preferred way to be."

"Why'd you steal it?"

"It's worth millions and I owed Donny, and therefore Wolf, a whole lotta money. Wolf wanted the Devereaux. I wanted to be done with him."

"How did the Carlisle end up with a forgery?"

"How should I know? Never been to the place."

"So you expect us to believe that the very same week that you steal the Devereaux from Ingram's house, a random forgery just happens to be donated to the museum."

The man laughed. "Crazy world, right?"

Logan didn't believe in coincidence. "Who are you covering for?"

"Why would I cover for anyone?"

Logan didn't have an answer, but Dodger's story was full of holes. He just hoped that Stokes had better luck at the museum. He rose and tossed his card on the stained coffee table. "I'm not looking to jam you up any more than you already are. I'm just looking for the truth. I think someone out there is passing off forgeries and I want to know who. Call me if you think of anything."

He left the smelly apartment and prayed the stench hadn't clung to him. In his car, he texted Mia the address of his favorite restaurant and suggested a time to meet. On the drive back to his house, the feeling that they were on the verge of fitting pieces together settled over him. Taking the night to clear his head would allow him to go at it fresh in the morning.

MIA SAT IN THE back of her car share ride and replayed all of Wade's hints for running a con. She was letting Logan win by going on this date, even though she knew nothing of his plans.

Even though all he'd said was to dress comfortably.

In something that would keep her cool.

That she wouldn't mind getting messy.

Which pretty much ruled out most of her wardrobe. But she was rolling with it because it also showed confidence. She could handle herself no matter where they landed. As long as it wasn't outdoorsy and athletic.

"Be confident. Use his name. Mimic his body. Let him win. Start small." She repeated the five rules like a mantra, no different than when she had to study for finals.

When the driver pulled up in front of a little Mexican restaurant, Mia just stared.

"This is the address you gave me. You gettin' out?"

"Yes. Sorry." She opened the door and stepped out, squinting in the early evening sun. She slipped her sunglasses on her face and repeated the mantra one last time.

The car pulled away and Mia looked around for Logan. Suddenly, he was there, stepping around a potted plant near the outdoor dining area. He waved and flashed her a grin that was charming and sweet. One that said he was happy she showed up.

No falling for the mark, she reminded herself as she walked closer. When she stood right in front of him, she said, "Logan." A short nod and small smile to deter him from leaning in to kiss her.

"I'm so glad you could make time for a date with me."

"Just to be clear," she said, pointing at the restaurant behind him. "You plan to woo me with tacos?"

"So little faith." He stretched out his arms to guide her toward the door. "It's Taco Tuesday and this is one of those hidden gems of the city. Only locals know about it."

He opened the glass door that held signs regaling the quality of their homemade salsa—Best in the city!—as well as their weekly discounted tacos. Logan put his hand on her lower back as they stepped into the restaurant. When they reached the hostess, he said, "Table for two." He looked down at Mia. "On the patio?"

"That's fine."

"Right this way." The hostess grabbed menus—plastic—and silverware—wrapped in paper napkins—and led them back outside through a side entrance.

The outdoor seating was quaint but crowded. Pitchers of margaritas flowed freely with this crowd. The space was bustling, but quiet enough for people to engage in conversation without yelling. The chairs were painted in bright blues, oranges, and turquoise. Logan pulled out the chair for her.

He sat and the waitress immediately arrived with glasses of water and rattled off the evening's specials. Instead of reading the menu, he said, "If you trust me, I'll order for both of us."

"All right." She smiled. *Another win for Logan.* This was becoming a bit tedious. She liked to win, too. Which reminded her of Wade's warning about patience.

Logan placed an order of what seemed like an overabundance of food. When the waitress left, his attention returned to her. "How was work?"

"Long. Busy. I had meetings all day for a big exhibit I'm planning."

"Really? What's the exhibit about?"

"Crime and punishment."

"Like the novel?"

"No, as in crimes people commit and the consequences they suffer because of them. Revenge. Retribution. Rehabilitation." She sipped her water. "I had the idea after my father left the country. I thought it would give me something to focus on, and now my small exhibit is going to be the major event of our fall season."

"Wow. So you've been planning this for years?"

"Yes. A lot of research is needed to figure out what we want the exhibit to be and then determine what pieces we have versus what pieces we'd like to borrow from other museums or private collections. We're at the stage now where we have to design the space and choose the most prominent pieces. We have an ancient Chinese tapestry that shows how prisoners were punished. The Met in New York is lending us a Vallotton lithograph from *Crimes and Punishments*."

He put his elbows on the table and leaned forward, nothing distracting him. He stared directly into her eyes, as if every word she spoke mattered.

Mimic his body language.

She, too, leaned forward with a smile. "Thank you for indulging me."

"Indulging you?"

"I know my job doesn't interest most people. But you're not rolling your eyes, cutting me off, or looking for something more interesting."

"In general, I find most people are shitty. And I find your job fascinating. People take the work behind an exhibit for granted. I've never given it much thought. You just go to the museum and stuff is collected there. I never considered how that collection actually happens." He held her gaze for a few more beats.

The waitress arrived with a bowl of chips and a selection of salsas. Logan leaned back, and when the waitress left, he pointed at each bowl. "Mild, medium, and scorch your pants."

She took a chip, broke it in half and went straight for the hot. "A little heat never scared me."

"Daring. I like it." He helped himself to a blend of medium and hot.

"And how was work for you, Logan?"

"Busy. I had to meet with some clients and we're still running down leads on where those forgeries came from."

"What do the police say?"

"Local police are pretty much out of it now since the Devereaux is with its rightful owner. The FBI will probably bring in experts to look at the forgery to try to figure out who made it. It's a strange coincidence that a forgery was delivered to the museum at the same time the original was stolen from Max Ingram."

"How is it your job as an insurance agent to run around chasing leads? Isn't that the job of the police?"

He didn't even blink at her accusation that he wasn't doing his job. He didn't know that she suspected he was law enforcement. She figured he might give a clue when she said that. But nothing.

"It boils down to using resources where they're needed most. Right now, there is no crime. The man who stole the Devereaux from Max Ingram is in custody. While Randall Scott says he was robbed, there's no evidence to support that."

Damn, I'm good. As long as Nikki's father didn't let anything slip, they were free. "Where do you go from there then?" She took another chip and ate even though his answers mattered far more than eating. But it was good salsa.

"We've pulled records of all of the policies we have in the area, and we're checking on them. We need to make sure it's not a whole forgery ring."

"Running audits?" If they were inspecting pieces, that would give her a timeline to make sure that Nikki stole them after Atlas authenticated them. Then when the men tried to sell, they would look like the criminals they were.

"Not quite. I can't get authorization to just go into people's homes and say we need to look at your art."

"I would think the policy would provide for some measure."

"It does, but the bosses don't want to ruffle feathers. If it is a forgery ring and we go in and authenticate a piece before they make the switch, we'll have egg on our face. It would make our company look like we have no clue what's real and what's not."

She sipped her water. "So you have to wait to be asked to authenticate?"

The waitress returned with two huge platters of food. Rows of tacos sat on one plate, and the other held heaping piles of rice and beans.

Mia opened her paper napkin and laid it across her lap. "Exactly how many people do you think you're feeding?"

"Just us. But they're really good tacos. Plus, they're cheap so we can take the leftovers home and have them for breakfast." He smiled as he loaded his plate with food.

Mia helped herself to a taco and some rice. She added a generous helping of salsa to the taco.

Logan held up a hand. "You are going to pick that up and eat, right?"

She looked at him, puzzled. "How else would I eat it?"

He shrugged. "Last time we shared a meal, you ate your pizza with a knife and fork."

"That would be more difficult to do with a taco." She folded the soft shell over and picked up the taco.

He rolled his eyes. "So you would prefer to eat that way?"

"Using utensils makes it less messy." As if to prove her point, a glob of salsa plopped onto her plate.

"Sometimes getting messy is a whole lot of fun."

She bit into her taco with another reminder: No falling for the mark.

LOGAN WAS HAVING A great time talking with Mia. She was still pretty formal, but she seemed more relaxed than usual. As far as he was concerned, it was a step in the right direction. They enjoyed their meal for a bit before he broached the subject that he wanted to run by her, even though he didn't have authorization to bring Mia in.

"You're right about the authentications. Right now, my bosses just want us to wait to see if something else happens, but I want to be more proactive."

She dabbed a napkin on her mouth. "How so?"

"At the gallery last week, you mentioned that Keaton Bishop was selling his Moreau painting. Do you think if he let you look at it, you would be able to tell if it's a forgery?"

Her eyes widened and she sat back in her seat. "I'm not sure."

"You looked at Randall Scott's Mathis and knew it was a forgery."

"There were obvious signs. I would think if the forger was really good, I wouldn't be able to tell. You'd have to run actual tests. Besides, what happens if it is a forgery?"

"We cancel the policy and don't pay out, unless he can produce a police report showing that it was stolen. Otherwise it appears that he's attempting to defraud Atlas as well as any potential buyer."

She leaned forward again and her bright eyes focused on his. "What if I'm wrong? I'm not a trained, certified appraiser."

"I'm not looking for a guarantee. If you raise a red flag, I can get an appraiser in. If you say it's real, then we can watch it. Wait to see if someone makes a switch. With any luck, we can catch them in the act."

She became quiet in a studious way, and Logan thought he'd lost her. He'd rolled the dice and if Taggert caught wind of him dating Mia and then asking her to step in like this, he might lose his chance at the permanent transfer to Chicago. It might even be a ding in his file. But he couldn't keep spinning his wheels. If he didn't catch a break in this case soon, he'd be bumped somewhere else anyway.

Mia crossed her arms and a sly smile slid across her face. "Logan, I think you are one sneaky insurance agent. This is far above and beyond your job description." She angled her head and her hair slipped down her back, revealing the column of her neck.

Logan had the urge to stroke the smooth tan skin. He

wanted to feel the pulse of her heartbeat under his palm.
The flutter of her breath against his lips. Speaking of
lips...hers were moving again and he didn't hear her.

"I'm sorry. What was that?"

She licked her lips and leaned her arms on the table,
bringing her face close enough to touch. He fisted his
hands in his lap to keep his impulses in check. Her smile
sparked brighter. The sun caught the deep auburn in her
hair that he hadn't noticed before, making it look warm,
begging for his touch.

"I asked why. Why do you care so much about whether
these men are trying to sell forgeries? I understand that
Atlas doesn't want to lose money. But this feels...personal."

Whoa. This was getting too personal. He'd spent the
last five minutes thinking about kissing her instead of
looking for evidence that she might be in on this scam.

He sat back in his chair to create much-needed distance. "I'm going to tell you the truth, and I hope what
I say won't offend you or ruin the rest of our night, because I am having a great time with you."

Her crooked smirk remained on her face, but her
eyes sharpened, as if she were expecting a blow and
braced for it.

"Remember how I told you that my great-grandfather
had a painting that was stolen?"

She nodded.

"That was all he had of value. I look at the rich men
who have more money than half the city, but it's like
it's not enough. They're willing to cheat and steal to
get more. They might not be stealing from a little guy
like my grandpa, but it bothers me on a personal level.
I can't stomach seeing them get away with it."

Her gaze softened. "Why did you think that would offend me?"

"You're friends with these men. You've spent your life around them and others like them."

She nodded. "And then there's my father, who is the supreme crooked rich man. One who did steal from the little guy."

"Well, yeah."

"I'll let you in on a not so little secret." She crooked her finger and it was like a string lifting him forward, pulling him into her mesmerizing bubble.

When he was close enough that the soft scent of her perfume surrounded him, she said quietly, "I hate what my father did. I think these men are as guilty as my father and uncle." She narrowed her eyes and gave him an assessing look. "Did you know they profited from my father's scam?"

"What? Why weren't they indicted?"

"They all claimed that my father simply invested money for them. It had been the luck of the draw that they profited while others lost everything. I guess the authorities had no proof that they are just as guilty." She finished her glass of water and sat back. "So, your reasons have no chance of offending me. And if there's anything I can do to help you bring these cheating, lying men down, count me in."

In that moment, Logan was positive that Mia Benson was nothing like her father.

"How do you propose we get Keaton to let me assess the Moreau painting?"

"I have no idea. I'm making this up as I go. After seeing you lay into Bishop's son at the gallery, I had the realization that those people are part of your world.

You can navigate it in ways I never could. But I've seen no signs that you're like them."

"If you had met me five years ago, your opinion might've been different. Having your entire life flipped upside down and inside out has a way of messing with your sense of self. Most of my life was a lie. My father's arrest and subsequent departure was an eye-opener for me. I began to see all of them for their true selves." She wrinkled her nose. "I didn't like what I saw."

"Well, I'm glad you had that epiphany because I definitely like what I see." He reached across the table and held her hand. "Are you ready for the next part of our adventure?"

"There's more than Taco Tuesday?"

He liked her snark. It was cute. He pointed at the bowls of salsa. "This is a themed evening."

Her forehead wrinkled. "I'm truly stuffed. I couldn't possible eat any more."

He waved the waitress over and asked for the bill and a to-go container for the leftovers. "The next phase of our evening will help you work off all the food you ate."

"Please tell me that you don't think I'm going hiking or playing some sport thing."

"Nope. I think you'll like this." He paid the tab, gathered his breakfast for tomorrow, and took her hand. It was small but strong and he couldn't wait to have her whole body in his arms.

He'd made a good decision to invite her into his plan for the forgeries. Hopefully, he'd be able to prove she wasn't involved, and then he could come clean about his real job.

And with any luck, she wouldn't hate him for lying about it.

ELEVEN

MIA'S HEAD WAS spinning with possibilities. If Logan, regardless of whether he was law enforcement or an insurance agent, could get her to authenticate the Moreau, she would be able to drive the timeline. Nikki could make the swap before Mia inspected it, and when she questioned the authenticity, Logan wouldn't have a choice but to call in experts.

She needed London to make an obvious error on the painting. As the ideas flooded her brain, she almost forgot that Logan was by her side, guiding her to his car. He put his leftovers in the trunk and opened the passenger door for her.

"How do you know I didn't drive here?"

"First, I saw you get out of the Lyft. Second, you told me you don't see the reason to drive in the city. It left me with the impression that you only drive when you need to. Do you even own a car?"

"For your information, I do. But you're right. I rarely drive it." She settled into his car, which was far from a luxury vehicle, but it was clean. "Where are we going?" she asked once he sat behind the wheel.

"Dancing."

She hadn't seen that coming. Most men would rather scoop out their own eyeballs before willingly dancing. "You're taking me dancing."

"You said you used to be a dancer. I figured it would

be a good way to spend some more time together, getting to know each other."

Mia suddenly had images of thumping music at a nightclub. "Where?" She couldn't keep the skepticism from her voice.

"Remember I said it was a themed evening? We had chips and salsa, and now we're going salsa dancing. There's a great little club in Humboldt Park that does weekly salsa nights."

She couldn't remember the last time she danced anything other than formal waltzes at events. "Do you know how to salsa?"

He shrugged. "I'm not winning any *Dancing with the Stars* trophy, but I can get by."

"You can get by as in you've seen it done on TV or you actually took lessons?"

"My sister Carmen taught me." He chuckled. "More like bullied me into it. She took one look at me dancing and rolled her eyes, talking about how white boys don't have rhythm."

"Your sister isn't white?"

"She's Latina. Foster sister. We grew up in the same foster home."

"Oh. I didn't know. Do you mind me asking how you ended up in foster care?"

He lifted a shoulder as if it didn't matter, but Mia saw through the nonchalant movement. "My biological mom had me really young. She had some addiction issues, couldn't hold down a job. She was in and out of rehab my whole childhood, and since she didn't have any family that I knew of, I flipped between her and foster care."

"How many siblings do you have?"

"By birth? None—at least none that I know of. But if you're counting foster family…a lot. My mom died when I was about ten, and I bounced around to group homes and foster homes for a couple years before landing with Mae and Joe. When I moved in with them, it was me, Isaiah, and our four sisters, Carmen, Hana, Sam, and Jill. There are a lot more if you count those who came before and after us."

Mia's eyes widened. "Five siblings? And you consider the ones you didn't live with siblings, too?" She closed her eyes because she knew she sounded dumb. "What I'm trying to say, and doing such a poor job, is that I assume if they moved in after you left, that they are much younger than you are."

"Some are, sure. And while I probably wouldn't call the younger kids close, we're still family. Mae gave us that. No matter where we go in life, we can always count on each other."

"You still keep in touch?"

"Of course. We're family."

She should've known better than to forget that not everyone walked away from family. "How many foster children have they taken in over the years?"

"Over thirty. They look for the kids no one else wants, so the kids are usually a little older and only stay for a few years."

"Mae sounds like an amazing woman."

"She is. I wouldn't be the person I am today if Joe and Mae hadn't taken me in."

Before she knew it, Logan was parking at a meter. After he parked, she turned and looked at him. "Thank you for sharing that. I'm sure it's not easy to talk about."

"You're easy to talk to, but I don't keep it a secret.

And I figure if I want to get to know you, I have to be willing to open up, too." He cut the ignition. "Ready to dance?"

"One more thing. Can you tell me more about your grandpa's stolen painting?"

"Why?"

"I have acquaintances all over the art world. I might be able to do some research to see if I can find out any information about it."

He shook his head. "It's long gone. That's why I didn't say anything when you texted."

"Any good thief would want the family to believe that. Whoever took it from your grandfather wouldn't have sold it right away, especially if it was noteworthy."

"It was right before World War Two. Art all over the world went missing."

"But much of it has popped up over the years. People wait until they think it's been forgotten. Or it's been passed down through a family and the younger generation has no idea where it came from. I'm not saying I'll get it for you. I'm simply offering to do a little research."

"Why?"

"Because, like you, it pisses me off when people are taken advantage of. In addition, it's a bit of an adventure." She smiled. "Like Indiana Jones."

He pulled his phone out and scrolled through. "All I know is that the artist was Camille Hurley. It was a painting of a young girl in a field. I don't know the name of the painting. I don't know that my grandfather did. What kid pays attention to things like that when their parents talk? But he did have this."

Logan handed her the phone. It was a grainy, ancient picture of a photo of a man with a young boy. In the background, a painting hung on the wall. Unfortunately, you couldn't make out much in the old black-and-white image. Logan had been telling the truth. This wasn't a part of his made-up persona. He was sharing a genuine part of his life. It made her want to really help him.

She handed him his phone. "Do you still have the original of this picture?"

"Joe might, but if he does, it's buried in a box in the attic."

"Send me this and I'll see what I can find."

"You really don't have to do that. Joe always told me that his father talked about that painting, but it probably wasn't worth anything. No one expects to ever see it."

"It can't hurt to look." She tilted her head toward the door. "Now, show me what you got."

Logan led her into the small club. With it being a Tuesday night, she hadn't thought a club would be crowded. The space was filled with people, but not uncomfortably so. The music was loud, which hindered conversation, but that was all right because Logan immediately led her to the dance floor. He twirled her out, away from him, and then brought her back, catching her. Their hands met and loosely held. His other arm wrapped around her lower back, but he kept distance between them. Mia gave him credit. The man knew how to salsa. The first two dances were fun, but...*proper* would be the best way to describe it.

They were not dancing like other couples on the floor. There was an intimacy between the other dancers that said they were couples. They danced close, hips swirling and touching in an erotic rhythm.

After the second dance, Logan leaned close and spoke in her ear, "Ready for a drink?"

She nodded and they made their way over to the bar. He ordered her a glass of wine and a beer for himself, along with two glasses of water. Mia drank the water first and eased up on a stool. Logan's gaze skated over her entire body, down to her feet and back up.

"I don't know how you can even walk in those shoes, much less dance."

She smiled. "I told you I'm a woman with many talents. I'm short and these enable me to be a little more in line with others, so people aren't looking down at me. Plus, they make my rear end and legs look phenomenal."

Logan laughed, almost choking on his beer. "You're not wrong, and I love that you own that." He nudged her glass closer. "Now drink up. I want another dance."

They finished their drinks and when they returned to the dance floor, Logan held her closer. She didn't think she imagined it, and maybe it was the alcohol hitting their systems, but for the rest of the dances, her body moved along the long lines of Logan's. When he brought her close and their legs interlocked a la *Dirty Dancing*, he stared into her eyes, and she felt as if he saw her in a way no one had in a long time.

They didn't speak, but their bodies communicated. Lust. Want. Desire.

And Mia knew she was in trouble.

Two and a half hours later, Logan was holding Mia's hand on the way back to the car. In fact, he'd had his hands on her one way or another the entire time they'd been in the club and he'd enjoyed every second. But it was getting late and they both had work in the morning.

"I'm glad you came out with me tonight. I had a great

time," he said. "And admit it, I'm a much better dancer than you thought I'd be."

"I will concede that you actually do know how to salsa. Kudos to your sister for teaching you rhythm."

"Seriously? Even after proving I can dance, I don't get credit. My sister does." This woman was always busting his chops. It should irritate him, but he was having fun.

"I had a good time as well."

He unlocked his car, but instead of opening the door, he leaned against it and pulled her close. "So have I succeeded in wooing you?"

Her gaze darted away. Her cheeks were flushed, as they had been since they started dancing. When she spoke, her voice was soft. "Being with you is definitely different than other experiences I've had."

"Closer to being complimentary, but still not quite there." He tugged her a step closer, until her body brushed his. "*Different* can be good or bad. I'm pretty sure your expensive college education gave you a better vocabulary than that."

"My vocabulary is excellent; however, I was also raised by a master manipulator to never reveal too much too early."

"Maybe in the boardroom, that makes sense. And most of the time you don't give an inch, but now that I've witnessed you on the dance floor, I know your weakness. You have a hard time hiding when you dance. I saw the way you looked at me. I felt the beat of your heart, the catch of your breath." He reached up and brushed her hair back, off her shoulder, and stroked the side of her neck. His thumb made a small circle. "Right here, your pulse spikes when I touch you. And don't get me started on your eyes. Like right now, your pupils are huge. You, Mia Benson, like me."

"So what if I do?" She cocked an eyebrow.

"God, I love your attitude. You could give whole seminars on how to keep a man in check." He levered himself away from his car, pressing his body to hers. Her crooked smile dropped as he lowered his mouth to hers.

When their lips met, her pulse under his palm kicked up again. She reached up and wrapped her hand around the back of his head as she angled her head, allowing him to take the kiss deeper.

This kiss blurred the line between professional and personal. Logan no longer knew which side of the line he was on. What was worse was that in this moment, he didn't care.

They kissed for long minutes out on the street, with cars whizzing by and pedestrians entering and leaving the restaurants and clubs on the block, but they were in their own time and place. Nothing mattered more than the slick of their tongues, their racing hearts, and Mia's breathy sighs.

As much as he hated pulling away, he finally did. "I should get you home."

"I can call a car."

"That's ridiculous." He paused and studied her face. "Unless you don't want me to know where you live?"

"It's not that. I don't want to inconvenience you. A car could be here in five minutes."

He touched her chin and tilted her face further up until her eyes met his. "You are not an inconvenience."

He'd like to know who had taught her that she was. Mia was no wilting flower, fading into obscurity because someone had talked down to her. No, she stood taller and took care of herself. He wondered if it had been her father who had done that.

She ran her hand down the front of his shirt. "Thank you."

Logan opened the door and waited until she stepped in. As he walked around the car, he tried to organize his thoughts. He'd asked Mia out because he genuinely liked her. She was smart and beautiful. He hadn't found proof of her involvement in the forgeries. In any case, she was useful to his investigation, and he couldn't afford to blow that. So maybe he needed to slow things down. Buy himself time to solve the case or at least know definitively that she wasn't involved.

He got in and started the engine. Mia put her address into the navigation system. As he pulled out into traffic, Mia stared out her window, her hand a fist next to her thigh. He reached over and smoothed her hand open before interlocking his fingers with hers. She turned and looked at their joined hands.

"Having second thoughts about our date?"

"Not at all." Something in her voice betrayed that she wasn't telling the whole truth. "I was thinking about what you said about getting me in to see Keaton's painting. What if I tell him I have a potential buyer? As I said earlier, I have many acquaintances in the art world. If I ask him for a private viewing, he would probably agree. A guaranteed sale without having to give the auction house a cut is very attractive."

"Would it be weird if I came with you?"

Her brow furrowed. "Yes, I would think it would be quite suspicious for me to arrive with his insurance agent to look at a painting."

"What if I went as your boyfriend? Maybe we go on our way to dinner."

"That might be all right. Although that would make the gossip circuit pretty quickly. I haven't had a boyfriend in years. Since my fiancé broke off our engagement when my father was indicted."

There was a lot of information in the brief statement. He'd read the file and knew her life had imploded with her father's arrest, but this was a lot. "The guy you planned to marry and spend your life with left you because your father is a crook."

She nodded. "Yes. He also worked in the financial world, and he felt that his association with me would reflect poorly on him."

"What a jagoff."

She chuckled. "No argument."

"More importantly, you haven't dated in five years?"

She sent him a sly look. "I didn't say that. I said I haven't had a boyfriend. I've dated. If you've learned nothing else about me, you should know that I know how to take care of myself."

"Is that your way of saying you have regular booty calls?"

"A crude way to put it. I wouldn't necessarily say regular, but when the urge strikes, I do know a few men who are discreet. Being the topic of the gossips is tiring. I prefer not to be in the spotlight. I've already had enough to last a lifetime."

"You are full of surprises."

"It keeps people on their toes." She returned to looking out her window but didn't extract her hand.

"What exactly does one have to do to get on the list of approved booty callers?"

"I have a lengthy application process," she deadpanned. "I'd be happy to add you to the queue."

He released a belly laugh. She was too much. Unfortunately, they were nearing her address and this date was coming to an end. "Would it be all right for me to park and walk you in?" he asked as he eyed the highrise condo complex. The sleek building looked no different than the others surrounding them. He didn't know what it would cost to live here, but he knew he would never be able to afford it.

"I appreciate the offer, but it's late and we both have work in the morning."

He pulled over and put on his hazards. "I wasn't asking to spend the night."

"I'm not so naïve as to think if I invite you in you wouldn't be spending the night."

"Are you saying you can't resist my charms?"

She leaned across the console and pressed a kiss to his lips. "What I'm saying, Logan, is that I've been adequately wooed."

Then she slipped out the door and into her building without so much as a glance over her shoulder.

Before he left, he pulled out his phone and texted her a gif: Did you just blow my mind? With a Magic 8-Ball saying, "All signs point to yes."

TWELVE

AFTER AN EXCRUCIATINGLY long night and an entire day of snapping at people, Mia was finally in a position to go to London's loft to discuss the Moreau painting. Mia had texted her late last night and told her to stop working on it until they could talk. She didn't want to attempt an explanation over the phone.

En route, she called Keaton Bishop to forge ahead with her plan. "Hi, Keaton. It's Mia Benson. Is now a good time?"

"Mia, how are you? Chad mentioned he ran into you at the gallery event last week."

"We did see each other." *For a few miserable moments.* "Actually, it was something I heard that night at the gallery that's the reason for my call. I heard you're selling your Moreau."

"I am. Goes to auction in a couple weeks. It's going to be a big one, too."

"I have an overseas friend who is a huge Moreau fan, and he's interested in the painting, but he won't be able to attend the auction. He might be interested in buying it preemptively." She'd never been much of a saleswoman, but she knew she had to make this an attractive option for Keaton.

"A preempt? That would be costly."

"As you said, the auction will bring out the big

spenders, what with a Picasso going up at the same time. I explained all this to my friend."

"I'll definitely entertain his offer. Give him my contact information."

"Can I ask a huge favor before I do that? I know it's not exactly the usual way of things, but he's asked me if, because of our personal connection, I could come over and take a look at the painting and send him some photos." She closed her eyes and prayed he would agree. They needed to catch a break. Having to only get one painting from the auction house would be easier than trying to get both.

"Absolutely. Let's make a night of it. I'll have Sheila make dinner and we can catch up. I can invite Chad..."

Unfortunately, his trailing off was full of innuendo. "While it would be fun to see Chad again, I'm currently seeing someone." The lies were so easily slipping from her lips these days.

"Oh, excellent! Bring him. I'd love to meet the young man who has finally caught your eye."

"Wonderful. When would you like to do this?"

"The sooner the better. How about tomorrow night?"

"If it's not an imposition on Sheila. I'd hate to put her out on such short notice." That part was true. Sheila was a nice woman. How she stayed married to Keaton, Mia had no idea.

"She loves to throw a dinner party. Say seven o'clock?"

"Perfect. We'll see you then."

She arrived at London's loft and texted Nikki and Audrey to ask them to meet her at the apartment for dinner. Bribing them with a good meal often made them more amenable to listening to her. As much as Nikki might balk at bumping up the timeline again, this was in their best interests.

London swung open the huge metal door. Her long, light brown hair was piled on her head and she was wearing paint-splattered jeans. "What's the problem now? I thought we were on a tight timeline. Why tell me to stop working on this thing?"

Mia followed London into her loft, the hallway noticeably quiet for a change. On the other occasions Mia had been here, the occupants in the building were extremely loud. "First, the timeline is out the window. I need this painting complete, dry, and ready to install by seven o'clock tomorrow night."

"Tomorrow?" London's bright blue eyes shot open and she started waving her arms. "I just lost all of today because you told me to stop working." She stalked to the easel holding the partially finished painting and picked up a paintbrush.

"Can you do it?"

London's gaze snapped to Mia's. "Of course I can do it. What's an all-nighter?"

"There is one more thing."

London crossed her arms, smearing paint on her sleeve.

"I need you to make an obvious mistake."

"What? That doesn't make any sense. You're paying me to make these forgeries good. Why would you want something obviously wrong with it?"

"Because Nikki is going to make the swap at Bishop's house tomorrow night while I'm there for a dinner party. Then, I'm going to look at the painting to take pictures for an imaginary potential buyer, and I have to recognize that it's a forgery."

London huffed. "What kind of mistake are you looking for?"

"I'm not an appraiser. I won't be running any tests, so I need it to be something that the average person might not notice, but something that as an expert in the field, I would at least question. I don't have to prove anything. I just need to make the accusation."

"This is getting pretty involved for you."

"I know." She didn't particularly like it, either, but she'd come to realize that she couldn't ask these women to continually take *all* the risks, even though she was paying them well. They had become a team, and loyalty and trust mattered.

"I'll figure something out. I'll call you and let you know what to look for."

"Nikki will be in touch tomorrow to get the painting. Thank you."

"No problem." London pointed the brush at her, luckily without splattering Mia's silk blouse. "What does this mean for you and hottie cop man?"

Mia blinked. "Hottie cop man?"

London waved the hand holding the brush, as if it were an extension of her hand. "Nikki told me all about the fake insurance guy who has the hots for you. She said you were going on a date with him to get information."

"I have, and it was his idea for me to get a look at the Moreau. He'll be joining me for dinner at the Bishops' tomorrow night."

London jumped up and down. "Oh my God. You're bringing the cops to the place where Nikki is going to steal the painting right out from under their noses? I am so going to be there for this."

"Aren't you normally there?"

"Mostly, yeah. But now it's can't-miss!"

"So glad I could provide you with additional entertainment. I'll talk to you tomorrow." Mia let herself out of the loft, with London still squealing excitedly behind her.

While she stood outside waiting for her ride, she placed an order for food that she could pick up on the way to the apartment. Then she texted Logan. She hadn't been in contact with him since she stepped out of his car last night, except for the gif he'd sent. The man had a thing for gifs.

Keaton invited us to dinner tomorrow night.

Us? You snagged me an invite? I feel special.

It was either tell him about you or be forced to sit through an entire meal with his son Chad.

Well, at least I'm better than Chad. I'll take it. What time should I pick you up?

Dinner is at 7, so 6-6:15. Will that work with your schedule?

It's fine. I'm looking forward to it.

She waited to see if he would say anything else, maybe send one of his silly gifs, but nothing came. Disappointment stabbed at her. Then she shook it loose. *It's silly to be disappointed that the man you are fake dating for information didn't send a picture.*

When she arrived at the apartment with dinner, she let herself in and found Audrey and Jared hovered over the computer. For a change, they weren't touching and kissing and doing other adorable couple things.

"Dinner is served." She set the bags of food on the table.

Jared looked up. "I'm trying not to be offended that you called Audrey to meet you here but said nothing to me."

"First off, she's always with you. Second, the things I need to discuss with them have to do with the actual heist, not the sale of the painting."

"Ouch. Are you saying that I haven't been pulling my weight in planning?"

"You know that I appreciate every bit of help you offer. I wasn't thinking about your involvement, that's all. It's not as though I'm asking you to leave."

"Is everything okay?" Audrey asked.

"Yes. Everything is going mostly according to plan. Just a bit quicker than I anticipated."

"Oh no. Nikki's gonna hate that."

The door opened and Nikki and Wade came in.

"Nikki's going to hate what?" Nikki asked. "Wade's staying for dinner, all right?"

"That's fine. I ordered plenty."

They all took seats while Mia busied herself gathering plates and utensils from the kitchen. While there, she started a pot of coffee and grabbed a bottle of wine.

Nikki was already unboxing the Thai food while Jared scooped up the photos and plans they had spread out. "Don't think I didn't notice that you haven't answered the question."

"I have an even more important question," Wade

interrupted. Pointing at the stack Jared held, he said, "Why do you have a picture of an FBI agent in your plan?"

"I knew it!" Nikki yelled as she jumped out of her chair. Then she spun. "Wait a minute. How do you know Logan's FBI?"

"Ah, shit." Wade sank to a chair.

"What is it?" Mia asked. Her heart sank. Hearing the truth of who Logan was jarred her. Knowledge that he had, in fact, been lying about who he was.

Wade pointed to the bottle of wine. "You might want to crack that open for this."

Mia braced herself. They'd guessed that Logan was law enforcement. What difference did it make that he was FBI?

"I know he's FBI because he came to Dodger's— Nikki's dad's—apartment to ask some questions about the Devereaux heist."

"Fuck," Mia said as she sat. Everyone stared at her. "What?"

Audrey said, "You hardly ever swear, and you never say *fuck*."

"She did that one time when she admitted she'd suck at being a thief," Nikki pointed out.

"I choose to be professional with people I work with. I'm still human. And correct me if I'm wrong, but if he showed up to speak to Nikki's father, he's probably much closer to putting the pieces together than we thought."

"Dodger wouldn't have told him anything, would he?" Jared asked Wade.

Nikki and Wade both said "no" a little more forcefully than necessary.

Audrey wiped her hands on a napkin. "Did you get his last name? I could do some recon."

"No," Nikki said. "The more Mia knows about him, the greater the chance for a slipup."

Mia ignored the food on the table and stood. "I agree. Does knowing he's FBI change anything? Do we know what he does know?"

Wade leaned back in his chair and crossed his arms. "Based on what Dodger said, it was a fishing expedition. Dodger admitted to stealing the painting. They're suspicious about the forgery at the Carlisle but can't figure out how to connect the forgery with Dodger's arrest."

"Then we're good," Nikki said.

"How so?" Mia asked.

"I ran the con at the museum, and I'm good at what I do." Nikki gave her a don't-doubt-me look. "When they go to the museum—which they will if they haven't already—all they're going to find is that a grad student named Alice Hyde interned for a few days and disappeared. Alice was with Roberta Wolcott when the switch was made and it was Roberta's ID that was used. We went old school. No hacking, no trace."

"What if they have security pictures of you?" Mia asked.

Nikki just laughed.

Wade patted Nikki's leg. "That's not really a concern. She was in disguise. She wore glasses that would cause glare to make facial recognition software useless. Besides, I'm sure there are a number of law enforcement agencies that have some version of a photo of her, yet she's never been caught. It's a dead end for them."

"So we can move forward as planned," Mia said.

"Cautiously," Jared added.

Mia bit back a smirk. At any other time she would agree, and she was cautious in all areas of her life, but at this point caution was slipping through her fingers. "We're going to take the Moreau from Bishop's house tomorrow night."

Audrey gasped. Jared's jaw dropped, and he gave her a cold stare.

"Before you get all up in arms, I will be there at a dinner party under the guise of seeing the painting for a possible private sale." That grabbed their attention. She laid out the situation and waited for their reactions.

Nikki gave her a round of applause, but Audrey was out of her chair and sitting at her computer mumbling to herself. Jared followed his girlfriend with a plate of food.

"I think I've successfully lured you to the dark side," Nikki said with an evil grin.

"We're not dark side anymore, babe, remember?" Wade said.

"Speak for yourself," Nikki said to him and then turned to Mia. "So what's the plan?"

"I have no idea. That's why we're here."

"Okay. Audrey, you're up. What do we know about the Bishop house?" Nikki stood and carried her plate of food over to the TV.

Jared rejoined Mia at the table. "Are you sure this is a good idea?"

"Good or not, it's what we have. If she can make the swap now, then we only have to worry about one painting at the auction house. If we pull this off, it takes the spotlight away from us and shines it on the men. The

FBI will take a closer look at their dealings. It buys us time."

"And Logan?"

"What about him?"

He lowered his voice, as if he wasn't going to tell everything to Audrey later. "Your mother called mine to tell her about you having a new man in your life."

Mia waved him off. "I had to cancel our weekly dinner and I didn't want to lie to her. I told her it wasn't serious."

"We're talking about you. You've avoided relationships since Derek. Any mention of a man in your life is a big deal to her."

"It's fine. I'll handle my mother." Whether she could handle Logan might be a different story. "Now, let's develop a plan."

LOGAN SAT IN THE conference room where he and Stokes had set up shop for the investigation. He was still trying to draw lines between all these men and figure out what, if anything, it had to do with Dwayne Benson. Stokes came into the room and threw her jacket against a chair.

"No luck at the museum?"

She had gone to the museum yesterday and spoken with people, but the head curator, Roberta Wolcott, hadn't been in. Stokes went back today to talk to her and check surveillance. "What a waste of a day. I skipped lunch and worked straight through reviewing video footage."

Logan reached into his coat pocket and tossed her a candy bar.

"You're a lifesaver." She tore into the wrapper and took a bite. "They have no record of any break-in. They have no idea how the forgery got in there. Dr. Wolcott was sure she had the original. The only suspicious thing is that they had a graduate intern arrive right after the Devereaux was donated. She was only supposed to be there two weeks. She made it less than one."

Logan stood and went to the board they had set up with who they believed to be key players. "What do we have on her?"

"A name—Alice Hyde. A vague description of tall, pretty, blonde. Wears glasses."

Logan waited. "Picture?"

"Nope. Conveniently, every shot of her she was either not facing the camera or there's a glare covering her face." She finished the candy and crumpled the wrapper.

"I'm guessing Alice is a bogus student."

"You win the prize. Dr. Wolcott thought nothing of it when Alice didn't show up for work. They go through a lot of interns and she said that Alice didn't like one of the lab guys. It sounded fishy to me, so I had Wolcott call her contact at the University of Chicago. Sure enough, there was no record of Alice Hyde." Stokes sank into one of the leather chairs and spun to face the board. "It doesn't make sense. Why give the museum a fake?"

"Unless they didn't." He pointed to the picture of Troy Evans. "Troy hires someone to steal the Devereaux from Ingram. Troy gives the painting to the Carlisle. You said Alice showed up at the Carlisle *after* the Devereaux." He wrote the name Alice on a piece of paper and stuck it to the board. "Alice swaps the original for the fake and gives it to Russo—Dodger—to give to Wolf."

"So Dodger and Alice are in cahoots. But how does that tie in to everything else?"

"No clue." He returned to his chair and continued to stare at the board. Every time one piece fit, three new pieces scattered. He'd managed to stop himself from reaching out to Mia all day because he didn't want to seem too eager, as an insurance agent or as a boyfriend.

While he and Stokes talked in circles to try to figure out the end game, his phone buzzed with a text from Mia. For a change, they'd caught a break. "We're on for checking out the Moreau painting that's supposed to go to auction."

"You're sure bringing Mia Benson of all people into this is a good idea?"

"She's either already a part of it, or it can't hurt. She knows these people. If her father is somehow behind this, I think she'd want to know."

Logan's gut rarely let him down, and his instincts told him that Mia wasn't one of the bad guys.

THIRTEEN

MIA HAD STAYED at the apartment far too late last night, and the brief dozing she did before coming to the museum was nowhere near enough sleep. After her morning meeting and sending a few emails, she told Jasmine not to disturb her, closed her office door, and lay down on the love seat. She'd never been one to nap, but she'd been sure exhaustion would take over. Of course, she had no such luck.

First, she ran through tonight's plan over and over, making sure she knew every precise move. When she was satisfied she had it committed to memory, thoughts of Logan filled her head. The press of his body against hers while they danced. The low chuckle in her ear when he liked her snarky comments.

Regardless of how she played it with Jared or Nikki, she liked Logan. She knew she shouldn't, but he was the first man in a long time who didn't care about her last name. Even if he was feigning interest—and she didn't think he was—she enjoyed the attention, the attraction, the banter.

She knew she couldn't trust him, but she hadn't censored her thoughts or words. She was being herself around him and it was freeing.

Giving up on the notion of sleep, she sat up and scrolled through her phone to the photo of the Hurley painting. She went to her computer and began a basic search on Camille Hurley. Hurley was an Irish artist who died not long after World War II. Her work was valuable. Mia looked at the clock. She didn't have time to do a full search for every painting the woman did.

Then she had a brilliant thought. She picked up the phone and had Jasmine call Anya to her office.

While she waited for Anya, she printed a really crappy, grainy copy of the picture.

Anya knocked on the door and stuck her head in. "You wanted to see me?"

"Come in." She waited for Anya to take a seat across from her desk. "I have a special assignment, if you're interested."

"For the *Crime and Punishment* exhibit?"

"No. This is more of a personal quest. You'd be doing me a favor. I just don't have time to tackle this right now."

"What is it?"

Mia briefly explained Logan's story. "I don't expect you to attempt to track the painting down, but if you could just take some time to find the name of the painting and any information about it, I would be grateful."

Anya smiled. "So if I dig up some useful information, you'll owe me one."

"Yes, I would, but don't get carried away."

"I'll have something for you by end of day tomorrow."

"Don't neglect your regular work for this. It's not a rush."

Anya rose. "Like I said, I'll have something for you by tomorrow."

"Thank you." With that off her plate at least temporarily, Mia could turn her attention to other things.

Although Logan hadn't expected her to search for his family's painting, she needed to know how much of what he said to her were lies. Just because she felt free and totally herself didn't mean the same was true for him. He was playing a role.

So are you.

Mia went through the rest of her day on autopilot, answering questions and replying to emails all while staring at the clock. She planned to leave early, so she could go to the apartment, pick up a comm, and see the mistake in the forgery London created.

She packed her things, let Jasmine know she could be reached by text, but she would prefer not to be bothered, and left. She arrived at the apartment, where Nikki was running London through the plan.

"Unfortunately, we have to go in fast, even though I won't have full cover of darkness."

"I'm sorry," Mia said. "He wanted a dinner party, and I thought it might be a tad suspicious to ask for a ten o'clock dinner."

"Not your fault. It is what it is." Nikki pointed at the sketch she'd created. "I scoped out the area earlier today. The neighbor has a huge lot filled with willows. Plenty of shadows."

"Are you sure the Bishops don't have security cameras all over?" Audrey asked.

"Just the camera in their doorbell. Unless they've done some kind of upgrade since I was there last." Mia set her bag on a chair and listened to Nikki go through the plan.

"When Mia gets there, she's going to go through and unlock as many windows as she can—first floor, second floor—whatever she can access without raising suspicion."

"But not in the room where the Moreau painting is. That room will remain locked. Just in case."

"While she's doing that, I'll skulk around in the shadows waiting for her signal. Then, I'll either go in through this den—" she pointed at the paper "—or, if they're having their hoity-toity predinner drinks in there, I'll scale the wall and go in upstairs."

"What happens if he has an alarm on the painting itself?" Mia asked. "We haven't planned for that."

"Maybe you haven't planned for it, but I have a bag of tricks. I'll just bring them all."

The front door opened and Audrey joined them.

Nikki smiled. "And one of my favorite tools will be on hand if something needs to be hacked."

"I am not a tool," Audrey said.

"I meant it in the best way." Nikki blew her a kiss.

"When dinner is over, and we've done adequate small talk, I'll ask to see the painting."

London flipped a canvas up to reveal the painting and laid the forgery on the table. They all huddled around it.

"It's even uglier in person," Nikki said.

"He just has this hanging in his house?" Audrey asked. "Why would his wife be okay with that?"

"Sheila is a lovely woman," Mia answered, "but she's spent most of her life being a dutiful wife. I doubt she's ever disagreed with Keaton."

Mia studied the painting. The shape, colors, and even the brushstrokes were dead on. It was a good forgery. But then she saw it—a weird blend of green and brown near the bottom, and a random daisy on the edge of the man's pocket. It was small and from a distance, it would barely be noticeable. In some light, it might even just appear to be a glare, but it was obvious enough for her to call it out as a fake. "This is amazing, London."

"Thank you."

"If everyone knows what they're doing, I'll take a comm and go. I have to get ready for my dinner."

"Are you going to have a camera? I really want to see the look on Bishop's face when you tell him," London said.

"That might cut down on the image of me talking to myself in an effort to give you information, since you'll be able to see for yourself."

Audrey handed her the earpiece. "How about the necklace you wore to the gallery if you want to let us peek at the events?"

Mia accepted the comm and pointed at London. "If you squeal in my ear, you'll regret it."

"Yay!" London gave a bounce and a clap, but at Mia's glare she sobered.

Audrey handed her the jewelry. "Keep in mind this comm is the more sophisticated one, so we hear everything without you having to press a button."

"I know. I don't want to look ridiculous always poking at my ear."

"It also doesn't give you any privacy," Audrey said in a low voice.

"That's fine. Thank you." She tucked both items in her purse.

"What are you going to do if Bishop wants you to inspect the thing before dinner?"

Mia waved a hand. "Sheila would never let him conduct business without feeding their guests first. If he had offered drinks, that would be one thing, but he planned for this to be a dinner party."

"You sure we won't need a plan B?" Nikki asked.

"Positive. I'll see you all back here tonight unless things get out of hand with my observations and I'm stuck there late. I have no idea what Logan's plans are once I say the painting is a forgery."

"Make sure you don't rush," Nikki said. "You have to sell this, so really inspect it. Keep suspicion off you."

"I know. I think I'm getting the hang of running a con."

Nikki snorted. "We'll see."

LOGAN CALLED MIA WHEN he was nearing her building. "Hey. I'll be there in about five. Should I park and come up?"

"No need. I'm ready, so I'll come down."

"A woman who is ready on time. Impressive."

"First, that's a very sexist thing to say. Second, I am impressive in many ways."

"My apologies. All of my sisters take forever getting ready for anything. Mae used to lie to them about what time we had to leave to make sure they didn't make us late."

"I'll see you in a few minutes."

They disconnected and Logan turned the corner and parked right where he had dropped her off two nights ago. Through the glass doors, he saw her wave to the doorman. When the door opened and she stepped out, he lost the ability to think. She wore a stunning red dress that wrapped around all of her tight curves and plunged into a deep V in the front. And, of course, incredibly high heels.

As she got closer, he came to, jumped from the car, and ran around to open the door for her.

The corner of her mouth kicked up in that crooked smile of hers. "Thank you."

"You look amazing."

Color rose in her cheeks, but she looked him up and down. He felt a little self-conscious in his everyday suit that was nowhere near the designer clothes she was used to seeing on men.

"You look pretty good yourself."

He leaned in to brush a kiss on her cheek, but she turned her face and captured his lips with hers. When she pulled away, she rubbed her thumb on his bottom lip.

"Sorry about that. Lipstick."

"Never apologize for kissing me. I don't mind getting a little messy." He held her hand as she slid into the passenger seat and then he closed the door.

"Do you have a plan for this painting?"

Her eyes widened. "What do you mean?"

"Do you know what to look for to figure out if it's a forgery?" He pulled into traffic and headed to the highway.

"I did a little research on Moreau and his general style. But really, there's no way to know what to look for if it's fake. Every artist is different. I plan to have a nice meal, share some idiotic small talk, and then look over the painting. I'll take some photos and send them to my *friend*."

"Who is your friend?"

"I'll send the pictures to my cousin. He might be a little confused when photos of a painting land in his inbox, but it's me, so he'll wait for an explanation."

"Is there anything I need to know or do? Or not do?"

"Act like my boyfriend so they stop trying to set me up with their creepy son."

"That's a task I can handle. It's a role I'd like to play for real."

"I'm not really in the market for a serious relationship right now. I have a lot going on with work. I can't devote time to building a relationship."

"I said nothing about serious. I can keep it casual. How thick should I lay it on tonight?"

She sighed. "I don't want them calling my mother and telling her we're headed down the aisle, but I also don't want them to think we're friends with benefits. Maybe something in the middle?"

He reached across the console and held her hand. "Anything you want to talk about?"

"About what?"

She seemed distracted suddenly. He hoped all the talk about a relationship—real or not—didn't give her cold feet.

"Whatever's on your mind. You seem preoccupied."

"I'm a little nervous."

"About pretending to be my girlfriend? Don't worry. I'll guide you."

She smiled, which was what he'd been going for. "I can handle faking that."

"Cold, Mia, really cold."

She laughed. "Haven't you heard? I am the ice queen of the Chicago social circles."

Whoever had dubbed her that didn't really know her. He understood the reasoning behind building walls for protection, and Mia had a veritable fortress. But nothing he'd seen indicated a truly cold woman. "I think

I might've melted some of that away because there's nothing icy about you when we kiss. In fact, it's downright hot."

"Yes, yes it is."

At least he wasn't caught up in some one-sided feelings. "So what is it then?"

"It feels like there's a lot riding on my inspection of the painting. What if I mess up? What if I think it's real and it's a forgery? Or I call it a forgery and it's not?"

He rubbed his thumb on the back of her hand while their fingers were still interlaced. "If you think it's real and you're wrong, it'll be found out when it gets to the auction house. If you call it fake and it's not, oh well, you're not an expert. Everyone makes mistakes."

She sighed.

"I really appreciate you doing this for me. I need some kind of evidence of what's going on. My bosses won't budge until my theory has legs."

"I'm glad to help, if I can."

They held hands in silence the rest of the way to Bishop's house. The neighborhood was quiet as shadows fell. When they pulled into the tree-lined driveway, Logan was flabbergasted by the size of the house. Even though he'd been visiting similar houses for the duration of this investigation, he continued to be amazed by the sheer luxury. Glancing at Mia, he asked, "You ready?"

"Of course." She offered a small smile.

Any doubt or unease she had been feeling was wiped clear from her face. This woman was a master at masking her emotions. He'd hate to be the agent who had to interrogate her.

He parked near the front door and before taking the key from the ignition, he twisted in his seat and pulled her close for a kiss. When he felt her melt against him, he whispered against her lips, "This isn't faking."

"No, it's not."

As cool as he tried to play things, he couldn't deny that her admission gave him no small amount of satisfaction. He cut the ignition and walked around the car to open her door for her. He helped her from the car and continued to hold her hand as they strode up the walkway.

She reached out and rang the bell. A moment later, Sheila Bishop answered the door, which surprised Logan. He'd assumed that they would have a butler or someone answer.

Sheila smiled. "Mia, it's so good to see you. It's been far too long." She closed in on Mia, so Logan finally released her hand. Sheila held Mia's shoulders and air-kissed her.

Logan didn't see the point.

"How is your mother doing?" Shelia asked.

"She's well. Thank you for asking. This is Logan Freemont. Logan, Sheila Bishop."

He held out his hand to shake. "Nice to meet you, Mrs. Bishop."

She barely touched his hand with the tips of her fingers. He couldn't decide if she was avoiding his touch or if it was just supposed to be a dainty handshake.

"Please, call me Sheila. Dinner will be ready soon. We're in the dining room enjoying a glass of wine." She led the way across the sleek marble floor in the foyer.

Logan lagged behind, looking around, a little in awe of the sheer size of the place. He couldn't imagine having the kind of money required to own a house this big. And there were only two of them living here.

He'd lived in Mae's house, which was less than half the size—maybe a quarter—of this one and on average three times as many people. How many kids would Mae have taken in if she'd had this much space?

Mia glanced over her shoulder. "Coming?"

"Yeah, just looking around."

"It's a beautiful house."

"Thank you," Sheila said without turning.

In the dining room, Keaton turned from where he was pouring a glass of wine as Sheila disappeared through another door. "Wine for both of you?"

"Thank you," Mia said.

"So this is the man who finally turned Mia's head. We've met, haven't we?"

Logan accepted the glass from Keaton. "Yes, Max Ingram introduced us recently at a party at his house."

"In fact, that's where Logan and I met. He works for Atlas Insurance, and we got to talking about art, and—" Mia let out a little sigh "—things just clicked."

Oh, she was good.

"Atlas, you say?" Keaton said. "That's the same carrier I use for insurance. Are you sure this is a social call?"

"Absolutely. I try not to mix business and pleasure, and when I'm with Mia, it certainly isn't business."

"I'm glad to hear it, but in case she didn't mention it, we do have a bit of business to tend to this evening." He said it like it was a conspiracy instead of Mia taking a look at a painting.

Sheila breezed back into the room. "Certainly, it will keep until after dinner."

Mia laid her hand on Shelia's arm. "Of course. There's no hurry. Actually, Logan was just admiring your beautiful house. Is there time for him to get a quick tour?"

"Oh, yes. Keaton?"

The man sighed.

"I don't want to trouble you." Logan couldn't imagine simply walking through his own house would be considered a burdensome task.

"Don't be silly," Sheila said. "Show the boy around, Keaton, and by the time you get back, dinner will be ready."

"Of course, dear," he said as he refilled his wineglass. "This way."

FOURTEEN

"MIA, THIS IS your chance. As soon as you see an opening, slip away and start opening things for me," Nikki said in the comm.

Mia took a deep breath and plastered a smile on her face. Nikki's incessant chattering in her ear was about to drive her mad. Luckily, Logan dismissed her distraction as being preoccupied about the painting instead of realizing that Nikki and Audrey were commenting on the status of their relationship and wishing the camera had a better angle to really be able to capture the kiss she shared with Logan.

Keaton guided them back to the foyer and crossed to the other side of the main staircase to show them the family room they had turned into a library after Chad had left the house. Floor-to-ceiling bookcases and beautiful untouched leather-bound editions of classic works of literature. "When Chad was small we used this as a playroom for him and as he grew, it became more of a family space to watch TV or play games. Many Sunday afternoons were spent watching football here."

"I can imagine," Logan said.

Mia walked the line of shelves, running her fingers over the volumes. She never understood having books that weren't read. If you enjoyed something you should be interacting with it, not just looking at it. These weren't works of art like paintings or sculptures. They were meant to be touched and read. Rather than say anything, she sipped her wine.

The men made their way back out of the room, and Keaton said, "I'm guessing you don't want to see the kitchen, so let's head upstairs."

As soon as they cleared the doorway, Mia hustled over to the window, flipped the lock, and inched it open. She wanted Nikki to have every advantage available. "Library, first floor, east side," she said quietly, hoping Nikki was paying attention. Then she hurried from the room to catch up to the men. They were halfway up the staircase, discussing the handmade rail and how long it took for it to be created.

When she joined them, Keaton turned and continued climbing the stairs. They just peeked in the master bedroom, as no one wanted to invade the Bishops' privacy. But Keaton enjoyed showing off the guest room they recently remodeled, and when they crossed the hall to his office, Mia's heart rate sped up. She hadn't seen the Moreau yet, so it made sense he would have it in his office.

Keaton opened the door and turned on the light. The room had a much warmer feel to it than she'd expected. The men started discussing the desk and the leather chair. Was Logan really that interested in the furniture? She had no idea what game he was playing, but she couldn't stay in the office and run the risk of them wanting to study the painting now.

"Excuse me, Keaton. The powder room?"

"It's right across the hall."

As she opened the bathroom door, Sheila called up the stairs, "Dinner is ready if you're done with the tour."

"I'm just going to freshen up. I'll meet you all back downstairs."

Logan came from the office and reiterated to Sheila how beautiful the house was. Mia locked the bathroom door and took a deep breath. The window in this room wouldn't help Nikki, as it was a small glass block. While she had privacy, though, she said, "Guest bedroom window is unlocked but not opened. I'm going to go back to the office and open that window for you. While it puts you in a position to have to scale the wall, you can be in and out without having to dodge anyone else."

"That's the room with the big casement crank windows, though. I don't think I can come and go without notice. The screen is on the inside and so is the crank for closing it. I think the den is my best bet."

"You'll have to carry the painting through the foyer to get upstairs. It's risky."

"I live for risk. Just keep them occupied. I'll be there in about three minutes."

Mia sighed again. "Make it ten. By then, I'll be downstairs and Sheila will have dinner served. How will you know it's safe?"

Nikki sighed. "If I'm clear say that something is delightful."

"And if it's not safe?"

"*Stop?*"

"How about *wait*? *Wait* might be easier to work into a conversation."

"*Wait* it is then."

Mia washed her hands and considered possible topics to bring up to keep everyone distracted enough that they would dismiss sounds coming from another area of the house. She left the bathroom, gave the office a fleeting glance, and went downstairs.

"Thank you for waiting for me. I received a call while I was upstairs. It took a little longer than I expected."

Logan stood and pulled her chair out for her.

"No problems, I hope," Keaton said.

"Not at all. I'm working on a big exhibit at the museum and a colleague had a question." She took her seat, with Logan guiding her close to the table. "It smells delicious, as always, Sheila."

Keaton, at the head of the table, picked up a platter of prime rib and stabbed two thick pieces of perfectly pink meat and slapped them on his plate before passing it to Logan. Logan turned to her and offered her a slice before taking one for himself. For a man who supposedly didn't belong in this world, he was fitting in just fine.

"Coming up on the house now. Yell if there's a problem," Nikki said in her ear. "But you know, don't really yell."

"So, how's retirement treating you, Keaton?" Mia asked, hoping the man would talk loudly because he had a booming voice when he thought he was being funny.

"I have to admit, it's killing me. I find myself still waking up early and getting dressed even though I've nowhere to go."

Sheila tittered. "He still goes into the office two or three days a week."

"It pisses Chad off, I'll tell you that. He thinks I'm there to check up on him, but in reality, I'm simply bored. I have no idea how Sheila has occupied herself for all the years since Chad started school."

Sheila pursed her lips. "I've been a member of many fine organizations. We've raised money for a lot of deserving charities. Maybe you should take up a hobby and you wouldn't be so bored now."

Mia stiffened. She had no idea that a simple question would reveal marital distress. The silence in the room was horrible.

A grunt came across the comm. "Damn window is tight."

Time to change the subject. Mia spoke louder than normal, her heart thudding in her ear, afraid everyone would hear Nikki. "Speaking of organizations, Sheila, tell me about the programs you have coming up."

"I'm in," Nikki whispered. "Keep up your boring conversation."

She patted Logan's leg under the table as she faced him. "Sheila is the queen of coordinating the best outdoor summer events." Turning back to Sheila, she added, "I've always thought you could sell your services. You handle every minute detail and make it look effortless."

"Actually, since you're here, maybe I could hit you up for some tickets to special exhibits at the Art Institute."

While Sheila talked about the upcoming event, Mia nodded and forced herself not to look toward the hall where she knew Nikki would be stealthily climbing the stairs. Mia ate her meal of prime rib and seasoned asparagus without tasting much. She tried to focus on the conversation, but her heart was racing. How did Nikki do this all the time without having full cardiac arrest?

"This thing is even more hideous than the pictures you showed us. How can people not only waste money on crap like this but then actually hang it where others can see?" Nikki whisper-ranted in her ear.

Mia started to laugh but covered it with a cough, and reached for her wine. She took a sip.

"Are you okay?" Logan asked.

"Yes," she said quietly and laid a hand on her chest. "Wrong pipe."

"Nikki, stop talking. You're making Mia laugh."

"Swap is done. Safe for me to travel back downstairs?"

Mia was about to compliment Sheila on the delightful dinner, but then Logan stood. Mia almost shot out of her seat. "Where are you going?"

"Excuse me," he said to Keaton and Sheila, "but I need to use the restroom." He paused, waiting for directions.

"Wait. I'll show you where it is," Mia said quickly, tucking her napkin next to her plate. She hoped to God Nikki was listening.

"Got it," Nikki whispered.

Mia walked with Logan back to the foyer. With a stealthy glance up the stairs, she walked a few steps down the hall and pointed. "First door on the left."

Before moving, he pulled her close and kissed her. Against her lips, he said, "I've been wanting to do that since we got here."

In her ear, Nikki said, "Bow-chicka-bow-wow."

Mia ran her hand down his lapel. "Save it for later." She waited until he turned and walked to the bathroom. When she looked to the top of the stairs again, Nikki stood there with a grin on her face. Mia shot her a dirty look, pointed, and mouthed, "Wait," and gestured to where Logan had just walked off to.

Nikki gave her a flirty wave and rolled her eyes.

Mia returned to the table and finished a few more

bites of food, chewing nervously, waiting for Logan to come back.

"Here comes lover boy," Nikki whispered.

A moment later, Logan returned to his seat.

"I'm heading out. Keep them all there," Nikki said.

"I hope you're all saving room for dessert," Sheila said.

Sheila to the rescue.

"Of course," Mia said. "Dessert sounds delightful."

"I'm stuffed," Logan said. "I don't know that I can eat another bite."

Mia smiled at him. "I hope you don't think I'll be sharing. In addition to being an excellent event planner, Sheila is known for being the best baker this side of the state."

"Gotcha," Nikki said. "Give me three minutes and I'll be gone."

"Mia, please don't say things like that," Sheila protested. "You'll make his expectations much higher than they should be. Baking is a hobby. Something I do to destress. I'm no professional."

"Don't let her fool you. Whatever the dessert is, you want some."

"I think you should just let me try a bite," Logan said in a low voice that felt like it was about far more than a sweet treat.

LOGAN WAS FULL FROM the fine meal the Bishops provided, but mostly he wanted to get this charade over with so he could be alone with Mia. He'd watched her work these people all night. She was so good, he wasn't even sure she was aware of how well she managed them.

When he asked to try a bite, her pupils dilated and

her breath caught, just barely, but enough for him to notice. Part of the problem was that he was spending too much time noticing everything about her. How she could converse on almost any topic broached. How her crooked smile was reserved for people she truly liked—he had been on the receiving end, but the Bishops weren't. How she touched him in ways that felt more intimate than their relationship warranted—not sexual, but careless in a way that expressed it was natural—and he wanted more of it.

To break her spell, and to prevent himself from touching her inappropriately at the dinner table, he stood. "Let me help you clear the table."

"You're a guest," Sheila said. "Please sit."

"I was taught that if someone else does the cooking, the least I can do is help clean up." He lowered his head a bit and asked Mia, "May I take this?"

She stacked her plate on top of his and wrapped her cool fingers around his wrist. "Thank you. But I'm still not sharing my dessert."

Sheila had already taken Keaton's plate, so he followed her to the kitchen. He set the dirty dishes on the counter near the sink.

"Please just leave them there. Our housekeeper will run the dishwasher."

"I really don't mind."

"I can see that. You're a sweet boy." She handed him a little white ceramic cup filled with some kind of chocolate pudding. "Now go take this in to your girl. Are you sure you don't want one?"

"It looks amazing, but I really am stuffed. Besides, I think I can talk Mia into sharing." He winked at the older woman and returned to the dining room. At the table, he set the cup in front of Mia.

"Oh, chocolate mousse."

She didn't even look up as he took his seat. She continued to stare longingly at the dessert.

"What I wouldn't give for you to look at me like that," he said quietly.

She glanced at him from the corner of her eyes. "Like what?"

"Like you can't wait to be alone to devour me."

The corner of her mouth kicked up. "Maybe I would if I had the satisfaction guarantee I have with this mousse."

"That is one guarantee I can get behind."

Instead of responding, she looked at Sheila as she set a cup in front of Keaton. "Sheila, this looks divine."

Sheila smiled and pointed at Logan. "He said he was going to talk you into sharing."

"He hasn't yet made an offer worthy of chocolate mousse."

"If that mousse is as good as you say, you can have whatever you want."

Mia picked up her spoon and scooped the tiniest bit out of the bowl. He stared as she slid the spoon into her mouth, wrapping her lips around it, and closing her eyes. The image caused his blood to heat and race and he wanted to put his hands on her.

She let out a little moan as she slipped the spoon out of her mouth.

"It cannot be that good." He leaned closer and whispered, "You're a tease."

"Yes, I am, but this mousse is magnificent." She scooped another bite and this time held it to his lips.

He opened and tasted the chocolate. It was a burst

of sweet, creamy dark chocolate on his tongue. He savored the flavor before swallowing. "I concede. It is that good."

Sheila put her napkin on the table. "Would you like one?"

He held up a hand. "No, thank you. It is delicious, but I really can't eat another bite."

While Mia finished her mousse—the woman took her dessert seriously—Logan spoke to Keaton about the Moreau painting. "Mia said you're selling your Moreau painting. Can I ask if there's a reason? I thought part of the purpose of buying art was to let it appreciate."

"It has appreciated in value and in all honesty, I've grown tired of it. In addition, Sheila has never been fond of it."

"That's an understatement. It's revolting. Have you ever looked at it?" Sheila fluttered her lashes. "Keaton wanted to hang it in the living room. I wouldn't have it."

"Well, it'll be gone soon enough. Maybe even before the auction. Isn't that right, Mia?"

Mia dabbed at her mouth. "Possibly. I'll take some good photos of it and send them to my friend to see if we can make a deal."

"Are you ready now, or would you prefer an after-dinner drink?"

"I'm ready." She shifted her chair back.

Logan rose. "Sheila, how about I help you clear the table while these two go conduct business?"

"I think this one might be a keeper, Mia. So sweet."

He looked over at Mia, who rolled her eyes at him. She stood and he leaned in for a kiss. It was brief, but he tasted the chocolate on her tongue. "I'll meet you upstairs."

FIFTEEN

THE COMM IN Mia's ear had been blissfully quiet for the last ten minutes. While Mia ate dessert and adequately teased Logan, Nikki had said she was clear of the house. Mia had finally been able to breathe freely. That, coupled with the delicious mousse, allowed Mia to relax. Now she just needed to do her part.

Keaton led the way back up to his office.

"I gotta say, Mrs. Bishop was right to hate this thing. Have fun keeping a straight face while pointing out a silly flower," Nikki said in the comm.

In the office, Keaton turned on the ceiling light as well as the desk lamp and the track lighting he had over the painting itself. Mia pulled out her phone, stood on the opposite side of the desk, and snapped a few photos. She texted them to Jared.

"Would it be all right to take it off the wall so I can inspect it? My friend is going by my word and I want to make sure I can let him know of any imperfections or issues I see."

"It's in perfect condition, but we can take it down. Give me a minute." He moved a stack of file folders from a side table.

Keaton removed the painting and set it on the table. Mia lifted an edge and peeked underneath. Then she used her phone to take a quick video. She bent over the painting and began inspecting it, inch by inch. But the stupid flower was glaring at her from the center of the canvas. She couldn't rush to find it, though, as this was not her area of expertise.

"Looks good, right? Pristine condition. I had professional movers deliver and install it for me."

She got to the flower and stepped back. Then leaned in and squinted her eyes. "Do you have a small brush or dust-free cloth?"

"What is it?" he asked.

"It might be nothing. Maybe a piece of dust caught in the paint, but I can't be sure."

He handed her a handkerchief.

"This might leave other fibers. Can you ask Sheila if she has an unused makeup brush?"

"Sheila!"

Mia started. She hadn't expected him to holler.

Logan rushed into the room. "What's wrong?"

"Nothing. I just need a brush. I think there's something on the painting," Mia said.

Sheila came in, wiping her hands on a towel. "What is it?"

Mia turned to her. "Do you have a new makeup brush I can borrow?"

Sheila pressed her lips together. "Possibly. I'll go check."

"What is it?" Logan asked.

"It might be nothing." She waved him over and pointed at the tiny flower.

He reached out as if to pick at it. She slapped the back of his hand.

"Don't. If it's something stuck in the paint, you can cause a chip. Let me try a brush."

Sheila returned and handed her a wrapped brush. It was fat and full.

Mia pulled off the plastic and then twirled the bristles over the flower. "Huh. Didn't work." She picked up her phone and zoomed in on the spot.

After snapping the picture, she stepped away, and with Logan looking over her shoulder, she studied the picture.

"It looks like a flower."

"It does. And I don't believe it belongs there," Mia said.

"Please turn to Bishop. I wanna see his face," London said in the comm.

Mia turned and handed the phone to Keaton. "It looks like a small daisy. It's easily overlooked, but Moreau wouldn't have added anything like that to his painting. Definitely not this one."

"What are you saying?"

"I don't think this is an authentic Moreau." She scrunched her face apologetically as she said it and reached for her phone.

"Impossible. Do you know what I paid for this? It was authenticated before it was insured." He jabbed a finger at Logan. "Your company said it was real."

Logan raised his hands. "I don't know anything about this."

Liar. Mia turned back to the painting. "Let me keep looking. Maybe I'm wrong."

"Pictures don't lie," Logan said.

She shot him a look. Was this what he was hoping for? If so, then she'd played right into his hands. Mia continued her inspection of the painting. When she neared the bottom, the incongruent brushstrokes stood out. The color was off and the paint layered on much too thick. She turned around again to face Keaton. "I see another issue. There are some brushstrokes that aren't right."

Keaton stepped closer and she pointed at the discolored paint.

"I'm sorry. I can't recommend this purchase to my friend. At least not without another certified appraisal."

"This is ridiculous. You must be wrong."

She crossed her arms. "I admit that I am not an expert, but I strongly urge you to have someone look at this before you send it to auction."

"I'll do one better than that," Logan said. "We'll have an appraiser here tomorrow. We carry the policy on this painting and if it's a forgery, the policy is void."

Keaton got red in the face and began to shake. "Are you accusing me of fraud? This is real!" He jabbed his finger toward the painting. "Bring your experts. You'll see."

Mia ducked her head to hide her smile. Now she understood why Nikki enjoyed this. "I think we should be going, Logan."

As she walked past him, she masked her joy and looked at Sheila. "Thank you so much for the lovely meal."

"I'm glad you enjoyed it."

Behind her, Logan said to Keaton, "My office will be in touch in the morning."

Logan walked beside her down the wide staircase with his hand on her lower back. She said nothing until they were in his car.

"I can't believe it. What's going to happen?"

Logan started the car. "How sure are you that it's a forgery?"

"Positive."

"You didn't sound positive in there." He stared into her eyes as if assessing her answer.

"I learned early in life that if you challenge men like Keaton Bishop, you better have the proof to make them fall. There is no room for error. Since I am neither certified nor an expert on Moreau, I let him yell and imply I'm stupid. But that painting is not authentic."

He wrapped his long fingers around the back of her neck and pulled her close. A moment of panic struck at the thought of him seeing the comm in her ear.

"God you're sexy." Then he brought her to his mouth and kissed her deeply, stealing her breath, and making every nerve tingle with awareness and thoughts of the comm disappear. "I've been waiting to do that again since dessert."

"That would have been totally inappropriate for the dinner table," she said against his lips.

"You might want to take your comm out if this is going to continue," Audrey said in her ear.

For a brief moment, she'd forgotten about being listened to. She slid back into her seat. "So if your appraiser comes tomorrow and determines that the painting is a forgery, what happens next?"

"We cancel the policy on the basis of fraud. He'll try to sue Atlas, but given that I didn't see adequate security on the painting, he'll have a hard time winning the suit." He pulled out of the driveway. "Unless he can show proof of a break-in, which isn't going to happen because what kind of thief steals a painting and leaves a forgery?"

"Us, bitches!" Nikki yelled in her ear. "'Cause we're fucking brilliant!"

Under the guise of looking out her window, Mia pulled the comm from her ear. She'd had enough of Nikki's commentary. She didn't need to announce her brilliance. As she dug into her purse to drop the comm and pretend to fix her makeup, she said, "So he won't be able to sell the painting, but then what?"

"What do you mean?"

"His plan to defraud some unsuspecting person failed, but he doesn't suffer any consequences for the attempt?"

"Not really. Assuming he still has the original, he'll be able to sell it and recoup his money. And if he's slick and brings the original back tonight, I look like an idiot to my bosses for claiming it's a forgery."

There was zero chance of that happening, but she couldn't let him know that. "I have the photos and a video recording. It will be time-stamped, so you have evidence of his scam."

Logan reached over and took her hand. "Thank you for that." Then he chuckled. "Did you see the look on his face when you pointed out the flower? I thought he was going to burst a blood vessel."

"Yes, that was quite a show."

He lifted their joined hands and pressed a kiss to hers. "Thank you for your help on this. It might be just the thing I need to take to my boss."

"What do you mean?"

"Your photos should be enough to get my boss to do a full audit of...clients in the area."

He stumbled on the word *clients*. What had he been

thinking? Criminals? Thieves? Her father's friends? He'd be right on all counts.

"Everything okay?" he asked.

"Yeah." She shook her head. "No. It feels very much like the stink of my father's crimes oozing its way back into my life. Keaton is one of my father's friends. They played poker together for years. Another crooked man in my life. It's disgusting. Do they seek each other out? Or compare notes on how to be a criminal?"

"Probably a little of both. I'm sorry this is dredging up uncomfortable stuff for you."

They drove in silence the rest of the way to her condo. Logan had held her hand the entire way, soothing her, offering comfort. But the kiss he'd given her when they got into the car had been sexy and exciting. She had no doubt he could offer her an escape from the miserable path her thoughts were taking. He pulled up alongside her building.

She decided to just go for it. "If it's not too late for you, you can park and come up for a drink."

"Just a drink?" He gunned the gas to turn the corner into the parking garage. "I'm always up for being with you. For drinks or anything else."

"I imagine there might be quite a bit more than just a drink."

THE LOGICAL VOICE IN Logan's head told him this was a bad idea. He was undercover and while Mia wasn't exactly a suspect, she wasn't totally clear either. She pointed him to where guest spots were located and he parked. He considered all the ways this could go bad:

She might be involved in the forgeries.

But she just nailed Bishop and didn't back down.

If she was in on it, she would've lied or he would've called her out.

She might be running some other scam.

To what end? She's been handed a raw deal with her father. She's led a law-abiding life.

You could fall for her. At some point she'll realize you've been lying to her and she's completely out of your league.

Mia opened her door to get out and glanced at him over her shoulder with that teasing crooked grin and he made his decision.

It's worth the risk.

He followed Mia into the building and then the elevator. Once the doors swished closed, he slid a hand around her hip and pulled her close, her back to his front. He brushed her hair from her neck and planted an openmouthed kiss at the juncture between her neck and shoulder. She gave a little shudder and leaned against him. The doors reopened and she straightened away from him.

She unlocked the door and set her keys and purse on a side table. "What would you like to drink?"

"Uh, whatever you have is fine." He took in his surroundings. Never before had anything so blatantly smacked him as much as this décor did. He was almost afraid to touch anything. A huge marble fireplace took up most of one wall. In front of it was a leather couch that probably cost a month of his salary. Everything was pristine and perfect.

A moment later, Mia was standing in front of him with a glass of whiskey. "Something wrong?"

"No." He accepted the glass and took a sip. The smooth burn was another reminder of how far out of his league she was. His brain scrambled to keep up. He'd known she had money. Even after her father ran and the government seized assets, Mia had an inheritance in trust from her mother's side of the family.

"Are you sure? If you don't want this, it's okay. It can be just two friends sharing a drink."

"It's just that... I knew you had money, but this place is amazing. I guess I didn't realize how rich you are."

"Is my wealth an issue?"

He knew it shouldn't be. Logically. "You know I don't come from money, right? I'm not part of your world. I'm a visitor that most people will overlook."

She reached up and stroked his cheek. "Then let's enjoy your visit. One of the things I like best about you is that you're not from my world. You have no personal feelings about my last name—you're not using it to get ahead or as a weapon against me. And right now, that's enough."

It probably wouldn't be enough for long. But Mia was an amazing woman, and if he had one shot to be with her, even for a little while, he would be completely stupid to pass it up.

"Would you like to sit down to finish your drink, or will you be leaving?"

"I'm not leaving. But I do have to make a quick call to set everything up at Bishop's tomorrow."

"Well, then." She slugged back the remaining whiskey in her glass. "While you take care of business, I'm going to change into something more comfortable."

"I'll hurry."

When she had turned the corner, he pulled out his phone and called Stokes.

"Don't you have a life, Ford?" she answered.

"I'll have you know I'm on a date right now."

She snorted. "Must not be going well if you're calling me."

"I'm with Mia Benson and it's going very well. She just called out Keaton Bishop's painting as a fake. I'm going to forward pictures to you. We need to get Atlas to send certified appraisers to Bishop's house tomorrow. This is our chance."

"You and Mia, huh?"

"Yeah." He paused and waited for her to tell him it was a bad idea.

"Are you sure she's clear of this?"

"She's done nothing but help."

"Just watch yourself."

"Will do." He downed the rest of his drink and set the glass on the table behind the couch. He loosened his tie as he walked the room, looking for some indication of who Mia Benson was. She had a steely façade that she showed the world, but he'd seen the cracks, and he wanted to know the real woman. But there was nothing in this living room. It was almost sterile. Too perfect.

Mia came back and stood beside the fireplace wearing a silky, champagne-colored nightgown. It went past her knees, but had a slit up the side. The smooth material clung to her curves in a way that made her appear to float. "Done with your call?"

"Yes."

She took a few steps forward. "So no more talk of business?"

"What business?"

She smiled. "May I take your jacket?"

"Sure."

She walked around him, reached up, and wrapped

her fingers around the collar to slide the jacket from his body. He turned around and watched her hang it up. Without her heels, she was really short. Like he would have to bend in half to kiss her. She walked back to him. Maybe not quite in half.

She moved her hands up his chest until they reached his shoulders. Then she went up on tiptoe to kiss him. His hands skated over the slippery material at her waist.

"You sure about this?"

"Yes. Bedroom's that way." She pointed over his shoulder.

"Lead the way." He opened his arms and she took his hand, truly leading him like a lost puppy. And he would gladly take any scraps she offered.

SIXTEEN

AFTER CATCHING HIS BREATH, Logan sat up and asked for directions to the bathroom. When he returned, Mia was still stretched out on the bed. She'd made no attempt to cover up. She looked at him with a sleepy smile.

He wanted nothing more than to crawl back into bed with her, but they hadn't discussed him spending the night.

"Are you staying or leaving?"

"Which do you prefer?"

She pushed up on an elbow and cocked an eyebrow. "I'm not into games, Logan. I have no hang-ups about spending the night with a man. I'm fully capable of sleeping with someone without thinking marriage is imminent."

"I wasn't accusing you of anything. There hadn't been an invitation, and I know better than to assume a woman wants a man to spend the night."

She patted the mattress beside her. "The invitation has been extended. Get your sexy butt back in this bed."

He twisted to show her said rear. "You think my butt is sexy?"

"Oh Lord. Fishing for compliments is not a good look." But she still cracked a smile.

He climbed into bed and kissed her before sliding his arm beneath her head and pulling her close. "Everyone needs to hear good things on occasion."

She threw her leg over his and the feel of her smooth skin against him was a turn-on. She kissed his chest and asked, "Are you spending the night?"

"I can, but I'll have to leave early enough to go home to change before going to the office. I want to be at Bishop's when the appraiser is working."

"Excellent. Be prepared for Keaton to yell at you all red-faced with neck veins bulging."

Logan reached for his phone and set an alarm. "My veins would be ready to burst too if I was looking at losing all that money. It's kind of a brilliant scam. To sell a forgery, make the money and still have the original to sell at a later date."

"He must not be all that brilliant if he's been caught," she said sleepily.

"True."

Mia dozed in his arms, but Logan couldn't sleep. His mind raced with all the possibilities. If Bishop did, in fact, still have the original, why get so angry? It would make more sense to demand a certified appraisal and make Mia look like an idiot. He could switch out the forgery for the original by tomorrow.

Unless he didn't have access to the original.

Or if someone was scamming him. Ingram thought he had the original and it was stolen, but the one that was supposedly stolen a forgery, or was replaced with a forgery. Something still wasn't lining up. He was close. He could feel it, but he couldn't see how things fit together. Maybe proving Bishop's painting was a forgery would be enough to get him to spill. If they knew who the forger was, they could find out if there were more counterfeits in the Chicago area.

He finally fell asleep thinking of puzzle pieces.

The following morning they had a shower together. Although they'd joked about him being a visitor to her world, part of him wanted to stay with her. Those burgeoning feelings made guilt rise in him because he was lying to her. As they dried off, he asked, "Do you have time for a cup of coffee? There's something I want to talk to you about."

She hung her towel on the warming rack. "That sounds rather ominous. But I'll go make a pot of coffee."

She strode from the bathroom totally naked, making him rethink how this might go. After wrapping a short silky robe around herself, she went to the kitchen. Logan gathered all of yesterday's clothes and redressed, preparing how to tell Mia the truth. It might be a mistake. It could blow his cover, but he didn't think she'd tell anyone, even if she chose to never see him again. He did believe, however, that not telling her the truth would ruin any chance he had with her.

As he walked to the kitchen, he rolled the sleeves of his shirt. He heard Mia talking but didn't hear anyone else's voice. He paused and debated whether he should wait in the bedroom to give her privacy.

She sounded upset, and then Logan heard the words that had him surging forward.

"No, Daddy. That's not at all what you asked."

MIA COULDN'T BELIEVE her ears. Of all the gall.

"It was quite the simple request, kitten. I told you I needed your art connections. The last thing I wanted was for you to try to tell my friend that he was holding a forgery. I know it's not a forgery, but now doubt will be cast. You need to go back to Keaton and tell him you were mistaken. Tell the insurance agency that you were… I don't know—thinking of a different painting or artist. Something to set this right."

"I'm not wrong."

Logan came into the kitchen, shirt sleeves rolled to his elbows in a careless, casual way that made her want him all over again. His face, however, was filled with concern. She forced a smile and held up a finger to let him know she'd be done soon. Then she gestured to the full coffeepot before heading out to her small balcony. She squinted into the early-morning sun and peered down the block and between buildings to catch a glimpse of the lake. The streets below were packed with rush-hour traffic, but she was high enough that she could talk on the phone and still hear. She lowered her voice. "Keaton's painting *is* a forgery, and I won't lie about it."

"Mia, sweetheart, I need this."

"Why do you care about Keaton's painting?"

She was met with a long pause. She thought they'd been disconnected again.

Finally, he released a long sigh. "The painting is mine. Keaton is holding it for me. When you said you hadn't gotten your inheritance because of your mother, I asked Keaton to sell it and send me the money."

Gotcha! "Why don't you just come home?"

"We've been over this, Mia. I can't. I need your help. I'm running out of money and into issues with my contingencies."

"What contingencies?"

"Keaton and that painting is one. If he can't sell it, I can't get the money."

"How many such contingencies do you have?" So he had always been planning to run.

Another exaggerated pause.

"If you had told me about Keaton, I wouldn't have offered to look at it. I wouldn't have been able to ruin your scam."

"It's not a scam. Keaton bought the real thing. If it's a forgery, then *he's* the one running a scam and it's going to cost me."

"What do you want from me?"

"I'll need help liquidating my other properties. Can I count on your help?"

Her stomach tightened in a knot and bile rose. She hated allowing this man to think she was on his side. "I don't know how I can help."

"Thank you, baby. I knew I could count on you. I'll be in touch with more information soon. Just help me make the sales. That's all, and I'll never ask for anything else."

"Does that mean I'll never see you again?"

"Of course we'll see each other."

"When? It's been five years."

"I had to give it enough time for the feds to give up on tracking you. Let's get some paintings sold and I'll meet you for a vacation."

She sighed. "Helping you is illegal."

"Only if you're caught, and no one will be looking at you. I'll make sure of it. We'll talk soon." He disconnected then.

Mia was filled with a mix of anger and hope. Her plan was coming together in ways she hadn't even considered. She smelled the fresh coffee wafting from behind her. "How much of that did you hear?"

"Enough," Logan said as he joined her at the railing and handed her a steaming cup. "Your father?"

She nodded. "He—"

Logan touched her arm. "Before you continue, there's something I have to tell you."

"What is it?"

"Maybe we should sit." He moved to one of the chairs she kept out here for when she wanted to relax with a glass of wine and a good book on a warm summer evening.

Instead, this morning, she was going to sit with a cup of coffee, serious conversation, and the cool morning air. At least the company was good. She sat and took a drink of coffee.

"When I said there was something I needed to tell you, it's important that I tell you now before we get any deeper."

"Are you married? Engaged? Have four baby mamas who are going to hunt me down?" She'd been trying for levity, but the conversation with her father dragged her down.

His laugh was dry. "My real name is Logan Ford and I don't work for Atlas Insurance. I'm an FBI agent."

Wow. She hadn't expected him to come clean on being undercover. She took another drink of coffee and let that sink in. If he was telling her, it must mean that he had zero idea that she was behind the forgeries.

"Mia?"

She set her cup on the small round table between them. "I knew."

His eyes widened.

She held up a hand. "I didn't know you're FBI, but I've had my doubts about you being an insurance agent for weeks now. You don't know enough about art to be in this line of work, and while you explained that away, you're more invested in these paintings and the forgeries than any insurance agent I've ever met."

He blew out a long breath. "I warned my boss that someone was going to figure me out." He gave her a smile. "Had a feeling it was going to be you, too."

What did that mean? Why did he continue to spend time with her if he knew she could possibly blow his cover?

"Why tell me now?" she asked.

"Well, first—" he reached across the table and took her hand "—after last night, I felt guilty. I know you said you want to keep this casual, but even a casual relationship is still a relationship. I wasn't comfortable keeping something so big from you. I wouldn't be giving us much of a chance."

Mia's lungs froze. Sure, they were having fun, but he couldn't believe this could go anywhere, could he? She stood, pulling away from him, so she could breathe. "Is there a second? You started with *first…*"

"I planned to tell you anyway, but then I overhead you talking to your father. I didn't hear much, but I heard enough to know he's asking you for something. I wanted you to know who I am, full disclosure, before you said something to me you might regret."

"So you're telling me this now because it gives me the option to not tell you about the conversation with my father and you'd be okay with that? If you knew he was calling me, but I didn't tell you the content of the conversation?"

"I might not like it, but I'd understand. Criminal or not, he's your father. And it's not my case."

This guy was too good. "Even though you work for

the FBI, who happens to be after my father, you're okay with me helping him?"

He pressed his lips together and leaned forward, bracing his arms on his legs. "I don't think you're a bad person. I would hope that you wouldn't want to help your father, and I would definitely try to talk you out of it because he'll hurt you, but I would do what I could to protect you."

Shit. Why couldn't he be like normal men? Or even a normal cop? Tell her that if she broke the law, he'd arrest her. She would know how to respond to that. Walking away would be much simpler. She stood and looked out over the city again.

"You can tell me as much or as little as you want."

"He wants me to help him. He needs money."

Logan stood and came to her at the railing. "What do you plan to do?"

"I don't know. I'll have to call the agents who are on his case and let them know."

"I can do that for you if you want. They'll want to talk to you and I'm sure they'll ask about tapping your phone."

"The answer to that will still be no."

He continued to study her. "Can I ask why? If he keeps calling you at this number, we might be able to figure out where to get him."

"Not wanting to give the FBI access to my phone doesn't make me a criminal. I value my privacy, especially in light of everything my father has done. And for the record, I've told the FBI where my father is. To my knowledge, he's still in Montenegro. There's simply nothing you can do about it." She pushed away from the railing. "Tell Halloran he can call to harass me this afternoon. I have a busy morning."

"You're very practical about all this. It's a little frightening."

"I was raised by a lawyer and a businessman. Practicality runs through my veins."

"One day soon, I'm going to witness you lose control and do something silly and impractical."

"Not likely."

"We'll see." Then he turned and left.

Mia immediately texted the rest of her team and called an emergency meeting. Things were heating up all over.

SEVENTEEN

Mia arrived at the apartment, where everyone was already waiting for her. Jared and Audrey were huddled over her computer and Nikki was playing a video game on the TV. When the door closed, they all looked up. "I don't have a lot of time to talk, so let's get through this fast. As you know, Nikki made the switch last night, and Keaton almost had a coronary when I told him his painting was a forgery."

"We knew all that," Nikki said, returning to her game. "We didn't need a meeting."

"You'll want to pay attention to this next part." She took a deep breath. "Logan came clean to me about being FBI."

"That's good, right?" Audrey said. "If he's telling her the truth, he has no clue she's part of this."

"That's my thinking," Mia said, still feeling satisfied both from her amazing night and Logan's admission.

Nikki spun around on the couch. "Or he told you to gauge your reaction. See if you got twitchy." She smirked. "Did you get twitchy?"

"No. I told him I already knew."

"What the fuck!" Nikki threw her game controller against the corner of the couch. "What's next? Gonna invite him here?"

"Don't get your panties in a twist. I didn't tell him

I knew he was FBI. I simply admitted that I suspected he wasn't really an insurance agent."

Nikki moved her head side to side. "As a bluff, not bad."

"A good con has hints of truth. Or so I'm told."

"I don't like it," Jared said. "How do you know he bought it? Like Nikki said, this could all be a setup."

Mia pressed her lips together. She didn't know how to explain, but in her gut, she knew. "You have to trust me on this." She paused and decided to come clean to her team. "There's something else." She waited until she had their complete attention. "After the Devereaux fiasco, my father called me."

Jared pushed back from the desk. He'd be extra irritated that she hadn't told him.

"I didn't mention it earlier because there wasn't much to say. He asked for money and I told him I didn't have any. Then he said he would need my connections in the art world. That was the entirety of the conversation."

"It would've been nice to know that the plan is working," Audrey said. "What we're doing is hitting him."

"Then you'll be glad to know that my meeting with Keaton was a hard hit. My father called again early this morning, angry because I told Keaton he had a forgery. He also admitted that he has more art to liquidate, and he wants my help. He's going to get me a full list."

"Wait a minute." Jared raised his hand as his eyes narrowed. "Where was Logan when this phone call happened?"

Mia licked her lips. She hadn't planned on telling them she'd slept with Logan. "In my kitchen." She crossed her arms. "I told the FBI about the first call, and I informed Logan this morning after I spoke with my father. That's part of the reason I believe he doesn't suspect me. He overheard that it was Dad on the phone, but he stopped me from saying anything until he told me about the FBI. He wanted to give me the option of what to tell him and what not to."

And he'd said he'd do whatever he could to protect me.

"Wait a minute," Nikki said with one hand in the air. "You're intentionally bringing the FBI in to investigate?"

"They're already investigating. They know my father wants my help, but as we've discussed, since Logan told me the truth, he has no clue about my involvement. Once I have the list of art from my father, I'll withhold it until we make all the exchanges. Then, I'll give the FBI the list. Right now my father thinks Keaton is running a scam to cheat him. If I keep Logan close, I can steer the FBI away from all of you."

Regardless of her feelings for Logan, she would protect them and the work they were doing.

Jared rose and crossed the room, eyeing her suspiciously. "Who are you and what have you done with my cousin? She made it clear that we were *not* going to be a team and that everyone was on her own."

"You're not very funny." She looked at Audrey and Nikki. "Regardless of how this all started, I assure you I will do everything I can to keep you from getting caught. You just keep doing your jobs."

"Speaking of…" Audrey said. "There's a truck set to pick up the Spenser painting from Small's house tomorrow. We need to decide where we're going to hit it."

Nikki leaned over the back of the couch. "As much as I'd love to take something from McNamara's, it makes more sense to take it from the house. It'll be quicker, less planning."

"Fewer things to hack," Audrey added.

"He isn't hosting anything at his house as far as I know," Mia said. "I have no reason to go there."

Nikki had a wicked smile on her face. "But Logan does."

"If Logan goes there, it's going to be with a certified appraiser. If you make the switch after that, insurance will pay out. The switch will have to happen before then."

"Field trip!" Nikki yelled as she hopped off the couch. Not much rattled that woman. And for that, Mia was grateful. "We'll go to Small's for recon today and determine the best way to grab it."

"Just don't get spotted."

Nikki snorted. "I'm good, remember?" Turning to Audrey she said, "Should we resurrect Barbie and Susie?"

"God, no," Audrey answered. "I have a fully equipped van now. We can park near his house and I should be able to figure something out."

"That's no fun."

"I'll leave you to it then," Mia said. "I won't be able to be back here until later tonight. I still have my job to tend to."

"And a sexy FBI dude to date," Nikki said flippantly.

Mia felt her face warm. "I am not going to discuss who I choose to sleep with."

The thief sobered quickly. "If it compromises us, we have every right to know."

"My actions will not compromise the mission. This plan has been the driving force in my life for five years. Sleeping with someone is not going to change that."

Nikki snickered. "You just admitted to sleeping with Logan. I hope it was good."

"It was phenomenal. Thanks for asking."

Jared groaned. "I do not want to hear this."

"I'm going to work. I'll be in touch." Looking pointedly at Nikki, she said, "Stay out of trouble."

Nikki flailed her arms with a huff. "Why does everyone keep saying that? I've been so good."

"We all know the potential for trouble is still there," Mia retorted. She picked up her purse and left the apartment.

Jared was on her heels and confronted her when she got to the elevator. "What's going on?"

"What do you mean?"

"You and Logan?"

"We have chemistry. We like each other. And if things were different, I might even take him seriously. But we both have jobs to do that are in direct conflict with one another. If I stay close to him, I'll have the inside track."

"I worry about you. You've barely given anyone a second glance in years, and now you set your sights on an FBI agent? The one who just happens to be investigating the forgeries we've put out in the world."

"Story of my life. Ridiculous relationships. I'm fine. Thank you for your concern, but I'm fine." As if repeating herself was more convincing.

"Okay." He wasn't buying it either. He turned and went back into the apartment.

Mia rode the elevator down to the street and really hoped that everything she just told her cousin wasn't a lie.

ONCE SHE GOT to her office, she switched gears, at least for a little while. She had meetings upon meetings to organize her exhibit. It left little time for her to conduct more research to try to find the last few pieces that would fill out the remainder of the exhibit. Between the thefts and Logan wanting to date, she had no after-work free time these days.

As she attempted to squeeze in a quick lunch at her desk, Anya knocked on her partially open door. *I knew I should've closed and locked it.*

Wiping her mouth with the tiny paper napkin from the cafeteria, she called, "Come in."

"Hi. I've been looking for you all day."

"Sorry. I've been swamped with meetings. What do you need?"

Anya took the seat in front of Mia's desk, clutching her tablet to her chest. "I found it. The painting you asked me to look into."

Mia had totally forgotten tasking Anya with trying to figure out Logan's missing painting. Pushing her sad salad to the corner of her desk, she said, "What have you found?"

"Camille Hurley created a painting entitled *Farm Girl Dreams* in 1922. I was able to follow provenance until 1934. Then it drops off the radar. If I have some more time, I can dig and maybe find out what happened to it."

"Thank you, Anya. But this very well might be a wild-goose chase. We know the painting went missing after World War Two. For all we know, it might've been destroyed."

"I don't think so. It's a treasure hunt."

Mia thought the same. She saw the glint in the woman's eyes. "I appreciate the offer, but you have a proposal to get together for the *Crime and Punishment* exhibit."

"It's almost ready. I would've had it to you by now, but it's missing the perfect final piece."

"It's better to take your time and get it right."

"Thank you." She got up and left the office.

Once she was gone, Mia took the notes on *Farm Girl Dreams*. The timeline fit the story Logan's grandfather had shared, and it certainly looked like it matched the grainy photo he'd shown her. She followed the same path of provenance Anya had, but after some more digging, she was able to get a little closer. Then the trail went cold. But she had a name. It was a start. Jared would probably know where to look from here. Mia wasn't in the habit of traveling the dark web to find art, but Jared was. If she could find the painting, it could mean a lot to Logan's family. It felt important. She didn't want to inspect the feelings behind those motivations too closely.

Later that afternoon, Mia called Nikki. "Have you and Audrey had any luck with plans?"

"Oh, yeah. But you're not gonna like it. Come here when you get off work."

She sighed. "Fine."

She might not like the plan Nikki and Audrey came up with, but at least they had forward movement. She texted Logan. Your great-grandfather's painting was titled Farm Girl Dreams.

How do you know?

Research, baby.

He sent a gif from the movie *Wayne's World* of Wayne and Garth bowing.

She responded with a Venus Williams princess wave from Wimbledon.

Then she put her phone in her purse because she was having far too much fun with her mark.

EIGHTEEN

BY THE TIME Mia got to the apartment to meet Nikki and Audrey, she was exhausted. Walking into the living room, she saw a wooden crate sitting in front of the couch. She went over and peered in. The Spenser forgery was packed inside.

"What is this?"

"While we were doing recon today, we saw a company come and crate up Caleb Small's Spenser painting to prepare it for transport. They set up in the driveway and built a custom crate. Using the pictures we took, we re-created it here," Nikki explained.

"I'm guessing your plan is to then switch the entire crate and hope no one notices."

"They won't notice. This is identical."

"What exactly is the part you think I will take issue with?"

Audrey tapped her tablet and brought up more images on the TV. "According to McNamara's, their preferred handlers will be picking up the painting tomorrow afternoon. We need to get in before then."

A pulse throbbed behind Mia's left eye. Even though she knew she would regret it, she asked, "What does that have to do with me?"

"We need access to the house, and you're our best bet," Nikki said, shoving a donut into her mouth.

"I have no way of getting you in."

"Mrs. Small is out of town. Caleb's been there all day. No sign of leaving. If you can lure Caleb out, we can get in. I'm not comfortable sitting and waiting for him to leave and hoping he doesn't come back before we're gone," Audrey said.

"He doesn't need to be gone. If you can just keep him occupied like you did the Bishops, I can work with that," Nikki added. "London is on call with the van as soon as we need her."

"Why would I want to go there? I need to have a valid reason." One that didn't involve bringing Logan because that would be far too suspicious. Then an idea sparked. "Forget it. I have an idea."

She checked the time. Late, but not rudely so. She dialed Caleb's number.

"Hello?"

"Hi, Caleb. It's Mia Benson."

"Mia, how are you?"

"I've actually been better. I was wondering if it wouldn't be too much of an imposition, I'd like to talk to you about something."

"Go ahead."

"Actually, this is better to be discussed in person. Are you available if I come over tonight?"

"Tonight? Uh, well, I suppose."

"Thank you. I'll be there within the hour." Then she disconnected. "Get your keys, girls, we have a painting to steal."

"What are you going to talk to him about?" Audrey asked.

"The truth. Keaton Bishop is angry and he wants to blame me for pointing out he has a forgery. Then my father called. These men have been in touch with him.

Even if he doesn't admit it, he'll know I'm not lying. I'll play the paranoia card I played with Darren Turner."

Nikki clapped. "That's it. We've brought Mia over to the dark side. Admit it," she said as she bumped Mia's shoulder with hers, "you like it."

Mia raised an eyebrow. "I don't dislike it."

Audrey asked, "How did you know he'd agree?"

"While I was being pushy, it would have been incredibly rude of him to turn me away in my time of need. I specifically asked him for help. He wouldn't want it to get around that he declined."

"You people have too many rules to live by," Audrey said.

"You people?"

"Rich people. The rest of us would be like, 'Hell, no. Call me tomorrow.' It's not like you were crying or really desperate or anything."

"It would have been far more suspicious if I had cried."

Audrey eyed her. "Yeah, I could see that."

"I'll get London here with the van," Nikki said. "Get your comm in because we don't know where the crate is and you'll need to direct us. Plus, you can give us a heads-up about what room you're in."

"Got it," Mia said and took the earpiece and the camera necklace. "My ride will be here in a few minutes."

"We're not going together?" Audrey asked.

Mia huffed. "Do you really think I would ever be seen stepping out of that van?"

Audrey's mouth dropped open. "The van is beautiful. It's a whole mobile command center."

"And it looks highly suspicious. But to save time, we'll all take the car together to get the van."

They gathered the crate and Nikki's tools and went out to the car. Mia got in the passenger seat and said, "Here's fifty dollars cash if you can take a quick detour and drop my friends off."

"No problem, lady. Where to?"

They gave him the address to London's loft and rode in silence. When Audrey and Nikki got out, Mia stepped out to move to the back seat. Before getting back in, she said to them, "Move fast and get in place so that as soon as I'm with Caleb, you can go in. I don't know how long I can keep him interested in my ramblings."

"Will do."

Once in the back seat, Mia made sure the driver knew where they were going and she texted Logan because they'd made tentative plans for drinks. I'm going to be much later than anticipated. Raincheck?

No problem. But I am a night owl.

I should be home in about three hours. And I do have a wonderful bottle of red wine.

You know I don't really need the nightcap, right? I just want to see you.

Of course she'd known that he wanted to see her again, but something about his message made her face flush. Pack a bag. I'll let you know when I'm home.

When the car arrived at Caleb Small's house, Mia tipped the driver and walked to the front door. "I'm here," she said for the comm.

"We're on the next block. As far as we know, there are no exterior cameras. Do you see any?"

Mia looked around. "I don't see anything." She made a point of moving in multiple directions so Audrey could see through the camera what Mia saw. She rang the bell and waited.

Caleb answered the door still wearing his suit pants and dress shirt, but no shoes. His tie was gone and his sleeves were rolled up. Mia had a flash of Logan dressed the same and what a turn-on it had been. Looking at Caleb, however, was like looking at her father.

"Mia, come in."

"Thank you so much for meeting me on such short notice." She stepped into the foyer and looked around. "Is Carole home? I haven't seen her in ages."

"No. She's visiting her sister in Arizona. Why the hell she'd want to go there in the middle of the summer, I'll never understand. Come in. Can I get you a drink?"

As they walked into the dining room, she saw the crate leaning against the wall. It did, in fact, look identical to the one Nikki had built.

Caleb saw her looking at it. "It's the Spenser I'm auctioning."

"Actually, that's what I want to talk to you about. If it's not too much of an imposition, can I have some coffee? I had a horrible evening and my day was jam packed with meetings."

"Sure. Let's go to the kitchen and I'll make you a cup."

"I forgot how lovely your dining room is. One day I hope to have a home with a formal dining room."

"Carole loves her dinner parties. The only reason that crate is there instead of sitting in my den is because she's not home. No one is allowed to do anything in this room. Or the kitchen for that matter. She sees them as her domain."

Mia chuckled. "You're just breaking all the rules while she's on vacation, aren't you?"

Caleb put a pod into his coffeemaker. One cup. He wanted her out of here fast. She made sure to take a seat at the far end of the kitchen breakfast counter, from where she could only see a sliver of the dining room, which meant Caleb wouldn't be able to see anything.

"The house is so quiet," she said.

"It took a lot of getting used to once the children were grown. I keep suggesting to Carole that we downsize, but she won't have it."

The smell of coffee filled the room and Caleb poured himself a brandy. He handed her the cup of coffee. "Cream? Sugar?"

"Black is fine."

In her ear, Nikki said, "Dude didn't even lock the front door. I'm going in. Keep him in the kitchen."

Mia's heart raced. How could Nikki think waltzing through the front door was a good idea?

"Have you talked to Keaton?"

"Not in the past week, no. Why?"

"I was at his house last night for dinner and to look at his Moreau for a private buyer."

"That's supposed to be part of the auction with my Spenser."

"I know. But an overseas friend heard about it and was interested. When I looked at it, I noticed that it was obviously a forgery."

"What?"

"Keaton was furious. I didn't know what to do. That's why I wanted to talk to you. First, Randall Scott asked me to look at his Mathis painting because the appraiser told him it was forged. It was. And now this. I feel like someone is after me."

"I'm making the switch now. Keep talking," Nikki whispered.

Mia forced her eyes down at her coffee to resist the urge to look in the direction of the dining room. "My dad called me this morning. Yelling at me for screwing up his deal."

When she looked up again, Caleb was staring at her with concern.

"He said the painting was his contingency because he needs money." She wrapped both hands around her coffee cup. "Something's not right. This many forgeries all at the same time?"

"What are you thinking?"

"Dad thinks Keaton is trying to cheat him."

"Keaton would never."

Sure. And my father is an upstanding citizen. "It's making me uneasy because I've been part of at least two declarations of forgery. I feel paranoid."

Caleb reached across the counter and put his hand on her wrist. "Your father will be fine. I'll talk to Keaton. We'll get to the bottom of this. You have nothing to worry about."

From the corner of her eye, she saw Nikki in the doorway to the dining room giving her a thumbs-up. The woman was impossible. Always taking unnecessary risks.

"I am worried, Caleb. About my father. About my reputation in the art world. About the effects of all of this on my mother. I'm just so overwhelmed." She rested her head in her hand. From the other side of the house, she was sure she heard the click of the front door. She needed to exit.

Keaton must've heard it as well because he looked over his shoulder. "I don't know what's going on, but know that your father is trying to protect you. I'll talk with the others and figure something out."

She slid from her stool and came around the counter to offer him a brief hug. "Thank you so much." She pulled away. "I should be going. It's late."

"Do you need a ride?"

"No. I'll call a car." She tapped a message to Nikki that she was leaving, then called a car. "My ride will be here shortly. Please tell Carole I said hi."

"Absolutely. We should have you and your mother over for dinner when Carole gets back."

"That would be lovely." Her mother was going to kill her for saying that. After every dinner party at the Smalls' house, Beverly would rant about the overdecorated rooms and the pretentious food. Carole had always tried to one-up each of her peers in dinner party flair.

Caleb walked her to the door, pausing to look at the crate. She followed his gaze, but it didn't look like the crate had been moved. He waited on the front steps until her ride arrived. They waved goodbye. As soon as she was in the car, she texted Logan to tell him she would be home in thirty minutes. Then she switched to her burner phone and texted Jared.

Nikki has the Spenser. Move it fast.

While the phone was still in her hand, Nikki called. "You were good. The painting is safe and we're on our way back to the apartment. Will you be joining us for a celebratory drink?"

"As lovely as that sounds—" and for the first time, she wasn't saying it sarcastically "—I have other plans. Jared will be by in the morning to handle that."

"See you tomorrow. Enjoy your *plans*." Then she hung up.

When the car pulled up at her building, Logan was already waiting in the lobby for her. She opened the door and he turned to see her. His face broke into a smile and her insides softened at an alarming rate.

He crossed to her, pulled her into a hug, and kissed her temple before stepping back.

"What was that for?"

"You looked like you needed it. You sure it's okay that I'm here?"

"Absolutely." She didn't want to admit how nice it was to be met by a smiling face after a long, stressful day. Pointing to the small container he held, she asked, "What's that?"

"Cookies." He bent and picked up a small duffel bag.

He planned to spend the night, which gave her another rush. She took his hand and led him to the elevator, waving at the doorman as they walked. "Why did you bring me cookies?"

She pressed the button for the elevator and the doors opened immediately.

When they stepped inside, he said, "They're from Mama Mae. She sent them as a bribe. We're having a birthday party for one of my sisters tomorrow and Mae wants to meet you."

"Oh." What was she supposed to say to that? Involving families would make it difficult to keep this casual.

"Before you decide, you have to try one." He opened the lid to the cookies as they arrived at her condo.

She reached over, took one, and bit into it as she unlocked her door. A chocolatey gooey deliciousness burst on her tongue. Chocolate dough with a mix of chunks and chips throughout. The edges were crisp but the center chewy. "This is amazing."

"Now you know why it's a bribe."

She put her keys and purse on the counter and took another cookie from the container he set down. "You want something to drink?" she asked without turning around.

Logan grabbed her from behind and pulled her flush to his body. "I just want you."

He kissed the side of her neck. She dropped the cookie back in the container and tilted her head to give him better access.

NINETEEN

LOGAN LAY IN Mia's bed, half dozing, with her body curled next to his. He ran his fingers down her back. "So, about the party tomorrow."

"Did you seriously ply me with cookies to get me to agree to attend a family gathering?" she murmured against his chest.

"Yes."

"We've only been on a couple of dates. Coming to a party with your whole family does not smack of being casual."

"I like you, Mia. And my family is important to me. I don't know how long I'll be in town. If I don't make headway on this case, I might get sent to a different field office. I want to enjoy my time while I'm here."

"And if you do get your transfer?" She angled her head to look at him.

"Then I get to spend even more time with you. Maybe we'll get serious or maybe we won't work out. But I want the chance."

She smoothed her hand over his chest. "You're a good man, Logan."

"I hope so. Mae would kick my butt if I wasn't." He continued to stroke her back, loving the feel of her silky skin beneath his fingers. "Are you working tomorrow?"

"I probably should, but no. I need a day off. How about you?"

"I have to run a few things down, but we should be done early. What do you plan to do?"

"I have to talk to my mother and let her know what's going on with my father. I don't want your FBI friends to show up to question her without warning."

"We work together, but I wouldn't say they're my friends."

"Agent Halloran's a jerk."

"He does seem to want you to be guilty of something, but I think that's mostly because your father slipped out of his hands. Your dad didn't call again, did he?"

"No. He said he'd be in touch."

He thought for a moment before continuing. He didn't want to mess up what they had going and he didn't want her to take things the wrong way. "I'm glad you're keeping us in the loop about your father, but are you really okay with it?"

"Yes."

No hesitation, no stopping to think. He'd like to think he'd do the same, but he couldn't imagine being in such an impossible position.

"I'm glad you came to spend the night," she mumbled and then her breathing evened out.

He was glad he came over, too.

When he woke in the morning, he reached across the bed, seeking Mia's body, but the space was empty. He opened one eye and checked his phone. He had to get moving to meet Stokes. He had one more thing to talk to Mia about—besides Paris's party later—so he climbed from bed, pulled his boxers on, and went to find her. He tried the kitchen first, but she wasn't there. He started a pot of coffee and went down the other hall.

As he neared a room, quiet strains of classical music floated through the air.

He peeked in the partially open door. Mia was dancing. She was graceful and beautiful as she twirled and leapt across the room. He leaned against the doorjamb to watch. When the music ended he clapped, and she jumped.

"Sorry. Didn't mean to scare you. I reached over and your side of the bed was cold. You're an amazing dancer."

"I'm an adequate dancer." She dabbed a towel on her forehead.

"You must dance often if you have your own studio."

"Not as much as I'd like. I hate working out, but I love to dance. It's also what I do when I need to sort my thoughts."

He wanted to pry and ask what had drawn her to dance this morning. She had plenty of reason between her father and the forgeries, but he wanted to make sure she didn't have doubts about them. "Everything okay?"

She nodded. "Is that coffee I smell?"

"I started a pot." As she walked by, he touched her arm. "You can talk to me if you want. Tell me what's on your mind."

She paused and for a brief moment, he thought she was going to tell him what was going on. Instead, she said, "Right now coffee's on my mind."

He followed her to the kitchen. "Can I make you breakfast?"

"You cook?"

"Another requirement when you live in a houseful of kids. I'm no gourmet, but I can hold my own." Without waiting for a response from her, he opened the refrigerator and pulled out ingredients for omelets. Before he had the chance to rummage through her cabinets to find a bowl, whisk, and sauté pan, she had the items on the counter.

Then she poured a cup of coffee and took a seat at the counter. "Show me what you got."

He cracked eggs, chopped vegetables, and shredded cheese under her watchful gaze. While the eggs cooked, he wiped his hands on a towel. "There's something else I need to ask about your father."

She set her cup down and met his eyes.

"When Agent Stokes and I went back to reinterview people, we got some interesting information about the Devereaux painting."

"What's that?"

"Ingram's provenance was bogus."

"I heard that. It all caused quite the stir in the art community."

"When we talked to Ingram, I asked to see the receipt of sale and he couldn't produce one. He said he won the painting in a poker game."

Her face went stony.

"He said he won it from your father. The thing is, if the Devereaux was your father's, why would he have a forgery and then give it to Ingram?"

Mia shook her head. "He's a scam artist. I wouldn't put anything past him at this point. But at the same time, Max is no saint."

"Did you know it had been your father's?"

"No."

She held his stare and he looked for any signs that she was lying. But even if she was, what did it mean?

Then she started to laugh. It began as a hollow sound

but rapidly devolved to hysterical laughter. He flipped the eggs and gave her a moment to compose herself.

"This is funny?"

"Yes. My father thought he had a perfect life with perfect friends. Now they're all turning on each other."

She was a little wicked and he was getting a little turned on. He plated the omelets and took a seat beside her. "So about the party later."

"I don't know that it's a good idea."

"It's really casual. Just a backyard barbecue for my sister Paris."

"How old is she?"

"Seventeen today. She's been working hard in summer school to make up credits so she can graduate on time after being in a series of bad situations. We're all really proud of her. I think you'll like my sisters."

"What time is the party?"

"It starts around two, but it'll go late. We don't have to stay for the whole thing. I can pick you up by three?"

She rolled her eyes. "Fine. What does one give a seventeen-year-old?"

"You don't have to buy her a gift. I got her something."

"I do not show up to a birthday party empty-handed. That would be an excellent way to make a horrible first impression."

"Aw…" He tucked a lock of hair behind her ear. "You want to impress my family."

"I like to impress everyone. It's who I am." She cut a piece of omelet and put it in her mouth.

Logan took a drink of his coffee while waiting for her verdict. "Well?"

"You can cook. I'll have to tell Mae that she definitely did something right with you."

He had a feeling Mae would spend ten minutes with Mia and fall in love with her. She wouldn't be the only one.

MIA SAT AT A window table at Big Jones waiting for her mother. When Mia called to talk with Beverly about what was going on, her mother suggested they meet for brunch. Knowing that her news would upset Beverly, Mia chose Big Jones because the restaurant served Southern cuisine. Logan was not the only one capable of providing a bribe. Beverly loved beignets. And the beignets at Big Jones were almost New Orleans good.

Mia sipped her coffee and considered how to tell her mother everything that was going on. Of course, she wouldn't be talking about her side project with Jared, but she needed to tell her the other things. Beverly arrived and brushed a kiss on Mia's cheek.

"I'm so glad you suggested coming here for brunch. It's been ages."

"I know it's your favorite."

The waitress arrived, refilled coffee cups, and took their orders. Mia was still stuffed from Logan's omelet, so she just ordered a fruit cup.

As Beverly added a half a pack of sugar to her coffee, she asked, "What did you need to talk about?"

"It can wait until the food comes."

"Uh-oh," Beverly said, setting her spoon down. "I knew I should've been suspicious when you wanted to meet here. You figured you could ply me with fatty, sugary dough and hand off your bad news. Just spill it, so you won't ruin my brunch."

Mia blew out a breath. "Are you sure? It's a lot."

"Tell me."

"As you know, there have been a few forged paintings discovered among the artwork of people we know."

"Yes."

"Well, you know the man I've been seeing? Logan? He works for the FBI and he's investigating the forgeries."

"You're dating an FBI agent." Beverly held her coffee cup stiffly and lifted it to her lips. Before drinking she asked, "He knows your history?"

"It's my father's history. And yes, I led with that when we first met, and he asked me out anyway."

"Excellent. When do I get to meet him?"

"That wasn't what meeting for brunch is about. Logan is actually undercover, so you can't tell anyone. He's pretending to work for the insurance company that wrote the policies for the forged pieces. He's trying to figure out where all the forgeries are coming from. He asked me to reach out to Keaton Bishop because Keaton was sending his Moreau to auction."

Beverly set her cup back down. "Don't tell me."

"We went over there for dinner, and when I looked at the painting, it was obviously a forgery."

"I bet Keaton blew a gasket. Poor Sheila."

"Keaton was *furious*." Mia turned her coffee cup in circles trying to figure out how to say the rest.

"I suddenly feel like I'm stuck in a late-night infomercial. But wait! There's more."

Mia chuckled. "Dad called me."

Beverly's face turned to stone, except for a fierce flash in her eyes. "What?"

"He actually called a couple of weeks ago to ask me for money because of my inheritance."

"Oh my Lord. If I ever lay eyes on that man again—"

"I told him you changed the parameters for access to my inheritance, so I still don't have it."

"Good girl. He knows better than to come to me for anything."

"He said he might need my help using my connections in the art world. I let him believe I would help, and I immediately called the FBI. But then, after I told Keaton his painting was a forgery, Dad called the next morning. The Moreau painting was actually his. It's his contingency and he's trying to liquidate. He was quite angry with me for ruining his sale with Keaton."

The waitress arrived with their food. Beverly studied her plate for a moment, then picked up a beignet and bit in. Once she swallowed the first bite, she said, "Is there more?"

Mia nodded and moved the fruit on her plate around with her fork. Part of her wanted to tell her mother everything about her plan, but protecting Beverly was her number one priority. "Logan told me that Max Ingram said that he won the Devereaux painting in a poker game from Dad. Did you know it had been his?"

"Of course not." Beverly took another bite of her beignet and smiled. "But I learned years ago not to put anything past your father. Is that everything now?"

Mia matched her mother's smile. "Yes." It was only a small lie. "I didn't want you to be blindsided if the FBI came to question you, or if Keaton called to tell you how angry I made him."

"I appreciate the warning, but I can handle both the

FBI and your father's tiresome friends. Now tell me about Logan."

Mia ate a couple of pieces of fruit to try to hide her smile when she thought of Logan. "There's not much to tell. We've only been out a few times. Although he grew up here, he's been living in New York." She left out the part where he hoped to move back.

"You've always liked New York."

Mia rolled her eyes. "We are nowhere near discussing moving in together."

"But I can tell you like him."

"I do." That much she could admit. She shouldn't like him as much as she did, which was why she shouldn't go to a family party this afternoon, but she'd already agreed to go. "Now, hurry up and finish your sugary meal and you can work off those calories helping me shop for a birthday present for Logan's seventeen-year-old sister."

Her mother sniffed. "And you say it isn't serious."

It wasn't. It *couldn't* be. At least not until she took her father down through any means necessary.

AFTER LOGAN KISSED Mia goodbye, he met Stokes in the office and they ran down the information again, trying to force the pieces of the puzzle together. At noon, he grabbed his suit jacket. "I have a family thing, so I'm heading out. You should, too. We'll start fresh on Monday."

"Does Bishop have a security system? He swears he had the original, just like Ingram and Scott. What if they're not the ones doing the forging? What if someone else is swapping them out?"

Logan sank back onto his chair. "We considered this,

but there's no evidence. Nothing suspicious. Other than these men themselves all attempting to sell art at once."

"But if I was part of their inner circle, and I knew they were going to sell, I could make the trade, sell the real thing, and watch them rant and rave and then cry." Stokes tossed her pen on the table, where it landed on top of the photos of the men in question. "If I had to put up with these pompous jerks, I'd want to see them fail."

Mia's attitude about her father's friends came back to him. She was angry and bitter that they profited. She'd laughed hysterically this morning at the thought of them turning on each other.

"With the added bonus of getting rich off them? It makes sense, but it's a stretch. That's a lot of moving parts. Not to mention having black market connections to sell a hot painting. As shady as these guys tend to be, I can't imagine them pulling that off." Mia had money. She didn't need more, and there was no evidence of her having the criminal leanings to know what to do with a stolen painting. He rose again. "Reach out to Cyber-crimes and see if they can detect any chatter about selling these paintings. If your theory is right, they have to be selling. Why go through all of that to just sit on them?"

"I would. Sometimes revenge is a long game. The art won't go down in value that much, right? Wait till things cool down and then sell."

Mia could afford to sit and wait. But he couldn't see her doing any of this. He trusted his gut, so he said nothing to Stokes.

"See what you can dig up and we'll talk more on Monday. Enjoy your weekend." He stopped to pick up ice and beer on his way to Mae's. He'd promised he'd help set up for the party, but he wanted to have time to change into something other than a suit before picking up Mia.

He went around back and bumped the gate open with his elbow. He heard Mae yelling from the kitchen. In the yard, Joe was unstacking chairs while Sam was setting up a folding table. Logan set the cases of beer down, and said, "Hey, I'll do that. Go grab the ice from my car."

Sam propped a hand on her hip. "You think because I'm a woman, I can't set up a table?"

"No, I'm just being nice. That table is almost twice as long as you are."

Her eyes narrowed. "Real funny. I'm not that short."

She wasn't, and he knew it, but he liked to tease her. In truth, she might be taller than Mia. As if to prove him an idiot, she flipped the table over just fine.

"It's about leveraging your body. But since you're here, you can climb up to the rafters in the garage and get the spare coolers and chairs."

Joe said, "I told you I'd get those."

"I got it," Logan answered.

"And ruin that fancy suit?"

"Nothing will be ruined. Cobwebs won't stain."

"Why are you all dressed up anyway?" Sam asked. "Hot date?"

"I went in to the office this morning. Working a big case."

"So the date was a bust, huh?"

"No, actually Mia is coming to the party. I'm going to pick her up after I help here and go home to change."

"Oh. You're moving fast."

"What?"

"Bringing a girl to not only meet the family but a

whole family party? You either really like her or you're trying to drive her away."

Logan shook his head, tossed Sam the keys for his car, and went to the garage. Helping Joe outside meant that he could dodge Mae's curiosity. Or so he thought. After lugging the coolers and extra chairs out, he saw Mae standing in the kitchen doorway.

"Not even going to come in to say hi?"

"I was helping. Plus, I'm going be here for the party." But he sighed and trudged up the stairs. "Hey, Ma. How are you?"

"Is your girlfriend coming to the party?"

"Yes. I'm going to pick her up at three. She enjoyed your cookies."

"Cookie bribes almost always work. Except for that one girl Isaiah brought home. She was vegan." Mae said the word like it was a disease.

"Do you need any help inside?"

"You know there's always something to be done. I have a bag of potatoes that need peeling for the potato salad."

Logan looked over his shoulder at Joe and Sam. "You guys got this?"

"For sure," Sam said. "You have fun peeling potatoes."

She was a little too cheerful in her dismissal and when he got into the kitchen, he knew why. The pile of potatoes was enormous. It had to be ten pounds.

Mae handed him a peeler. "Get to work or you'll be late to pick up your girl. What's her name?"

"Mia."

"Hmm." Mae turned back to the counter, where she was husking ears of corn.

"I'll trade you."

She shot him a look over her shoulder. "You said Mia works at a museum?"

"Yeah, the Art Institute."

"And where did you meet?"

"At an event for work. I'm undercover as an insurance agent and we've attended some of the same events."

Mae turned around. "Does she know you're not really in insurance? You know how I feel about liars."

"Yes, I told her the truth, but my job sometimes requires me to lie. It's for the greater good."

She waved an ear of corn at him. "When you're chasing bad guys, that's fine. But when you're starting a relationship, it shouldn't begin on a bed of lies."

"Ours did. I couldn't introduce myself with the truth, but since we've been seeing each other, and she's helping the investigation, I told her the truth."

They worked in silence for a while and Logan made headway through the mountain of potatoes.

"Do you really like her?"

"I do," he said simply. It felt foreign to admit that he liked someone as much as he liked Mia.

"What happens if you have to go back to New York or somewhere else?"

"We'll go our separate ways. Her whole life is here."

"And if you come home for good?" She gathered a pile of husks and shoved them in the trash.

He shrugged. "I told you. We just started dating. We like each other, but we're not getting too serious yet. We both have a lot going on at work, so it's not the best time to start a relationship."

"Child, there is never a good time to start a relationship. You either want it or you don't. If you do, you put in the time to make it work, and if you don't, so be it." She took the potato peeler from his hand. "I'll finish this. You go home and clean up. I'll see you soon."

"You sure? I can finish the potatoes."

"You move like a damn snail. Anybody else would've been nearly done. I don't have all day to wait on you. Part of me thinks you're still doing it on purpose like you did when you were thirteen."

He smiled and kissed her cheek. "But it never worked back then. You need me to bring anything else? Sam is putting the beer and ice in the coolers."

"I think we have it all covered. Thank you."

"See you in a couple hours."

"Don't be getting distracted with your girl. I expect to see you here before food is served."

"Yes, ma'am."

In his car, he texted Mia to make sure three o'clock still worked for her. She answered yes and he considered what Mae had said. How badly did he want a relationship with Mia? Did she even want one with him? They'd only known each other a few weeks.

One thing at a time. Solve the crime then deal with his personal life.

TWENTY

MIA WAS QUIET on the way to the party. While the conversation with her mother went better than planned, and they chose a beautiful silk scarf for Logan's sister, Mia was beginning to doubt the purchase. That doubt doubled as Logan turned down the street toward the house. The neighborhood was pleasant but tired. The buildings were old. Most had window air-conditioning units running and dripping onto the sidewalk between the houses.

Children were squealing and jumping through sprinklers. People were sitting on their concrete steps chatting with neighbors. Mia had heard of neighborhoods like this, but she'd never experienced them. She clutched the prettily wrapped gift and realized it was probably a mistake. She set the box near her feet.

"You're quiet today. How did brunch go with your mother?"

"As well as could be expected. I told her my father called, and that I've already let the FBI know."

"Having second thoughts then?"

"About telling you about my father? No."

"About coming to the party."

She looked over at him. "I'm having second, third, and fourth thoughts. I don't think I'm going to fit in here."

He smiled and took her hand. "You're with me, so you'll fit in fine."

"That's kind of you to say." She looked at his T-shirt and jeans and considered her own outfit. She wore a simple black sundress with spaghetti straps. The neckline was edged in white. But it was still expensive.

Logan parallel parked into a tight little spot between a pickup truck and a rusted sedan.

"That's another reason I don't feel the need to drive in the city. Parallel parking."

"It's like riding a bike. Once you learn to park in these neighborhoods, you never forget. Ready?"

She took a slow breath and looked at the smile on Logan's face. If nothing else, she was sure to enjoy herself being around him. "Let's go."

He walked around the car and met her at her door. "Don't forget the present."

"I think it might be better to just say your gift is from both of us."

"Why?"

"I no longer think my gift is appropriate."

"Did you buy her drugs, tobacco, or alcohol?"

She laughed. "No."

"Sex toy?"

"No!"

"Then it's probably appropriate."

She rolled her lips in. How could she explain without sounding like a snob? "It's a silk scarf. It's quite pretty and I thought teenage girls like to accessorize…"

"But?"

She looked down the street. "I don't want anyone to feel bad or think that I'm trying to buy acceptance."

"No one will think worse of you for spoiling my sister a little. People can tell when someone is being condescending, and the fact that you're willing to leave the gift here says plenty. Bring it. I'm sure Paris will love it."

She reached in and grabbed the box. After she closed the car door, she asked, "Where's your gift?"

He pulled an envelope from his back pocket. "Cash is something every teenager loves."

"But it requires no thought or consideration."

"Sure it does. I *thought* she would like to go spend money she didn't have to work for. I *considered* that I have horrible taste when it comes to understanding teenage girls." He took her hand and led her down the block.

Mia braced herself for whatever she might face. If nothing else, her con artist lessons should come in handy again. Facing Logan's family couldn't possibly be worse than showing her face after her father's arrest and disappearance.

Two hours later and Mia had forgotten everything that had worried her. Logan's family was something she'd never seen. It was sprawling and diverse and loud and rowdy and fun. It was everything her family wasn't.

She was sitting in a plastic chair at a wobbly folding table watching seventeen-year-old Paris school Uncle Phil on the proper use of pronouns. He groused and her voice rose. Mia braced for scathing remarks, but it was just a heated exchange. Logan smiled and waved from the grill, where he'd taken over cooking because Joe, his dad, had been looking a little tired from standing over the heat.

A woman plopped down next to Mia and said, "Hi. I'm Logan's sister Jill. You must be his date?"

"Yes. I'm Mia. Nice to meet you." Jill. Another sister.

She'd already met Sam, who was a short blonde with a loud laugh, and Carmen, a curvy Latina who took credit for teaching Logan to salsa. "I think you all should wear name tags because I'm going to lose track of all the siblings. I'm an only child and I have one cousin. You have aunts, uncles, cousins, and neighbors on top of… I lost count of how many siblings."

"You're not alone. Mae raised us and she messes up our names all the time."

"I heard that," Mae yelled from the kitchen window.

"She hears everything. Just can't remember our names," Jill said jokingly.

"Heard that, too, smart aleck."

Mia had no idea how Mae managed to hear over the noise of the radio and people yelling and laughing.

"Logan sent me over here to check on you. Do you need a drink or a snack?"

"I'm fine thank you. I was thoroughly enjoying listening to Paris teach Phil how today's world works."

"Whew. Sorry I missed it." She glanced over, but Paris was making her rounds, chatting with the guests. "When that girl gets riled up about something, watch out."

"I got that impression. She will be a force to be reckoned with as an adult. You can go back to enjoying the party. Tell Logan I'm fine. I don't need a babysitter."

Just then, Sam sat down, holding three bottles of beer and two decks of cards. "Who's up for a game of Bullshit?"

Suddenly a crowd swarmed the table. Mia shifted to get up to allow someone to take her spot, but Sam pointed at her.

"Nice try. You have to play."

"I don't know how to play."

She opened the decks and shuffled the cards. "We'll teach you."

Carmen brought a chair over and sat on the other side of Mia.

Mia got the feeling that this game had nothing to do with entertainment and everything to do with vetting the new woman in their brother's life. She was not one to back down from a challenge. "What are the rules?"

LOGAN COOKED UP BURGERS, brats, hot dogs, and chicken, all while watching Mia kill it at Bullshit. As good as his sisters were, Mia had had a lifetime of masking her thoughts. But after witnessing the first few rounds, he saw what he'd been looking for: her tell. When she lied, she always glanced up from under her lashes, almost coyly, before making full eye contact.

He filled the final platter and handed it off to Anton. "Take this in to Mama Mae and see where she wants it set up."

Anton followed Logan's gaze to where the girls played cards. "She's hot."

Logan gave him a shove. "Have some respect. That's my date."

"Not your wife. So maybe when you're done with her…"

"You couldn't handle her. I'm not even sure I can. Get moving." He crossed the grass and stood behind Sam.

Sam reached up and waved an arm wildly. "No cheating. Your girlfriend doesn't need help."

"You're right. You're the one who needs the help."

Mia's eyes went wide. "You cannot help Sam either. She roped me into this game and now she's being a sore loser."

"Only because she hasn't figured out your tell."

"Food's ready!" Mae called from the porch. "Come and eat before it gets cold."

Sam tossed the cards on the table. "She doesn't have a tell. She's like a robot."

Mia stiffened.

Sam snickered. "I could've used your help when I was a teenager. This one—" she flicked a thumb over her shoulder at Logan "—is like a human lie detector. Maybe you can give me lessons."

"You are the *last* person who needs to become a better liar," Logan said.

Carmen stood. "It was a fun game. I think later we should up the stakes and play a drinking game. I bet all the stoicism will be tossed out the window if we get you drunk," she said to Mia.

"And why would you like to see me drunk?" Mia asked with an arched brow.

"We have to vet you for Logan. It's like our sisterly duty. Plus, we can tell you all his embarrassing stories."

Logan walked around the table toward Mia. "As if you need to be drunk to try to embarrass me." He held out a hand to Mia. "Ready to eat?"

She took it and rose. "Sure." With a wink at Carmen, she added, "I would love to hear all your stories about Logan."

Jill came up on Mia's other side and looped an arm around hers, tugging Mia from his grasp. "First, know that the whole uber-gentleman thing is all an act. He wants to impress you. A more typical image of him is sitting on the couch half-dressed with a bag of Cheetos and a bottle of beer, belching and farting through a football game."

"Really? That is not at all how he's presented himself to me. Do tell more." With a glint in her eye, she let Jill lead her away and into the house.

"Thanks," he said to Sam and Carmen.

"For what? We were checking her out no differently than you have our dates."

"I haven't met anyone you've dated in years. I've been in New York. And we're not kids anymore. I'm pretty sure we all have the capacity to make sound judgments."

"I like her," Sam said. "I mean, she's obviously not from around here."

"Her dress!" Carmen said. "That is not a dress from Target or Kohl's. And her perfume? It might as well be called Money because I'm sure each spritz is twenty bucks."

"But she didn't run and hide from us or stand at your side waiting for you to protect her." Sam pushed her chair back under the table. "And she's a damn good Bullshit player. Next game, I want her on my team."

As much as he should've hated his sisters all ganging up on Mia, this was the most at home he'd felt in a long time. He'd missed the noise and nosiness that came from his family. "Hell, no. I brought her, I get to keep her."

"I taught her the game," Sam called over her shoulder as she headed toward the house. "I'm starving. You better not have burned the food."

Even though his relationship with Mia was new, something felt right about having her here with his family. It was definitely the start of something good.

As the evening wore on, Logan had barely left Mia's

side. Not that she wasn't handling herself just fine with his family, but he wanted to enjoy this respite from work and art and forgeries. Today, they were just a couple hanging out and having a good time. Until her phone started buzzing incessantly. The first couple of times, she barely glanced at the screen, but it didn't let up.

"Something wrong?" he asked.

"I don't think so. Work stuff."

"On a Saturday?"

She glanced down and then back up. "Unfortunately."

Maybe he'd had one too many beers, but that looked like her tell when she was playing Bullshit. The look from under her lashes. Why would she lie about work calls? Unless it wasn't work. Maybe it was one of her friends with benefits looking for a booty call.

He tried not to be irritated by the possibility. They didn't have an agreement about monogamy.

She walked toward the gangway between the houses and checked her phone. Logan came up behind her. "Is everything okay?"

"Um, no actually, I think I should be heading out."

"Oh, uh, let me give Paris her gift—"

"No, you should stay. I can call a car."

"No way. We came together. I'll drive you home."

"Logan. You should stay with your family. It's all right."

He studied her face. "Are you seeing anyone else?"

Her brow furrowed. "Where did that come from?"

That wasn't an answer, which didn't make him feel any better. "You've had a bunch of texts and now you want to leave without me. I know we haven't discussed monogamy, and there's no pressure. I just want to know where I stand."

She wrinkled her nose. "Right now, you're standing like an idiot. I'm not seeing anyone else. If you recall, when you asked me out, I told you I had a lot going on and I'm not looking for anything serious. Where would I find time to date more than one man?"

"I'm sorry. Sometimes my imagination runs."

"Thinking about me on a date makes you jealous?"

"I invoke my Fifth Amendment right."

Her crooked smile lit up. "A nonresponse is often an answer."

"Call your car and then let's have Paris open your gift before you go."

"I've had a good time today. I'm glad you invited me."

"I'm sorry I almost spoiled the night with my stupidity." He stepped closer, backing her to the wall.

She tilted her face up. "We all have moments of stupidity," she said quietly.

"Can you forgive me?" He lowered his mouth to hers and kissed her. He held her hip and his fingers flexed, wanting to touch more of her.

She patted his chest. "For a kiss like that I can forgive quite a bit. But I do need to go."

He sighed and stepped back. "Let's go find Paris. I'm guessing seeing you tomorrow isn't going to happen, given that your phone hasn't stopped ringing."

"Probably not. And for that, I'm more sorry than you know."

"I think I do know." He'd thought they'd spend the night together tonight and maybe even tomorrow. A real weekend. But it wasn't in the cards.

TWENTY-ONE

MIA HAD A hard time walking away from the party. Paris loved the scarf and thanked her profusely for it. Everyone was gracious as she said her goodbyes, and Mae offered her a plate of food.

Logan walked her to the front of the house to wait for her ride. "Thanks for coming with me. I know they're a lot to take in."

"They are a lot, but it's obvious they love you. It's a pretty amazing family you have."

"They like you, too."

Her phone vibrated in her purse again.

"What's going on?"

"Some of the texts coming in are work, but I just got word that a family friend died, and I didn't want to mention it at the party."

"I'm sorry. Was it someone close?"

"No." *Just one of our marks, so my plan is blowing up again.* "Word travels in our community. I'm sure you know how it is."

"Yeah. I have sisters."

A car pulled up. "That's my ride."

Logan walked her to the car and opened the door. Mia put the container of food on the seat. When she turned to say goodbye to Logan, he slid an arm around her waist and pulled her into him, planting another hot, wet kiss on her. When he released her, he said, "Let me know if there's anything I can do."

"Thank you." She got in the car and waved after he closed it behind her.

As the car drove off, she called Nikki. "What's going on?"

"Where have you been?"

"I couldn't answer. I was with Logan and this didn't seem like something I could discuss in his company."

"You heard Jerome Bauer died?"

"Yes. My phone has been going off nonstop. You, Audrey, my mother." She felt overwhelmed having two phones go off, not sure which to check, if any. And she couldn't afford to have Logan question why she had two phones. "I got the message. I'm on my way to the apartment now to discuss options."

"We're kind of screwed here."

Mia rolled her eyes. "You've said that before, and we've managed."

Although this time she had no idea how they were going to pull off the heist. Jerome was the owner of the Hardison painting that would be their biggest score yet. And now he was dead. She texted her mother to let her know she'd heard, and asked Beverly to let her know if she had any details. When she got to the apartment, everyone was there, including London, which was a little surprising, given that the forger didn't need to be there to strategize.

"What do we know?" Mia asked as she set the plastic container of food on the table.

"What's this?" Nikki asked.

"Leftovers from the party I came from. Help yourself." The woman was always hungry.

Jared stepped away from the computer and Audrey. "The gossip sharks are circling on this one. Jerome died in a car accident four days ago. His wife, Candace, told no one other than close family because as it turns out, Jerome was with his mistress when he died. They are not having a public funeral because Candace doesn't want the scrutiny. They were already on the way to divorce, which explains why they had nothing on their social calendars. Candace was in rehab, and based on the advice of her therapist, she's moving out of town."

Mia stood in the middle of the room, stunned. "How did you find all of that out?"

"People tell me things," he said.

"Where does that leave us?"

"That's where things get interesting," Audrey said. "Mrs. Bauer has decided to sell everything her husband amassed. Her bags are packed and she's headed to Florida. Guess who she contracted to handle the estate sale?"

"I have no idea."

"McNamara's Auction House. Nikki and London did a drive-by a little while ago and took pictures." Audrey cued up the TV and pictures of the Bauers' house flashed on the screen. A box truck from McNamara's was in the driveway.

"Are they packing up everything and taking it?" Mia asked.

"No." Audrey crossed the room with her tablet. "From what we can tell, the truck is for donations. They're clearing out the crap, but the estate sale will happen at the house."

"So Nikki just needs to go in and make the swap when they leave."

Nikki snorted. "Sure. Except when we did our drive-by today, I snuck in. They're in the process of tagging every pricey item with magnet security. Unless Audrey can figure out how to bypass it, I won't be able to move the painting."

"We can find a workaround for that," Mia said. "I know how the technology works. I've seen it used in some smaller galleries."

"That's good," Audrey said. "Because she tried to explain it to me, and I'm totally confused."

"When is the estate sale live?"

"I've heard next weekend," Jared answered. "But McNamara's hasn't advertised yet."

"Do we know how they're handling authentication on the artwork?"

"Nope," he said.

"So we need to figure out how to circumvent the new alarm and get Nikki in before it's open to the public *and* before they authenticate it." Mia's stomach turned, and all the delicious food from the party sat like a brick. Maybe they should walk away from this one. But it was worth more than many of the others. This one would hurt her father. Even more than the Devereaux.

Mia stared at the TV and the photos of Jerome's house.

Jared stepped next to her. "Maybe we let this one go. I doubt Candace has any intention of sending our fathers money."

"I was just thinking that, but you know what this one is worth. He needs this payday. He'd find a way to get it."

"Hell, no, we're not walking away," Nikki said. "London has the painting ready to go. They've only been in the house for a day or two. Maybe they haven't even tagged the painting yet."

Mia shook her head. "McNamara's knows what they're doing. They'd protect the highest priced items first, probably at the same time they marked the things for donations. With no one living at the house, they wouldn't risk not having an alarm on the items. Of course, if McNamara's has taken over, I wonder if their insurance would cover the painting if it comes up a forgery."

"Their liability would kick in if it's stolen, but if they're covering the painting and it's a forgery, they'll authenticate first," Jared said.

"What if I get Logan to pressure them to authenticate? Would that help or hurt?"

The room dropped into silence. She either had a brilliant idea or it was so stupid no one wanted to call her on it.

"I don't know," Audrey said. "Let's run it down."

The pictures on the TV disappeared and were replaced with a digital whiteboard. Audrey drew a line down the center of the screen and marked each column, pro and con.

They each threw ideas out and Audrey recorded them, but ultimately, it could go either way. It would only be safe for her to get Logan to force authentication if she was positive Nikki could go in before the expert. It was a gamble. Nikki, of course, was always willing to gamble.

"What's the worst that happens? The expert says it's the real thing before I can make the swap and we miss out on this one. You're already considering that.

If they sell the original, it also gives us cushion. We all know Logan is suspicious about all of these forgeries."

"Giving him one that's not counterfeit would poke a hole in his theory," Mia said. Her heart squeezed a little at the thought, because ruining Logan's investigation could cost him his transfer.

"But if it works, we get the painting and your daddy gets zip."

"Okay. I'll get you the information I can dig up on the magnetic alarms, and you two figure out how to get into the house." She looked at Nikki and Audrey. "Now that McNamara's is on-site, they might have changed all the security."

"What about me, boss?" London asked.

"You have the list of art we need. Whether we miss out on this one or not, we'll need the other pieces."

"On it. Do you have a preference for order?"

Mia rubbed the spot between her eyebrows. "Right now, thinking about how to retrieve the Hardison is all I can handle. It doesn't seem to matter what my plan is anyway, everything keeps shifting." She pulled out her phone and screenshotted her calendar. To Audrey she said, "I just sent you a copy of upcoming events that we can use to gain access to the various homes. You and Nikki discuss where to go next."

Jared reached over and touched her forehead. She swatted him away.

"You must be sick. You just willingly gave someone else the power to plan. You never relinquish that kind of control," he said.

"What can I say? I'm trying to be a team player," she said a tad too cheerfully.

Nikki was gnawing on a chicken leg from the leftovers. "Okay, you've totally creeped me out. Maybe you should go home and get some rest."

Mia picked up her purse. "I'll be in touch tomorrow."

When she left the apartment, she suddenly felt exhausted. All of the hours of planning and socializing were catching up to her. Tomorrow would be a Logan-free day and she could get her plans back on track.

In the car on the way home, her phone dinged with a message from Logan. A gif of a monster giving a little girl a hug along with a message telling her he was available if she needed anything.

So much for being Logan-free.

SINCE MIA WAS DEALING with work and family stuff, his plan for hanging out with her all weekend was blown. Instead, he spent it with his family and then going over all of his notes for the case. Monday morning, he arrived at the office ready to find some answers. Stokes showed up not long after he did, and they bounced ideas off each other. When his phone rang with a call from Atlas, he put it on speaker.

"We have another forgery," said Greg, the head auditor for the company.

Stokes slapped the table. Logan took a deep breath.

"I just got a call from McNamara's Auction House telling me they refuse to keep Caleb Small's Spenser painting in the auction because their experts have deemed it counterfeit."

"How did this happen so fast?"

"When it came out that the Moreau—which was supposed to be in the same auction—was forged, they inspected it immediately. It was delivered Saturday afternoon. Experts looked at it first thing this morning."

Logan looked at the clock. It wasn't even eleven. "What does Small have to say about this?"

"He's no different than the rest, screaming about how he purchased the original and he has no idea how he ended up with a forgery."

"We'll head out now to check it out. Is this enough to be able to request an audit of all local holdings?"

"I hope so." He disconnected.

Stokes looked at Logan. "Is it possible this has something to do with Atlas?"

"At this point, anything is possible. I've always considered that there might be an inside person, but they're not paying out on these claims. If the owners come after Atlas, it'll be long drawn-out court cases." He stood and grabbed his notebook. "Do you want McNamara's or Small?"

"I'll take McNamara's. I'm tired of talking to all of these liars."

"Yet you chose to work for the FBI where you deal with liars and criminals every day."

"Go figure. I expect the lowlife criminals to lie to me when I have them sitting in cuffs. But when we're just trying to figure out what's going on in a way that should help these guys—assuming they are as innocent as they claim—their deception makes me reconsider my stance on going by the book."

"Noted. Stay off Stokes's bad side."

"Don't turn into one of these lying assholes and you'll be just fine. See you back here in a couple hours to compare notes again."

He briefly considered disclosing his full relationship with Mia. Would Stokes consider him a liar for not telling her? Maybe. But he didn't want Stokes to doubt his ability to do the job.

When he arrived at Caleb Small's, the man was pacing the front of his house, talking on the phone, gesturing wildly. Logan got out of his car and waited, trying to glean any information from one side of the conversation. Caleb was pissed and yelling about provenance and premiums, so he was probably talking to someone at Atlas, which meant that his sudden arrival might look sketchy.

Small looked at him and said into the phone, "Looks like he's here now." He disconnected and slid his phone into his pocket. "You're from Atlas?"

"Yes. Logan Freemont." He extended his hand and Small reluctantly shook.

"You people better figure this out. You appraised the painting when I purchased it. It's been hanging in the same spot for almost five years, until it was crated up to be delivered to McNamara's."

Logan nodded. "Can we go inside and talk? I'd like you to run me through everything."

Small sighed and led him through the front door. "What do you want to know that I haven't already explained to your office?" he asked as he closed the door behind them.

"I understand you filed a claim. But as I'm sure you've heard, there have been a number of forgeries popping up in the area. Sometimes doing a walkthrough helps me see possibilities. Can you show me where you had the painting hanging?"

The man took a deep breath, but said, "This way." He led Logan upstairs and pointed to a painting on the wall. "It hung in this spot up until three days ago."

"Do you mind me asking why you decided to sell now?"

"It was time. The auction house is selling a Picasso and it will bring a lot of attention. I wanted to cash in on that, get the most money."

"So you arranged to have a company come and pack it?"

"Yes. McNamara's gave me the names of their preferred vendors. I called one. They came out on Friday afternoon to crate it up. They took photos and submitted them to the auction house. Then they sent the delivery truck on Saturday to pick it up and bring it to McNamara's."

"Why two different days? Why didn't they just take it on Friday?"

"They have one crew that goes around crating up and another that just handles delivery. Something to do with the trucks and the materials being separate from deliveries as a precaution against damage."

Logan pulled out his phone and texted Stokes to have her ask about the procedure while she was at McNamara's. He looked at Small again. "Were you here the entire time they worked?"

"Yes. They came in, measured the painting again, as if they couldn't trust the measurements I gave. Then they went to their van and custom built a crate for my painting. They brought the crate upstairs, put the painting in, and nailed the crate shut. They asked where I wanted the crate until the truck arrived to pick it up. I had them take it downstairs to the dining room. That way, I wouldn't have delivery people roaming all over my house."

They walked downstairs together and Small pointed

to where the painting was set until the delivery truck came on Saturday.

"Was anyone else home when they were crating the painting?"

"No. My wife is out of town. I monitored the process myself."

"Does anyone else have access to your house?"

"Without my being here? No."

"So no one else could have been here between the crating of the painting and the pickup on Saturday?"

"No. I was home the entire time."

"Did you have any visitors?"

"Actually," Small said, with a furrowed brow, "A family friend stopped by pretty late on Friday."

"Was he left alone with the painting at all?"

Small chuckled. "*She* was not."

Did Small just refer to his mistress as a family friend? "I don't mean to pry, Mr. Small. What you do privately is up to you, but if you were entertaining a guest, she might have information."

The man shook his head. "I was not cheating on my wife, Mr. Freemont. I meant a family friend. Mia Benson."

Logan froze. Mia had been here? She hadn't said anything about it. She'd told him she was working late. Was she coming from here when they met at her place? Logan blinked to regain control of his thoughts. "What was the nature of her visit? You said it was late Friday?"

"She came by to seek my counsel. She informed a friend that he was holding a forgery, but I'm sure you're aware of that, seeing that you were with Mia when she made the discovery."

"I was."

"Then I'm sure you know she wouldn't have done anything. She's had a rough go of it, but she was shaken by Keaton's outburst."

Logan looked around the room. "No one else was here while she was visiting?"

"No. She was looking for some fatherly comfort. That's all."

"Did you show her the painting? Did she handle it?"

"No. I pointed out that the crate was waiting to be picked up, but we walked by and went to the kitchen."

"And when she left?"

"I finished my glass of brandy, locked up the house, and went to bed."

"Alarm?"

"Set at night when I went upstairs."

"No breach?"

"None."

"Hmm." Logan didn't know what was going on, but it stank. The whole situation. And now his heart and mind were beginning to battle. All this time, he'd been sure Mia had nothing to do with these forgeries. If that were true, why lie to him about working late on Friday? Why not tell him she'd been here? He hoped there was some logical explanation.

"Thank you for your time, Mr. Small. We'll be in touch."

"You should know that I've called the police and I plan to file a complaint. Someone must've made the switch. I don't know when or how, but I own the real Spenser, and I will fight this."

"Understood." Logan let himself out and drove back to the office. He listed everything he knew. Mia had now been with three different forgeries, calling two of them as such. Then she suddenly goes to see Caleb Small at the same time his painting is conveniently crated and sitting in the dining room waiting to be picked up.

If she were going to steal it, why not just take it then? Why replace it with a forgery? It didn't make sense. Maybe her visit really was a coincidence.

As much as he didn't believe in coincidences, he wanted to give her the benefit of the doubt.

TWENTY-TWO

MIA HAD SPENT most of Sunday working with Nikki and Audrey to develop a plan to get the Hardison. They figured out a way to get in and out of the house, but they didn't know if the Hardison had been moved from the first-floor library, where Jerome had kept it for years. If McNamara's thought it would show better in another room, they wouldn't hesitate to move it. The sale was priority.

Leaving Nikki and Audrey to work the kinks out of the route to get into the house to locate the Hardison, Mia went to work. She had to get information on the magnet alarms McNamara's was so fond of using. She'd seen them and the security department at the museum had considered installing some for smaller, temporary exhibits.

So, after lunch, she visited the security office. "Hi, Jeff. How are you?" she asked the head of security.

"I'm doing well. What brings you down here? I was told we had weeks to develop the security protocol for your exhibit."

She waved a hand. "Oh, you do. This is personal. I have a friend who's invested in some valuable artwork and she needs some security information. We were discussing some possibilities—she's so overwhelmed by it all—and I mentioned the magnet-type security that we looked at a while back."

He nodded. "I remember."

"Well, I was wondering if you still had the samples so I could show them to her?" She added in some extra I'm-sweet-and-innocent to her question.

"Whew, boy. I'm not sure if I kept those samples."

"Shoot. Would you have saved the specs? Anything I can share with her so she knows what questions to ask?"

He rose and walked around to a massive file cabinet. He rifled through two drawers and came up with a file. "Look at that! Past Jeff was a genius." He handed her a file with the magnets attached.

"This is perfect!" She opened the folder and glanced over the paperwork. She removed the page with museum-specific information. "Can I take this with me if I leave you the museum pages?"

"I don't see why not. I'd appreciate you bringing it back, though, in case anyone asks."

"I'll have it back first thing in the morning. Thank you so much."

"Hey, if your friend is single, maybe you can fix us up."

"Sorry. She's newly widowed and not ready to date, but I'll keep you in mind as soon as she's back in the market." Mia left, congratulating herself on another mission accomplished with no problem.

Then she realized she was happy about becoming a quality liar and something about that didn't sit right with her.

She tucked the paperwork and the magnets into her purse to take to Nikki and Audrey as soon as she wrapped up meetings for the day. They'd been at this for less than two months, but she couldn't remember what it was like to only work her museum job. She felt like she was constantly running—and running behind.

She barely got settled behind her desk when Anya rapped on her door. Without waiting for a response, she stuck her head in. "I saw you just got back. Do you have a minute?"

Mia waved her in.

"It's about *Farm Girl Dreams*."

"I thought I told you to drop it."

"I was going to, but I couldn't help myself. I picked up sightings of it in the late '60s when it appeared in a traveling exhibit. The trail goes cold again after that, but I have the name of the family who loaned it to the exhibit."

Mia had gotten that far in her own research, but she let Anya have the win. "That's above and beyond what I asked for. Thank you."

"No problem. I loved it. Like I said, it feels like a treasure hunt. And here's a little tidbit: I think the reason it went quiet is that it was pulled from the exhibit before the tour was done. There were rumors of falsified provenance." She handed a piece of paper to Mia. "I haven't tracked down current family members or made any calls. I didn't know how far you wanted to take this."

Mia stared at the paper. "This is more than enough. Thank you. I really appreciate it."

Mia's afternoon just became booked.

"You're welcome." Anya flashed her a bright smile, and for the first time, Mia felt it was genuine.

"Do you have the information on the pieces you'd like to include in the *Crime and Punishment* exhibit?"

"I'll have it on your desk first thing in the morning."

"I look forward to it. If you've put half the effort into curating a valuable experience there as you have in this research, I'm sure it will be amazing."

Anya looked damn near giddy as she left Mia's office. Since Mia had some time before her last meeting of the day, she researched the information Anya had gotten. Even though this exercise had started as a means to test whether Logan was lying to her, it had become something she wanted to see through. She wanted to find this painting for his family. Mia made the last of her calls and left the museum around dinnertime. She let Nikki and Audrey know she had the magnet alarms, but they only had them for the night, so they needed to work fast.

LOGAN PACED THE conference room, waiting for Stokes. She got waylaid by an agent on another case, which was good for him. He was still processing what Small had told him.

Stokes finally came in juggling a legal pad and two coffees. "Figured we'd need this."

"Thanks. What'd you get from McNamara's?" He took a seat across from her.

She flipped her pad to the right page. "They're locked on. If there's something shady happening there, we'd have a hard time proving it. They have a total system from pickup to drop-off. Once on-site, the crate is on camera until it's taken to the lab for inspection. No cameras in the lab rooms, but all over the hall. No one is walking out with the painting undetected. I talked to the delivery crew. They said the crate was completely sealed and didn't appear to have been tampered with."

"So no help."

"How'd it go with Small?"

"More of the same. He supervised the crate up, and it was sitting in his dining room overnight waiting for pickup. Wife is out of town. No breach in the security system. He's pissed. He thinks someone screwed up somewhere. Definitely the kind of guy who will sue Atlas if he can."

"Can they all be that good at acting?"

"How do you mean?"

"If they're all playing a game, trying to sell forgeries, is it possible for them to all be so good at faking outrage?"

"I don't know."

"I doubt it. We're four forgeries deep. We've talked to each of these men and we haven't seen any cracks. No slips."

"You think someone is screwing with them. They either bought a forgery, and the Atlas rep was in on it, or someone replaced the original." As soon as he said the words, he thought of Mia again.

But he'd been with her when she looked at Bishop's painting. They'd been together all night. Except when she went to the bathroom. There hadn't been enough time for her to switch the painting, and he definitely would've noticed her leaving with one. And Small said he'd been with her in his house. She *couldn't* be behind this.

"These are rich, powerful men," Logan said. "I'm sure they all have their fair share of enemies. I think we need to start looking for who they have in common."

"They all work in different fields. How is that possible?"

"Heck if I know. Let's start at the top."

She started shuffling papers on the table and pulling together information on each man.

Before they were able to dig into anything, Logan's phone rang. "Another call from Atlas? This can't be good." He accepted the call and immediately put it on speaker. "Hi, Greg. You're on speaker. I'm here with Agent Stokes. Please don't tell me there's another forgery already."

"No, thank God. I'm calling because I just received word from McNamara's about an estate sale they're handling. One of our clients, Jerome Bauer, died last week. His wife is selling everything in the house, including a Hardison painting we insure."

Stokes flipped through the files and grabbed the information they had on Bauer.

"When is the estate sale happening?"

"Thursday."

"That's fast. What's the rush?"

Greg cleared his throat. "I don't want to gossip about clients, but Mrs. Bauer has already moved out of state and just wants to get rid of everything."

"Sounds like she's not too distraught over her husband's death. What can we do?"

"McNamara's has people working almost around the clock appraising items and preparing them for sale. They've already removed the items they felt they couldn't sell and donated them. They called us to make us aware of the impending sale. Mrs. Bauer didn't provide them with provenance and she hoped we would have a copy."

"Have they authenticated it?"

"No. It's not something Mrs. Bauer wanted to pay

for. I'm sending our expert there on Wednesday. It's the earliest McNamara's would give us access."

"It would be better to have access immediately. Do they have a security system set up?"

"The Bauers have one, of course. McNamara's is adding alarms to individual pieces."

"Do they have monitoring?"

"Only on the main system."

"Do we have any reason to suspect that the painting in the house is a forgery?"

"Nothing specific."

"Did Bauer plan to sell the Hardison?"

"Not that I'm aware of. His wife would probably know."

"All right. We'll be in touch." Logan disconnected and looked at Stokes. "What do you think?"

She was already pulling up information on her laptop. "Bauer's death was a car accident, so this sale probably wasn't planned. If we go with the theory that when the sale is announced, someone trades the original for a forgery, it might not have happened yet."

"The man died days ago. Anything is possible."

"The wife kept it quiet. Not a secret, but no big service. No half-page obit. She had McNamara's move in fast. You want to ask Mia Benson to take a look at it?"

Logan thought for a moment. He couldn't risk bringing her in if she played a role in the forgeries. He didn't want to believe it, but he couldn't ignore the possibility, especially in light of her being at Small's house Friday night. "I don't think it's in our best interest to bring her in again. She's not a certified appraiser, so regardless of what she says, it won't really hold up. McNamara's has no reason to listen to her."

"I guess you have a point. You pulled it off once with Bishop. I'm not sure it would work again. I think we should sit on the house and see who shows up."

"We have to ask Taggert to authorize overtime."

"I'll check with him. It's only two days. You prefer day or night?"

"I have something I need to take care of tonight, so if you can do tonight, I'll relieve you first thing in the morning."

"Sure. In that case, I'll talk to Taggert and head home for a bit. Can you notify McNamara's that we'll be around? I'd hate for them to call the local cops on me."

"No problem. Get some rest."

After she was gone, Logan reviewed their notes, this time looking at Mia as a suspect. She knew all of the victims—but based on how he'd heard her talk about them, she wouldn't consider them victims. She had the art knowledge to know what to go after. She might have the knowledge to create a passable forgery.

He logged into his computer and searched Mia's financials. He was bending the rules to access the information, but he didn't want this to be official. At least not yet. Right now, he just needed to know who he was dealing with.

THAT EVENING, MIA handed Audrey the specs for the alarms as soon as she walked into the apartment. Then she sat at the table with Nikki to explain how they worked. "This sensor connects with a magnet. The sensor gets stuck to the wall behind a painting, and the magnet's on the back of the painting or the frame. Once engaged, the painting can't be moved more than a few inches at most without setting off the alarm."

She set the sensor and the magnet close together and engaged them. Then she shifted the magnet away until it triggered the alarm.

"Does it matter how close they are when they're engaged?" Nikki asked. "Or is it a standard three inches or whatever they can be moved?"

Mia turned to Audrey. "I think it's a little of both, correct?"

"Yeah," Audrey responded without looking up. "It's a range of two to six inches, but environmental factors play a role."

Nikki picked up the small magnet and moved it away from the sensor. An inch and the alarm went off. Mia showed her how to reset it. "You push them within that six-inch distance to make a connection. The light goes on to show they're connected. My hope is that Audrey can rig something to interrupt the signal without making it think it's been interrupted."

"What if I take the magnet and the base together? Like rip them from the wall?"

Mia shook her head. "If they're removed from the premises, where the system is located, the alarm will trigger."

Nikki got up and paced. "So I need to be able to reach my hand behind the painting, pull the magnet off, but hold it in place, remove the painting, replace the new one, and attach the alarm. I'll need like three extra hands."

Audrey joined them at the table holding the papers with the alarm specs. "We'll figure this out. We always do." She held up a screwdriver and grabbed the sensor.

Mia held up a hand. "You cannot destroy these. They're on loan from the museum."

"You use these?" Nikki asked.

"No, so don't get any ideas."

"If you get fired, I lose this gig."

Mia cringed. "These were given to our security department as samples, but I'm expected to return them."

"You'll be able to bring them back. And they'll even look like they haven't been tampered with. I'll do my best not to really screw them up." Audrey popped open the sensor and inspected the tiny wires. "They use RF signals. According to the specs, some ferrous metals can interfere. I just need to figure out what we can introduce to the room to make it go haywire."

"How does that help?" Mia asked.

"Kind of like what we did to Darren Turner," Nikki said. "Make the system go crazy, and they'll turn it off."

"Exactly," Audrey agreed. "My signal jammer might work for this. It's a pretty simple design." She snapped the cover back on the sensor and made a connection with the magnet again. "See? Still works."

Then she crossed the room and dug around through the piles of stuff on the desk. Once she found her jammer, she pressed the button. Nikki slid the magnet along the table, away from the sensor, and the alarm went off. They reset it, Audrey stepped closer, and they tried again. It still didn't work.

"Maybe it's not as simple as you think," Mia said.

"It's also not that complicated. I just need the right frequency and the right distance."

After about ten more trials, it worked. Mia blinked as she stared at the sensor. "Wait a minute. Try it again."

Nikki reset the sensor and they stared at the red light. Audrey hit her jammer, the light turned off, and Nikki slid the magnet away.

Audrey executed a fist pump.

"Don't get too excited," Mia told them. "You're a foot away. If Nikki is standing there, jamming the signal, it might send a message to the system. Bare minimum, it notifies the owner, in this case McNamara's, via phone call or text."

"What if someone goes in and tests it?" Nikki asked.

"How?" Something told Mia she wasn't going to like the answer.

"If you go in and use the jammer, you'll know immediately if they're notified. If they are, they'll need to do a reset, which means the painting comes off the wall. You'll be able to see the placement and let me know. If you leave the jammer tucked somewhere, it will keep interfering until they think they have a bad sensor. Then I swoop in, make the swap, and leave before they come back with a new sensor."

Mia's head spun. "You think that will work?"

Nikki shrugged. "It's worth a try. We've done crazier things. The real question is, can you get in? The estate sale starts Thursday."

"I don't know. I can try."

"Let's do it tomorrow afternoon," Nikki said.

"All right." Mia stood and picked up the sensor and magnet. Looking at the specs, she asked Audrey, "Are you done with these?"

Audrey pulled out her phone and took a few photos. "For reference."

"I'll call you when I'm leaving work and heading to the Bauer house." Mia left the apartment wondering how she'd just gotten roped into playing yet another role in these heists.

When the car pulled up to her building, Logan was

standing in the lobby again. She checked her phone. She hadn't missed any calls or texts. A sinking feeling settled in her chest.

TWENTY-THREE

LOGAN THOUGHT ALL afternoon about how to approach Mia. He cared for her and he wanted to try to make their relationship work, but not if it was based on lies. If she was involved in the forgeries, he couldn't stay with her. He would have no choice but to arrest her.

Asking her about her visit to Small was all he had to go on, and he hoped it would be enough to put his concerns to rest. When she strode through the door of the building, he took one look at her and hoped he would hold on to his resolve.

"Logan. What are you doing here?"

"I hope it's okay that I just showed up. I needed to see you."

"Of course it's all right. Have you been waiting long?"

Quite a while, since I went to the museum first and you were already gone. "Not too long." He bent and kissed her cheek.

"Have you eaten dinner?" she asked as they stepped on the elevator.

"Not yet."

"Good. I'm starving. I'll cook us something."

"You cook?"

She angled her head and looked up at him. "Why do you sound so surprised?"

"You were shocked when I offered to cook. I thought that was because you don't. You strike me as the kind of woman who would rather order in than make a mess cooking."

The elevator dinged at her floor and they stepped off. "It's not messy if you know what you're doing."

"If you say so."

She unlocked her door and set her purse on the table. "Come on in and make yourself comfortable. How does a salad and pasta sound?"

"Anything would be good. I'm hungry. Had a busy day at work."

She disappeared around the corner to her kitchen, but her voice still carried. "Really? Any ideas on where the forgeries are coming from?"

He stepped into the kitchen and leaned against her island to watch her work. She already had water on the stove for pasta and was chopping vegetables. "Anything I can do to help?"

"Wash and cut the lettuce." She pointed at it with her knife.

He rolled up his sleeves and went to work. It felt very homey, and he liked it in ways he shouldn't. Right now, he could be making dinner with a suspect. He kept telling himself that she wasn't a person of interest, but his doubts were growing. They worked side by side in silence for a while.

"What did you want to talk to me about?" She turned away from him and added salt to her boiling water. She put the pasta in the pot and began creating a sauce. The smell of garlic and tomato filled the kitchen.

"It will keep until we're sitting to eat." He needed to be able to see her face, look into her eyes. He was good at reading people. He was sure he could read her. "How was work for you?"

"The *Crime and Punishment* exhibit that I told you

about is moving quickly. Unfortunately, that means that my days are filled with meetings and emails and conference calls to make it all happen."

"Does not sound exciting."

"This part isn't, but when the pieces on loan start to arrive and we're building the set design and creating the best positions to tell stories…that's magical."

She was still at the stove, stirring the sauce, but at her last statement, she turned her head to look at him over her shoulder. The excitement was plain on her face. She loved her job.

"If you weren't a curator at the Art Institute, what would you do?"

She set her spoon down on the edge of the pan and turned around. "I would probably work for another museum. I had plans to work in New York after I got my doctorate, but then my father was arrested."

"What if you couldn't be a curator at all?"

Her eyes widened and she bit her lip. "I don't know. It's not something I considered when I was in school. My education was designed to get me exactly where I am. I could probably get a job at a gallery. Why?"

"Just curious. You seem to really love your job. You can learn a lot about a person from how they would react to losing something that's important to them."

"What would you do?"

"If I couldn't work for the FBI, I'd probably be a local cop."

"No law enforcement at all."

"That's not fair. I didn't say you couldn't do anything in art."

"That's not my fault. But I'll answer." She turned back to test the pasta. As she carried it to the sink to drain, she said, "I would work in marketing or something similar for the Joffrey. I love ballet and being part of that world would keep me interested."

She plated some pasta for each of them and topped it with sauce. Then she set the plates at the counter. "Is this okay, or would you prefer going to the table?"

"This is fine." He set the salad in front of their dishes. "If I couldn't be like Indiana Jones, I would probably work private security. I have a brother who's starting his own business now that he's retiring from the Marines."

She wiped her hands on a towel. "Were you military?"

"No. College and then FBI." He looked her up and down. Not a spot on her. "You didn't wear an apron or anything and you're still perfect."

"As I said, if you do it right, it's not messy." She gave him a soft smile and handed him a bottle of wine to fill their glasses. They walked around the counter to sit.

He put a little bit of salad on his plate mostly because he'd taken the time to make it, but he wasn't much of a salad guy. He preferred something heartier. He twirled some pasta on his fork and filled his mouth. It was good. "Is there anything you can't do?"

She chuckled. "Plenty. I've simply learned to only perform the things I am good at. It makes me appear far more impressive than I am."

He reached over and brushed her hair away from her face. Her skin was warm and soft. He cleared his throat. "There's another forgery."

"What?" She set her fork down. "Where?"

"Caleb Small's Spenser painting was delivered to McNamara's Auction House and they said it's a forgery."

"No." She pressed her hand to her lips and shook her head. "I was there," she said quietly.

"Where?"

"At Caleb's Friday night before I met you here."

She was either a hell of a liar or she was honest. She'd offered up the information he wanted. He scanned her face for signs of deceit. "That's what I wanted to talk to you about. Why were you there?"

She sighed. "After what happened with Keaton, I went to Caleb to talk. While I don't regret helping you with looking at Keaton's painting, you must realize how bad it looks for me. I saw that Randall Scott's painting was a forgery. Then, I tell Keaton his is forged as well. These people talk."

She pushed her plate aside and drank some wine. Logan thought maybe she wouldn't say more, but after a moment, she continued.

"After my father was arrested, people offered their support. We still had friends. But when he ran...my mother and I were shunned. It didn't matter that we had nothing to do with his crimes, that we didn't know what he was doing. I've spent five years rebuilding my reputation to hold my own in this community. People will start talking about how I'm calling paintings forgeries to ruin these men. Or that I'm bad luck. Have Mia look at a painting and it will magically become a forgery."

"That's ridiculous."

"People are ridiculous." She maintained eye contact and he saw no hint of a lie. She was vulnerable when it came to this.

"Did you see the painting while you were there?"

"Not directly. It was in a crate in the dining room. He made a joke about how angry his wife would be if she knew the crate was there. But I didn't see *inside* the crate."

"Was anyone else there?"

She shook her head. "Not that I'm aware. The house was quiet. Their children don't live at home anymore. We were in the kitchen the whole time talking. I didn't see any other part of the house."

He kept looking for a sign that she was lying, but he saw nothing. But then he doubted his own ability to spot it. He *wanted* her to be innocent.

She smiled, leaned close, and ran a finger down his tie. "What are your plans for the rest of the night?"

"I don't have any."

"Will you stay?"

He shouldn't. He was compromised. But he wanted to stay with her. "I have to leave early tomorrow."

"We'll set an alarm."

They finished eating dinner and cleaned up together. With the exception of his mild suspicions, things with Mia were easy. He hadn't expected that with her. He thought they'd have some fun and go their separate ways, but he enjoyed being with her. He just needed proof that she was innocent and his instincts were searching for the nonexistent.

Hours later, Logan was lying in Mia's bed where she was sound asleep. Those nagging feelings from earlier crept back in, and sleep eluded him. Why would Mia go to Caleb Small of all people for reassurance? While her father had been friends with the man, Logan saw no other connection. It wasn't as though Small was like an uncle to her. And she'd made it clear that she kept her distance from her father's friends because of the way they'd treated her.

He slipped from the bed and went to the living room to snoop around. He didn't know what he was looking for—he figured he'd know it when he saw it. The problem was, nothing was out of place in her home. Everything was neat and organized, much like Mia herself. He looked in a few drawers, but even they were ruthlessly organized. Nothing that screamed, "I'm part of a forgery ring!"

He was about to turn back to the bedroom when he caught sight of her purse near the door. Mae's voice rang in his head, telling him to never go into a woman's purse without permission. He shoved that voice back. This wasn't the same thing. He crossed the room and opened the bag. Inside, he found the specs for a small magnet alarm and a sensor as well as a second phone.

He pushed the items back in and sat on her couch. Why would she have alarm information in her purse? Was there any plausible reason? She worked at the Art Institute. Maybe they were considering using this system.

But she doesn't work in security.

Maybe she had something here she planned to install it on. He stood and looked at the painting over the mantel. It didn't look like a masterpiece, but then again, neither did most of the pieces that had been forged. And that wouldn't explain the second phone. He returned to the couch and stared at the painting.

His suspicions were still raised, but he didn't have the proof either way.

Mia shuffled into the room, looking soft and sleepy, wearing her short pink robe. "Why are you awake?"

"Couldn't sleep and didn't want to bother you."

"Is something wrong?" She stepped closer.

He reached out and tugged her to his lap. "I feel like you're keeping something from me."

She looked up at him from lowered lashes. "I've been honest with you. What do you want to know?"

That glance of hers looked like her tell. Was it the position she was sitting in or was it a lie? He should just ask if she knew anything about the forgeries to see what she would say, but he couldn't tip his hand. He needed more evidence. "Why do you keep associating with your father's friends?"

She lifted a shoulder against his chest. "They're part of my parents' social circle."

"But you said they haven't treated you well since he left."

"They are rich, powerful men with many connections. Being part of their circle, even tangentially, is worthwhile. Criminal or not, my father was a ruthless businessman. He knew how to make money honestly even if he chose to steal. He built his business from the ground up. He taught me to never doubt the power of networking. You don't have to like the people you do business with."

"So you stay as a means to an end instead of looking for new friends?"

"I guess. More than that, it's what I've always known."

She was being honest, which just made this harder. He couldn't discern whether there was truth to her lies or if the lies were nonexistent. His brain ran in circles. "Come on. Let's go to sleep."

He followed her to the bedroom and hoped sleep would come. Tomorrow would be another day to search for answers to satisfy the nagging doubts.

When Mia woke the following morning, Logan was already gone. He'd left a note on the bedside table saying that he'd call later in the day. She stretched and replayed the night before. Something wasn't right with Logan. She couldn't explain what was off, but something was. The way he'd questioned her made her uneasy, as if he was suspicious.

Getting close to him might not have been the best idea after all. Maybe it was time to step back. What they had felt like they were building a relationship instead of keeping in casual, which was what it was supposed to be. Their involvement was a means for her to know what the FBI was doing. Her heart was getting involved and that was a mistake.

She knew this, but she didn't know what to do to change it. Before getting ready for work, she reached behind the painting above her mantel. The file she kept about her father's friends and their art was still there, undisturbed. To be safe, she asked Jared to stop by her place sometime today to make sure there weren't any listening devices or surveillance. While she wanted to believe Logan had just been sitting in her living room, it was possible that he'd intentionally planted bugs because he suspected her involvement. They couldn't afford to have Logan spying on them.

While drinking a quick cup of coffee before heading out, she read messages from Nikki. She and Audrey had a plan to move on the Hardison this afternoon. Mia questioned the idea of going in broad daylight, but Nikki said she'd seen enough to know she could get in and out during the day without raising suspicion—at least any more than what Mia would cause.

Mia went to work and plowed through meeting after meeting. She finally got approval to get Magritte's *The Menaced Assassin* and Caravaggio's *The Cardsharps* for her exhibit. Granted, cheating at cards wasn't quite the level of crime she expected for the exhibit, but how could she say no to a Caravaggio?

Just before four o'clock, she let Nikki know she was heading to the Bauer house. Before leaving the museum, she stopped by the security office and returned the sensor and magnet.

"Did your friend like this model?" Jeff asked.

"She didn't think it would be enough to stop someone from stealing. Thank you for letting me borrow this, though."

Jeff smiled. "I don't have much faith in the system either. A magnet? It just seems like it would be too easy to mess with."

That's what we're counting on. "Have a good night. Thanks again."

The midsummer afternoon sun was low in the sky, and dark, threatening clouds hovered overhead. She dashed off a quick text to tell Nikki to make sure the painting was protected in case of a storm. The crisp smell of incoming rain filled her nose. By the time her driver had them stuck in traffic leaving downtown, an ominous rumble rolled in the distance.

She hoped it wasn't a sign of things to come.

TWENTY-FOUR

LOGAN RELIEVED STOKES first thing in the morning. She said that no one had approached the house except Mc-Namara employees. No strange vehicles had been roaming the neighborhood. He parked in her spot, across the street from the Bauer house in a neighbor's driveway.

While he sat in his car, he researched the sensor he'd found in Mia's purse. He watched videos that showed how the sensor and magnet worked to provide a closed circuit alarm. The website that sold the system touted it as an excellent and inexpensive way to secure items. Logan wasn't so sure.

He hadn't done many stakeouts in his time, but this was beyond monotonous. He texted a bunch of his siblings and caught up. He played games on his phone to the point of boredom. Anything to stop thinking about his suspicions. Everything he'd considered, Mia was able to explain away logically. Then again, logic wasn't what was leading him down this path any more than it had led him to Mia in the first place.

The neighborhood was quiet. A few people walked their dogs and their kids. A couple of random joggers bounced by. People didn't sit outside and talk with their neighbors. No swapping gossip from the front porch. Then again, these front doors were too far away from each other to carry on a conversation. He'd take Mae's run-down, overcrowded, loud neighborhood over this one any day.

By late afternoon, dark clouds started rolling in. Lights flicked on in the Bauer house. Logan decided it was the best time to leave to grab something to eat. McNamara's people were in the house, so it was unlikely that the painting—or anything else—would be stolen. A typical thief would wait until the house was empty for the night. He drove out of the neighborhood and went in search of food.

MIA HAD THE CAR drop her off near the Bauer house and she walked down the long driveway. When she got to the door, she took a deep breath and rang the bell.

A young man who looked fresh out of college answered. "Can I help you?"

"Hi," she said, stepping forward. "My name is Mia Benson. I'm a curator at the Art Institute and a friend of the Bauers. Mrs. Bauer said I could come by and get a sneak peek at the items up for auction."

"Uh, I don't think we can do that."

"Why not? Would you like to call Mrs. Bauer and check with her?" Mia hoped he wouldn't call her bluff. She hadn't actually spoken to Tara Bauer. She was banking on the woman being difficult enough that they wouldn't want to bother her for such a trivial thing. Mia pulled a business card from her purse. "I really am from the Art Institute."

The man looked over his shoulder and then blew out a breath. "Megan is in charge. I'll need to call her and make sure it's okay."

"Whatever you need to do. Can I at least step inside?" She pointed to the sky behind her that appeared even more menacing than when she left the museum. "It looks like a huge storm is coming."

He opened the door wider and took out his phone. He stepped into the dining room just off the foyer, so Mia took that as invitation to wander in the other direction to the library, where she assumed the Hardison would be. The painting was there, but surprisingly, it wasn't hanging on the wall. They'd opted to place it on an easel. Mia reached in her purse, pressed the button on the jammer, and waited.

No sirens blared. The sensor on the painting didn't even beep. "Any signal going to McNamara's?" she whispered.

In her ear, Audrey said, "We're clear so far."

"Where are you?"

"London and I are on the next block. Nikki's jogging through neighbors' yards on the way to you."

"The painting is right where we expected. Sitting on an easel." Mia stepped closer and circled the painting. She placed the jammer in the cushions of a chair beside the fireplace, directly behind the painting. She reached over to the window, unlocked it, and pushed it up a fraction to make it easier for Nikki to open all the way.

She studied the back of the easel, where she could see the tiny magnet stuck to the stretcher bar. However, she didn't see the sensor. It was probably affixed to the easel.

"Oh my gosh," the man said as he entered the room. "Please don't touch anything."

Mia narrowed her eyes. "Who do you think I am? I told you I work at the Art Institute. I'm around priceless works of art every day. I know not to touch anything. I'm simply viewing the Hardison to see if it's something we'd like to acquire."

"Megan approved you to walk through, but seeing as we're not ready for the public, I have to supervise."

Mia waved a hand. "That's fine. You must protect the merchandise. I'm sorry, I didn't catch your name."

"Chris."

"It's nice to meet you, Chris. I'm sorry if I was a little brusque." She circled the painting again. "Why an easel and not hang it?"

"That is a rare Hardison that has never been re-stretched. The frame and stretcher bars are original to when he created the painting. We wanted guests to be able to see the quality of the frame and know that it was Hardison's own hands that put it together."

Mia nodded. Still no sign of a signal jam. "Do you have a pair of gloves I can use? I'd like to lift it and see the full back to look for damage."

"I'm sorry, but we can't move it." On cue, his phone pinged repeatedly. He answered. "I'm looking right at it. Nothing has moved. It hasn't been touched."

Lightning flashed outside, followed by a boom of thunder. The lights flickered. As worried as she was about the painting being damaged by weather, a power outage would help conceal Nikki.

"I'll reset it. Give me two minutes." He disconnected from his call. "Can I ask you to step back into the foyer?"

"Certainly," she said with a smile. She walked back to the foyer and whispered, "He's attempting a reset."

Mia paced the length of the foyer three times before hearing muttered curses from the library. Then Chris was on the phone again. "No. It's not working. It won't reset. We've had some power surges with the storm coming, but that shouldn't interfere with this." He lis-

tened for a moment, and she stepped closer to the doorway. "What about the curator? Okay. I'll let her know."

When he came from the library, he slid the pocket
doors closed behind him. "I'm sorry, but I have to close
this room off. Is there something else I can show you?"

"I'd love to have a tour of everything." She leaned
close to him with a wink. "While I wanted to see the
Hardison for professional purposes, I remember that
Tara Bauer had a beautiful armoire in her bedroom that
I'm interested in personally."

He gave her a sharp nod. "Right this way."

She followed him up the stairs. "This must be a huge
undertaking for McNamara's. And on such a quick turn-
around. Not to be a gossip, but I'm sure you've heard
the reason for the fast sale."

"I don't discuss clients' personal lives, ma'am."

"I wasn't trying to get you to tell me anything. I'm
sorry if I overstepped."

In her ear, Nikki said, "I'm in. Making the swap now."

Chris opened the door to the master bedroom and
they both walked in. No armoire. Mia happened to
know that Tara sold it three years ago after deciding
that none of her bedroom furniture brought her joy.

"Hmm," Mia said. "Is it possible they moved it to
another bedroom?"

"Keep him busy," Nikki said. "This wax they used
to stick the magnet on is tougher than I thought."

"I don't remember seeing an armoire," Chris said.
"But we haven't inventoried all the bedrooms yet. Let's
take a look."

Thunder rumbled again. A moment later, rain began
to splatter against the windowpanes.

They crossed the hall to the next bedroom. This one only had a bed.

"I made the swap and I'm leaving."

Lightning lit the room, and the clap of thunder shook the windows.

"It's getting really bad out there. I think I should head out before it gets worse. Thank you so much for your time, Chris. If you come across the armoire, let me know, okay?"

"Sure." He walked her downstairs.

In the foyer, she called a car and peered out the sidelights. She didn't want to sit here any longer than necessary, but she didn't want to get stuck in a storm either. The car was five minutes out.

"I'm in the van and we're going to the apartment to crack open the champagne," Nikki said in the comm.

Mia removed the earpiece and tucked it in her bag. Then she turned to Chris. "The car is close, so I'm going to meet it."

"You can wait here," he offered.

"It doesn't look too bad right now. Thanks again for the hospitality."

"The art world is pretty small. We take care of each other."

"Let me know if I can ever return the favor."

She opened the front door and wished she'd looked at the forecast before leaving the house this morning. There was no way she was going through this without damage.

LOGAN HAD PARKED BACK in the neighbor's driveway just as the first raindrops splattered against the windshield. He left the car running so he could keep the windows clear. For the first time in hours, a car drove down the street and stopped at the end of the Bauers' driveway. It was a Lyft driver.

A moment later, the front door opened and a woman came rushing out, head down against the rain. Logan leaned forward in his seat. It couldn't be. But when she got to the end of the driveway, she lifted her head as she opened the door.

What was Mia doing at the Bauer house?

Every suspicion he'd been harboring for the past week thundered through his head. He wanted to snatch her from the car and march her back into the house, but he feared what he'd find. She obviously hadn't stolen the painting. She had nothing but her purse with her. He pulled out and followed the Lyft car. When they got off the highway near River North, he knew she wasn't going home.

If she was going to wander galleries again, he was not in the mood. But the car turned and stopped halfway down the block. He sped up and pulled in front of a fire hydrant. He jumped out of his car and met her on the sidewalk. She hadn't even noticed him until she almost walked into him.

She stepped back, startled. "Logan? What are you doing here?"

"I followed you."

"You what?" The rain was picking up and her hair was now drenched and plastered to her head.

"I was staking out the Bauer house. I followed you. We need to talk. Now." He grabbed her arm and pulled her to his car. He opened the door and waited for her to get in.

When he got behind the wheel, he realized exactly

how wet she was. Her silk blouse was nearly transparent, and she shivered. He huffed, reached behind his seat to grab a sweatshirt and put it on her lap. "What were you doing at the Bauer house?"

"Why are you following me?"

"I didn't start out following you. I followed when you left the house. Now why were you there?"

She pulled his sweatshirt over her head. It swallowed her. "Thank you," she said quietly. She took a deep breath and looked at him from under her lashes. "I found out that the Bauers were having an estate sale and I went to check out the Hardison that they have. I thought it might be something to add to the collection at the museum."

Even if he hadn't known her tell for lying, he would still be able to call b.s. on that. "I've never heard of a curator making a house call to look at a painting."

She licked her lips. "The Bauers are family friends. When we were at the party on Saturday, word of Jerome's death was what had my phone ringing nonstop. I used my family's connection and my position at the museum to get in early to the estate sale."

"Stop lying to me."

Her brow furrowed. "I am not lying. Do you want to go back and talk to Chris? He took me on a tour of the house."

"You know Atlas insures that painting. Jerome Bauer was one of your dad's friends. Are you seriously going to tell me that when they try to authenticate that painting, they won't discovery it's a forgery?"

"How should I know what they'll discover?"

"How stupid do you think I am?"

She waved her arms, his sleeves flapping over her hands. "I don't think you're stupid at all."

"Why did I find security tags and a second phone in your purse last night?"

"Oh my God. Now you're searching my things? Have I been some kind of suspect all along? You took me to bed to gain access to my house?"

"Don't fuck with me. You know that's not how it is." If it had been, he wouldn't be struggling right now. He'd call her a liar and find a way to get a search warrant, tap her phones, follow her around until they found proof. But he still wanted her to be innocent.

She pursed her lips and narrowed her eyes. "The security tags were on loan from the museum. I borrowed them with the full permission of the head of security. His name is Jeff, if you'd like to check. And I have a second phone because I don't trust the FBI. Halloran keeps asking for permission to tap my phone. I deserve privacy."

Everything she said made sense, and he still wanted to believe her, which made him utterly stupid. Either she was a brilliant thief or she was completely innocent and he was ruining the best thing he'd had in a long time.

"What exactly do you want from me?"

He stared at her in silence for a minute. She looked small in his sweatshirt but not weak. He was falling for this woman, even though he knew she was lying about something. He also knew that she wasn't going to break from a simple question. She was too tough for that.

"I hoped for the truth. I can help you."

"I told you the truth. If you don't trust me, that's your issue." She grabbed the door handle. "And as I've told you repeatedly, I can take care of myself." Then she slipped out the door.

He watched her walk down the block and disappear between two buildings. She was in trouble, but he had no way of helping her if she didn't let him in. He'd just have to find the proof of her involvement.

TWENTY-FIVE

MIA SEETHED IN the gangway between buildings to give Logan time to leave. Who did he think he was to make such accusations? Even if he was right. She'd protected herself and the plan. This was her payment for getting close to him. She should've known better. When she was relatively sure Logan was gone, she let herself into the apartment and walked into a full-on celebration. Before she had a chance to say a word, Nikki pressed a glass of cold champagne into her hand.

"Looking a little like a wet puppy there, Mia. Shoulda moved faster out of that house," Nikki said with a chuckle. She was completely dry.

London squinted her eyes and angled her head. "What's wrong? And where did that sweatshirt come from? That is not part of your wardrobe."

Mia gulped the champagne and set the glass down. The realization hit her that while she'd thought they were safe, everyone was now at risk. She had to figure out how to protect them and the plan. It began with honesty. She didn't have time to be angry at Logan, so she shoved the emotion aside. "Logan knows."

Nikki paused with the glass midway to her mouth. "What now?"

"He was staking out the Bauer house and followed me here. He knows something's up and he's sure I'm part of it."

Audrey refilled Mia's glass and handed it to her while London dragged her over to the couch.

"Sit. Tell us exactly what happened," Audrey said.

Mia still couldn't wrap her head around it. She'd been careful. "When I left Jerome's house, I called a Lyft. It was storming and I ran to the car, obviously getting drenched on the way." She held up her hands to point at her wet clothes. "The car pulled up here, and when I got out, I almost crashed into Logan. He pulled me into his car to talk." She picked at the edge of the sweatshirt that smelled like Logan.

"What does he know?" Nikki pressed.

"He wanted to know what I was doing at the Bauers'. I told him that I was looking at the Hardison as a possible acquisition for the museum."

"That's good," Audrey said. "It's plausible."

"He didn't buy it. He wanted to know if, when they inspect the painting tomorrow, they'll find it's a forgery. He knows. He just doesn't have proof. But he's going to keep looking." She swallowed hard. "He also found my burner phone and the sensors in my purse last night. The phone was locked, so he couldn't access anything. And I offered plausible explanations for both. But he knows."

"So cut him loose," Nikki said. "He doesn't trust you, so break up with him. You need distance and you need it fast."

Her words made sense, but they still felt like a punch to her solar plexus. "I don't think that will stop him."

Nikki plopped on the couch beside her. "It's been a good run. Do I need to pack my bags?"

"No." Mia drained her glass again and stood. "I'll deal with Logan. You stay the course. He knows about me. At most, he might suspect Jared because we're cousins. I don't think he has a clue about the rest of you."

"That you're aware of." Nikki waved her glass. "You also didn't think he knew about you. How good do you think he is at his job?"

"Very. I'll talk with Jared and we'll come up with a plan. You do not need to worry about me exposing you."

"Why don't you stay and drink with us?" London asked. "It's still a celebration. Look at the Hardison. We did it. That sucker is gonna help a lot of people on your list."

That was the reason she kept going, even though part of her wanted to back off. It was getting exhausting, juggling the half-truths and multiple jobs. She had to believe they were making a difference in the lives of the people her father had hurt. "Thank you for the invitation, but I'm wet and cold, and I need a clear head to figure out what to do about Logan."

She turned and left the apartment, but Nikki followed her into the hall.

"Hey."

"Yes?"

"Look, as one woman with daddy issues to another, it's okay to walk away if it's what's best for you."

"This isn't about me."

"Maybe it should be. You obviously care more about Logan than you'd like any of us to believe. And as I said, it's been a good run. The Hardison can be it. Go out with a bang, no one can prove anything. The forgeries stop and Logan might believe he was wrong about you."

Mia gave her a weak smile. "We're not that lucky."

"Speak for yourself. I'm the luckiest girl I know."

Mia chuckled and stepped onto the elevator. "I'll be in touch."

On her way home, she tried to focus. She texted Jared to meet her at her place. He didn't even question her. His car pulled up right after hers.

"Are you okay?" he asked when he met her on the sidewalk.

"Yes."

"You look like hell."

"Thanks. That helps because being caught in a storm and then being almost caught red-handed by my—" she'd almost said *boyfriend* "—by Logan wasn't enough to ruin my night. You have to point out how bad I'm actually handling it all."

"Come on. You know payback's a bitch. I believe we had a very similar conversation earlier this summer about me and Audrey." He put an arm around her shoulder and they walked into her building.

"Not similar. My mistake is much worse than yours." They rode the elevator upstairs.

"You must really be miserable. You just admitted to screwing up."

She unlocked her door and tossed her keys on the table. "I'm going to get out of these wet clothes. I'll be back in a minute." She paused in the hall. "I assume when you checked, there were no surveillance devices here?"

"Nope. All clear. Wine?"

"Sure." She changed quickly and folded Logan's sweatshirt. How bad would it be for her to keep it? She glanced at her bed and a barrage of memories of her short time with him raced through her head. She stripped the sheets and shoved them in her hamper. The faster she removed reminders of their relationship, the easier it would be.

Walking back into the living room, she checked her email on her phone. A message from an account she didn't recognize stared at her. She opened it to see it was from her father.

Sweetie—here is the list of artwork I need sold. If you can do anything to aid my friends in making this happen, I would be so grateful.

She tapped to download the list. "Oh my God."

"What?"

"It's so much bigger than I thought." She moved to the couch and curled her legs under her.

"What is?" Jared handed her a glass of wine.

"Daddy just sent me the list of art he needs to have sold to fund his disappearance. I had a list of twelve. He's sent me no fewer than thirty names and pieces." Her stomach turned. She'd thought she'd made him desperate. She'd barely made a dent.

"Let me see."

She handed Jared her phone and sipped her wine. This made it worse. On the ride home, she'd considered what Nikki had said. Walk away on a high. Help as many people as possible. Hurt her father. She was such a fool to think she'd made a difference.

"What do you want to do?"

"I want to destroy him." Bitterness coated every word from her mouth.

"What about Logan?"

The million-dollar question. She shoved aside the emotion and any comments from her heart and focused on the reality of her situation. She pulled out her inner ice queen and wore her like a gown.

"What about him? He's on my trail. If I step back, you can continue to run things. Or maybe just let Nikki and Audrey run it. If forgeries keep popping up with Logan watching my every move, he'll have to give up."

"Do you want him to?"

"Of course."

"You know what I mean."

She sighed and told her stupid heart to shut up. "In a perfect world, things would be different. This list changes everything. Promise me that no matter what, you'll keep going."

"That depends on what you plan to do."

"I've been thinking about it since I left his car. The best thing might be for me to turn myself in."

"What?" Jared's usually calm demeanor disappeared. "That exposes all of us."

"If I use what he thinks he knows about me to leverage a meeting with the FBI, I could offer them our fathers."

Jared rubbed his chin. "It's risky."

"Everything we've done here is risky. We knew that going in."

"Maybe it would be better to give it a little more time."

"That gives him the chance to dig. Although I trust that you covered your tracks, it will be worse if he finds anything. I can preemptively end his investigation into us by offering up our fathers."

"Is there anything I can say or do to talk you out of this?"

She shook her head. "He might think other players

are involved, but he doesn't have anything. He suspects me. If I remove myself from the equation, he has nothing."

Jared's face filled with resignation. "Do you want me to go with you?"

"No. It's better if I handle this." She patted his leg. "Now go home to your girl. Sell the Hardison and take a copy of this list. Have London make as many as she can and move fast while Logan and the FBI are focused on me."

"Why are you throwing yourself under the bus here? There has to be a better way."

She hoped their fathers would be enough of a lure, but they both knew better. She would be putting herself at risk. She'd possibly face jail time. She'd definitely lose the one man who'd allowed her to be herself.

"How could I live with myself if I'm a hypocrite? I can't run around angry because our fathers and their friends don't suffer consequences for their actions if I'm not willing to. This was always *my* plan—not the parts of getting involved with an FBI agent and being a suspect—but I always knew getting caught was a possibility." If she had no other role in this endeavor, it was as the mastermind, to guide the mission. Now it was time for her to guide attention away from the team.

Jared snapped a picture of the list on her phone and said goodbye. Mia studied the list and considered her options.

They could walk away. That was the safe route. Life would go back to normal. But she no longer wanted normal.

She could keep going as they were and they would probably get away with it. Logan couldn't be everywhere all the time, and her team was damn good. But he'd never give up. Hunting them down would ruin him. He wouldn't be the charming, happy man she knew. And that would make her no better than her father, leaving devastated lives in her wake.

The third option was the most frightening, but after some internal deliberation, she made the call that would definitely end things with Logan.

WHEN HIS PHONE RANG, the last name Logan expected to see was Mia's. "Hello."

"I'm ready to talk."

That was fast. He'd thought for sure he'd need damning evidence for her to open up. He'd barely started digging into who she might be working with. "How official do you want it?"

Her laugh was dry. "I'm not looking to be brought in in handcuffs, if that's what you're asking."

"Do you want to come to the office tomorrow to talk?"

"I am willing to make it official, but I'd prefer to talk to you first."

"Are you planning to run?"

She scoffed. "I am not my father. I face the consequences of my actions."

He dropped into silence. Part of him felt bad for thinking she might run, but right now he was all twisted up. He'd trusted her, shared his true identity, brought her to meet his family. She'd betrayed all of that.

"Can we meet somewhere? I have your sweatshirt to return."

He sighed. His sweatshirt was the last thing on his mind. It might be a mistake to give her this chance.

She might still be playing him. But he couldn't say no. "Tell me where."

She sent him the name of a coffeehouse and he agreed to be there within the hour. He left his place immediately, not bothering to put a suit back on. He wanted to beat her there in case her crew showed with her to watch. He had no idea who she was working with, but there was no way she was pulling these jobs on her own. While he didn't fear her, she might bring more trouble, so he wanted to be prepared.

She wasn't a danger to him, at least not physically.

The small coffee shop was dead when he arrived. No other customers filled the space. He ordered a large coffee and took a seat at a corner table that gave him a clear view of the front windows and the street outside, as well as the back of the café.

His coffee sat in front of him untouched while he studied the street, quiet after the storm. As surprised as he was that Mia had called him, he wasn't sure how he wanted this to play out. He couldn't remember a time he'd been so wrong about a person. He couldn't reconcile the image of her being so bitter about her father and his crimes and the idea that she was doing the same. She never struck him as a hypocrite.

A car pulled up, and Mia got out of the back. She strode into the coffee shop looking unlike herself. The rain from earlier had ruined her sleek hair, and she now had it pulled back in a ponytail. For the first time since he'd met her, she was dressed casually in stretch pants, a plain shirt, and sneakers. She wore a light cardigan and carried his sweatshirt.

She nodded at him with a weak smile and ordered herself a coffee at the counter before joining him. Sitting across from him, she handed over the sweatshirt, which he shoved on the chair beside him.

"Why did you want to meet me?"

"I want to make you an offer."

He huffed. "You obviously don't understand how this works. I'm supposed to offer you a deal."

"Hypothetically speaking, let's say your suspicions about the forgeries are right. What if I could offer you something—someone—bigger than me?"

"I don't need anyone bigger. You've stolen millions in art."

"Allegedly. And you would have a hard time proving that since you were with me when Keaton's painting was swapped for a forgery." She took a drink of coffee and looked at him with solemn eyes. "I've had good reason to do what I've done. It hasn't been for personal gain."

"Every thief steals for personal gain."

She licked her lips. "What if I told you that all of the art that has been counterfeited belonged to my father? That the art is part of his contingency plan to stay on the run?"

The pieces in his head that he'd been puzzling over started to fall into place, but he didn't want to jump the gun, so he stayed quiet.

"If, hypothetically, I were to steal a painting and replace it with a forgery, my father's friend wouldn't be able to liquidate it to send Daddy money. If he runs out of money, he'll get desperate."

"You're telling me that you've been stealing art that actually belongs to your father."

"Hypothetically."

"Why didn't you tell the FBI that he had these holdings? They would've seized them like the rest of his assets."

"On paper, they belong to the men who are in possession of them. The FBI won't be able to prove he owns them. I didn't know for sure until he admitted it to me."

"If you didn't know for sure, why did you start?"

"Hypothetically, I would've started because those men all profited from his crimes and suffered no consequences for it. It wasn't right."

"I hope you understand that simply saying *hypothetically* repeatedly doesn't actually save you."

"I don't need saving."

"So you're issuing your own brand of vigilante justice."

"That's one possible way to look at it." She cradled her coffee cup and smiled.

An actual smile. And it pissed him off.

"You think this is funny?"

Her eyes narrowed and she leaned forward. "No. I think this is justice. My father and his cronies should pay for what they did to all of those innocent people. The FBI hasn't been able to do it, so I took matters into my own hands." She leaned back in her chair again. "I wasn't counting on you."

"Sorry to spoil your fun. I want the names of the people in your crew."

"I work alone."

"I thought we were being honest here."

"I'm here to give you a career-making arrest. I've gained my father's trust. I think I can get him to meet me and you can bring him in. That should allow you to get your transfer here to be close to your family. Such an arrest is far more impactful than charging me with crimes you can't even prove occurred."

She was smart and really good at this. Everything she said was right. And it pissed him off. "What if I just keep coming for you instead of taking your so-called deal?"

"You could hope to catch me in the act, but it won't give you the satisfaction you're looking for." She stood and slid a piece of paper from her purse. "Before you decide what to do, here's some proof that it wasn't personal gain driving me."

He opened the paper. "What is this?"

"Names of my father's victims. Check on them and see how they're doing. I'll wait to hear from you." She turned and left the shop.

He stood, picked up his sweatshirt, and shoved the piece of paper into his pocket. Earlier tonight, he'd wanted to help her, sure she was in some kind of trouble. Finding out she had a revenge plot going didn't sit well with him, even if he could understand the motivation behind it. Now she was reaching out for help under the guise of helping him.

Back home, he sifted through the files on Dwayne Benson and his victims. He worked all night to figure out what Mia wanted him to know. It took until morning when he could make phone calls. Three calls to three different victims of the Benson and Towers scam and he found the truth.

Mia Benson was playing Robin Hood.

TWENTY-SIX

After pulling an all-nighter, Logan wasn't any closer to knowing what to do. He had genuine feelings for Mia and those emotions were clouding his judgment. She'd come to him for a deal, though, and he couldn't ignore that. They made deals all the time with much worse human beings. She at least had a good reason for committing these crimes.

But she was still a criminal and he was FBI. They weren't a couple of fictional star-crossed lovers. And he had a job to do and a plan to create.

He had no idea where this would lead them when it was all done. He wanted to believe that if her father was brought to justice, Mia would no longer be dealing in forged art. That she was only a criminal because her father managed to escape. That if given the choice between their relationship and being a criminal, she would choose them. *Him.*

But first things first. He called Mia.

"Hello," she answered.

"Come to the FBI office later this morning. I'm going to bring in Lewis and Halloran to figure out how to get to your father."

"Should I bring my lawyer?"

"Not unless you want to wear the cuffs and be processed."

"Then I guess you investigated where the money is going."

"I did. What you're doing is still wrong."

"But for a good cause. I can live with that."

The question was, could he? "Off the record, if we catch your father, would you keep doing this?"

"I don't know."

He'd been afraid of that answer. He'd wanted her to say that she couldn't wait to get away from crime, but she didn't. That honesty he'd admired early on in their relationship was not offering him comfort now. "The FBI is still going to want your crew."

"I told you I work alone."

"We both know that's a lie."

"Then arrest me. Take my deal off the table and prosecute me. But I'm the only person you'll ever know about."

Naturally, her adamancy made him wonder who she was protecting. Her cousin, definitely. That man was shady. Beyond that, she had no one. He couldn't imagine her mother was part of this. "Let's see how today goes."

"Thank you."

He didn't know what to say to that. Should he be happy that she thanked him for helping her conceal her illegal activities? Doing this could cost him his job. He didn't even know why he was helping her. "I'll see you at ten."

They disconnected and he went to the office.

He called Stokes into the conference room before reaching out to Lewis and Halloran. She came in carrying coffee for both of them. "Quiet day at the Bauer house. McNamara's experts came in first thing this morning."

"It's a forgery."

She sat down and her brow furrowed. "How do you know?"

"I just do. I'm not sure how and when the switches are being made, but it's not the current owners doing it. These paintings belong to Dwayne Benson."

"What?"

"Mia Benson informed me last night that while she told us about her father calling her, she withheld some pertinent information. He owns the paintings his friends are selling. It's all part of his plan to keep raking in money while on the run. The forgeries are preventing him from getting his hands on cash."

Stokes leaned back in her chair and crossed her arms. "She's doing it, isn't she? Mia."

Logan sighed and sank into a chair. "We have no proof of who is swapping the art. However, she wants to help us take her father down." Or maybe the truth of the matter was that they were helping her.

"So she knows we're onto her, and she's trying to avoid prosecution."

"Definitely. But she's good. I don't know that we'd be able to build a case."

"Be able to or want to?"

The accusation raised his hackles. While he hadn't been totally open about his relationship with Mia, he hadn't exactly hidden it either. "I've consistently done my job. Regardless of my relationship with Mia, I've worked hard on this case."

"Are you sure she hasn't clouded your judgment?"

"You can trust me to put this case first." He twirled a pen and he thought about how to bring up the next part. "That being said, part of how I got her cooperation is a deal for her. We stop investigating her and get her father. If we tell Halloran and Lewis she's behind the forgeries, they'll press it."

"As they should."

"You've been with me on this since nearly the beginning. You know that there is no evidence, just a truckload of suspicion and hunches. It's a waste of resources to try to get her. Her goal is to force her father's hand and make him come out of hiding."

"Where are the originals?"

He smiled and shook his head. "As far as I know, they've all been sold and the profit from the sales have been passed on to Benson's victims. Mortgages and medical bills have been paid off, mysterious full-ride scholarships handed out."

He unfolded the paper Mia had given him and passed it to Stokes. She read his scribbled notes. As she read, Logan added, "I spoke with each person."

It was Stokes's turn to sigh. "I get it now. She's not evil incarnate. She's doing good and righting his wrongs with his money." She smiled. "It is pretty ingenious."

"You're okay with riding with me on this?"

"We'll get to close one of the biggest cases this city has seen in decades. It's like letting the street hustler go in order to grab his dealer. We might not like it, but it makes the most sense."

"That's what I was thinking. I'll call Halloran and Lewis."

A little while later, Halloran and Lewis came into the conference room. They looked at the board Stokes had set up with pictures of the forged art.

"What does this have to do with our case?" Halloran asked. "Other than Mia Benson."

"Dwayne Benson admitted to Mia that the paintings that have come up forged are his. When Mia announced that Bishop's painting was a forgery, Benson called the next day. He was at least as pissed off as Bishop was. He said the painting was one of his contingencies to stay liquid and on the move."

Lewis leaned on the table. "Where does the forgery fit in?"

Logan shifted in his seat. "Someone is switching the originals with counterfeit pieces. Benson thinks his buddies are trying to screw him over. Make the swap, and if they're caught, they can throw up their hands and tell Benson he's outta luck." Logan was working hard to skate the line of truth.

"And what's Mia's take on all this?" Halloran asked. "She think they're trying to screw over Daddy?"

"She doesn't care about his friends. She's trying to lure her father out of hiding. She said he's getting desperate. She thinks she can get him somewhere we can grab him."

Lewis's face lit up. "Five freakin' years and we're finally going to get the son of a bitch."

"Don't get too excited," Halloran said. "There are a lot of ifs in that plan. If he calls her again. If she can convince him to meet her. If it's a country with extradition. If she don't screw us over."

"She won't," both Lewis and Logan said.

Logan took a breath. "She wants to work with us. She brought this idea to me. He wants her help to sell more paintings to get cash."

"Whatever you say, man," Halloran said. "I've worked with plenty of scum that didn't look half as good as her, so I can suck it up and do the job. I ain't gotta like her."

Logan's back went up at the way he talked about Mia, but it wasn't his place to jump to her defense. Not to mention, she was good at taking care of herself. "I think we should flesh out a plan to propose to her when she gets here."

"What are you thinking?"

Stokes leaned back in her chair and twirled a pen. "I say we let her sell the paintings and tell him she'll only give him the money if he meets her."

"That's a little on the nose," Halloran said. "Benson's smarter than that."

"But," Lewis said, "not if he's desperate. He's calling her because whatever he had planned is falling apart. It's been smooth sailing for five years. Something happened. If we can push him a little more, he'll come out. He'll be too desperate not to do whatever she asks if she's throwing him a lifeline."

Logan agreed. He just hoped sending Benson a lifeline wouldn't bring Mia down. Guilty of theft or not, she shouldn't have to pay when her father wasn't.

AN HOUR LATER, Logan stood at the conference table. "Mia Benson is on her way up."

Stokes shifted their board back and removed any photos they didn't want Mia to see. She was being cautious, and he couldn't really blame her. It made sense to keep their cards close. He went to the elevator bank to meet Mia.

When the door opened, she stepped into the hall looking like a woman on a mission. "Mia," he said. "You ready?"

"Yes." She was fully shut down, no hint at the connection they'd shared.

"This way." He led her to the conference room, where he pointed at each agent. "I believe you know Agents Halloran and Lewis. This is Agent Stokes. Please take a seat."

"Hello." She wheeled a chair out and sat, keeping her purse on her lap.

"Ford tells us you're willing to help lure your father out of hiding and into custody," Lewis said.

"I am."

Halloran huffed.

Mia pinned him with a glare. "Look, Agent Halloran. I know you don't like me and you trust me even less. Forgive me if I'm wrong, but I'm the best chance you have of catching my father after five years. If I was part of his scheme, I wouldn't be here now. I wouldn't have come to you when he called. That was my choice. And if you don't want my help, you can go to hell." She stood, sliding the chair back and nearly into the wall.

Logan stood and put his hands out. He leveled a look at her, reminding her of their deal. If she walked out, he wouldn't be able to do anything to save her. "Now, hold on. We know you didn't have to come to us. I'm sure you can understand Agent Halloran's frustration. As you said, your father has eluded the FBI for five years. Please, sit. I think what Agent Halloran is questioning is why now? You've never offered help before."

She pulled her chair back and sat again, avoiding making eye contact with Halloran. "I have. They know I spent my own money to find him. But now I have a way. He's told me that he has artwork scattered all over the city as his contingency. Keaton Bishop's painting isn't the only one. Randall Scott's and Max Ingram's paintings also belonged to him."

Everyone around the table stared at her slack-jawed.

She pressed on. "Those forgeries are making him panic. He's asked for my help in selling what he has. He's flat-out asked me for money."

"Where do the forgeries come in?" Stokes asked, knowing that Halloran and Lewis probably wanted to know. "That's the piece that doesn't make sense."

"My father thinks Keaton Bishop was trying to cheat him and got caught."

"What do you think?" Lewis asked.

She pressed her lips together. "Bishop knew what my father was doing. They all did and they profited from it. They're all crooked, so I wouldn't put it past them to screw my father over. Serves him right after what he's done."

Logan smiled. This woman was a formidable opponent. Not one lie passed her lips. She would outsmart her father. No way would the man come out unscathed.

Halloran actually laughed. "So how do we catch him?"

"He said he'll meet me. Where can you get him?"

"How do you know he'll show if we set the trap?" Halloran pushed.

"He'll come if he thinks I'm bringing him money. He needs to be just the right amount of desperate. Rash enough to risk meeting me, not so hopeless that he burrows deeper out of sight. I'm the key to that. He believes I'm on his side and I'll help him."

"Why should we trust you?" Halloran asked.

"I know you think my mother and I knew what he was doing. I have no way to convince you otherwise.

But understand this—we've been paying for his crimes. Our reputations have been called into question constantly for five long years. Not a day goes by where I don't have to wonder if the person I was expecting to hear from isn't calling because of my last name. Or worse, if they want to befriend me because of it. If he's locked up, then the victims will have closure and I can go on with my life without having to worry about him popping up and causing another mess."

Stokes reached across the table and slid a picture to Mia. "This is a supposed grad student who was interning at the Carlisle when the Devereaux was there and found to be a forgery. Does she look familiar?"

Mia studied the photo. "It's a very poor photo. Should I recognize her?"

"She was there less than a week and no one has any record of her. Name appears to be phony. University of Chicago never heard of her."

"We routinely have grad students working at the Art Institute, but I don't meet them all, and I've never headed the program that organizes them, so if we ever crossed paths there, I don't recall." She handed the picture back to Stokes.

"What about Jack Russo? Do you know him?"

Mia's forehead wrinkled. "I don't believe so."

"He goes by the name Dodger."

Logan couldn't be sure, but there seemed to be a flicker of something in Mia's eyes.

"Silly name."

"He was the one who called in the tip about the real Devereaux."

"I knew nothing about any of that until I saw it on the news."

Still no sign of a lie. Either she was getting better at hiding her tell or she was speaking the truth. It didn't add up. Not if she really was behind all the thefts and forgeries.

"You inspected Randall Scott's Mathis painting when Atlas told him it was a forgery, right?" Stokes was definitely leading Mia down a path.

"He called me. He said the appraiser was wrong and he basically wanted a second opinion. I reminded him that contemporary art is not my area of expertise, but he was sure I could at least help him contest the appraiser's findings." She shrugged. "But I couldn't."

"Why would he call you?"

"My father's friends are all wealthy businessmen, but art is not in their wheelhouse at all. Ever since I was in college, they would ask my opinion on some purchases. It's the equivalent of having a friend who's a carpenter. He might not be able to build your house, but you'd ask him questions to guide you. In the past, they would ask my father, who would then rope me into attending a dinner party so his friends could ask me questions."

"I assume you can't get him on US soil," Logan said.

"I keep trying, but he knows if he comes home, he's going to prison."

"What about a new identity?" Lewis said. "If you offered to get him and your uncle new passports and IDs, would he take them?"

"Maybe."

"If he does, we can trace him and nab him at whatever airport he's at."

"Next time he calls, I'll offer it up and let you know." She stood, gave Lewis and Halloran a quick nod, looked at Stokes, and said, "Nice to meet you."

"I'll walk you out," Logan offered.

MIA WAS SURPRISED LOGAN accompanied her. She figured he couldn't wait to get her out of his sight. He was silent on the way down in the elevator. She looked up at him in the lobby, but he kept walking, so she followed him outside.

The humidity was oppressive after yesterday's storm. Logan stood for a moment, hands in his pants pockets, face solemn in a way she'd never seen.

"So you're working with the blonde who pulled the Devereaux job for Dodger."

"I told you that I don't know this Dodger character."

"But you know the blonde." He shook his head. "Don't say anything. I don't want to hear another lie."

"I haven't lied to you." Had she? She'd omitted information obviously, but she didn't think she'd outright lied. Her heart felt heavy and her lungs couldn't quite expand. She was so torn between protecting her team and protecting him. She was every bit the disaster her father was.

"Was I always just a mark to you?" He asked the question while staring out at traffic.

The heaviness in her chest squeezed tighter, but he deserved the truth. "Not at first. Once I figured out you weren't really an insurance agent, yes. I wanted to gauge how much you knew, how close you were. But I would be lying if I said it stayed that way. I have feelings for you I hadn't counted on and that's what led us here. You were the first person in years I felt comfortable enough to completely be myself around and it allowed you to see past my defenses."

"Do you regret it?"

"Slipping up and getting caught? Yes," she said with a smile that broke his heart a little more. "But I don't regret being with you for a second. If I wasn't who I am or you weren't you, I would've fallen deeply in love with you, Logan Ford."

She didn't wait for a response because she feared he hated her for using him. As she turned and walked away, she blinked back tears and focused on her mission.

She called Nikki on her way to work.

"What's up?"

"The FBI does, in fact, have a picture of you at the Carlisle. You're blonde and it's a bad photo, but it's you."

"You only recognized me because you knew it was me. I told you Wade's glasses prevented facial recognition."

"They also have your father's name. They're trying to piece it together, but they don't have it yet."

"Are you sure?"

"The agents in charge of my father's case were there. They neither like nor trust me, so they would absolutely withhold details. But the information about you came from another agent. Stokes was her name."

"Yeah, that's the one who cut a deal with my dad. I met her when I went to visit my dad with his lawyer. She didn't recognize me, so I think we're good."

"You might want to ditch the wig and come up with a different disguise."

"Will do. How did things go with Logan?"

"About as well as could be expected."

"Anything I can do?"

Inspiration struck. She might not be able to repair her relationship with Logan, but she could offer him something. Make things right in her own way. "Actually, I can use some help. There's a Camille Hurley painting titled *Farm Girl Dreams* that I want you to steal."

"London hasn't mentioned that one."

"It's not one of my father's. This one is a straight-up theft and it belongs to Logan's family."

Nikki barked out a laugh. "Now we've done it. We *have* pulled you fully over to the dark side."

Mia disconnected with Nikki's laugh echoing in her head. She might spend a little more time in the criminal world these days, but her heart still wanted to make things right.

TWENTY-SEVEN

LATER THAT NIGHT, after Logan had worked to develop documents for Mia to show her father, he went home to see Mae. She hadn't been expecting him, but whenever he was in trouble, home was where he went. He walked through the back door and yelled, "Who's home?"

Mae turned the corner, clutching her chest. "Boy, if you don't stop doing that, I'm going to hurt you."

"Sorry, Mae. Old habit." He bent and kissed her cheek.

She looked up at him with narrowed eyes. "What's wrong?"

He didn't even try to lie to her. She saw through everything. "It's Mia."

"You broke up already?" She shook her head. "Have a seat and tell me what you did."

"What makes you think *I* did something?" he asked as he sat at the kitchen table.

"I know you, don't I?"

"I'm innocent this time. Mia, on the other hand, isn't."

Mae poured them each a cup of coffee. "What is she guilty of?"

"Why is it so quiet around here?" The house was unusually quiet, and it was a little disturbing.

"Joe took the kids to a baseball game." She pinned him with a look. "What did Mia do?"

"She's a thief."

"What? Like a real thief? Someone who belongs in cuffs?"

Logan nodded. "It's a little more complicated than that. The case I've been working on—the art forgeries? She's involved in that. She's been stealing art and replacing it with counterfeit pieces."

Mae stiffened. "Did she target you?"

"I don't think so. But when I showed interest, she used it to her advantage."

"You have feelings for her."

He nodded.

"But she's on the other side of the law, something you've been working most of your life to uphold."

It wasn't his place to tell Mae Mia's secret, but he needed someone to guide him. "There's so much going on, Ma. The art she's stealing actually belongs to her father, who is a criminal. She's doing it to draw him out to bring him to justice."

"Well, that doesn't sound so bad. Still breaking the law, but for a good reason. Kind of like when a cop on TV lies to the perp to get him to confess."

Logan chuckled. They'd had numerous conversations about how his job was nothing like what she saw on TV. He blew out a heavy breath. "And the money she gets from the art she gives away to people her father screwed over."

Mae full-on laughed. "That girl is definitely going to give you a run for your money. She'll keep you on your toes."

"It's really not funny. She's breaking the law. In fact, she's the person I've been searching for, and she knew it."

Mae hummed. "Are you mad that she's a thief or that she fooled you?"

"Both. How could I let her sucker me like that?" He drank his coffee in an attempt to swallow down his own bitterness.

"You were falling for her. There's no shame in that. What happens now?"

"She offered to help us bring her father in."

"That's good. You said he was a big case."

"That's in exchange for me looking the other way on her crimes."

"Cops make deals all the time."

"I know." For him, the problem was that he wasn't sure if he'd agreed to her terms because it was the best decision for the case or because it was personal.

"Then what happens?"

"What do you mean?"

"If she helps you get her father, then what? Will she keep stealing?"

"I don't know." He didn't think so, but he'd been wrong about so much.

"If she stops, is this something you could get past?"

"I'm not sure. That's why I came home. I've always found answers here."

"Honey, I stopped telling you what to do years ago." She sipped her coffee and leaned back in her seat.

"You taught me lying is bad, yet you sit here with a lie on your lips without even blinking. You love telling every one of us what to do." But he hadn't truly expected her to make life decisions for him. He just needed the comfort of home to try to get his head on straight.

"I could tell you that no one is perfect. We all make mistakes, some bigger than others. Sometimes the choices we make are difficult. Seems to me her intentions were good. Is she a good person?" Mae stood and grabbed the coffeepot to top off their cups. She also slid a tray of cookies in front of him.

"I thought so." He picked up a chocolate chip cookie and bit into it. It tasted like childhood. "Realistically, if the FBI had kept her father in custody, I don't think she would've become a thief. And she's protecting her crew. I know she's not working alone, but when I mentioned I wanted her crew, she said she'd walk away from the deal and I could arrest her."

"Loyalty matters."

Mae made excellent points, as always. Unfortunately, it didn't give him a direction. He had feelings for Mia, but her criminal activity could cost him his career, no matter how noble she thought she was being. And she didn't say the stealing would end with her father's arrest.

"The last questions I have for you about this are whether you believe she also has feelings for you. Were you part of her plan to steal art? Did she put you at risk?"

"I don't know what to believe."

"Well," she said, standing again. "You have to figure that out before you can make a decision. Or you can cut her loose and go on your way. You haven't known each other long, so walking away is still doable." She moved around the kitchen to prep dinner. "Unless you think the relationship is worth fighting for."

"Still not helping, Mae."

"What can I say? I like her. Are you staying for dinner?"

"Of course. Who would be dumb enough to say no to one of your meals?"

"Then wash up and go chop the vegetables."

FOR THE NEXT two days, Mia kept her head down and focused on her work at the museum. She felt so isolated, which irked her because being alone had never bothered her before. She'd stayed away from the apartment, and obviously far from Logan. She was lonely in a way she hadn't expected. Nikki and Audrey had called, but she'd ignored them. She was pretty confident the FBI didn't have the number to her burner phone, but she didn't want to take any chances. Right now, her team was clear, and she intended to keep it that way.

Of course, dodging them meant red flags to Jared, so it wasn't surprising that he was waiting for her to get off work. He'd texted to let her know he'd ordered dinner, so she wouldn't freak out about someone being in her house. Although he had a key, her cousin rarely used it without warning.

When she arrived at home, he had sushi from her favorite restaurant spread out on her dining room table. She looked at the food and then at him. "I'm fine."

"No one said you weren't."

"Yet you've come to my house uninvited and brought my favorite meal." She set her purse by the door and strode across the room to pour herself a glass of wine.

"We both know that I haven't been invited because you're hurt and sulking. You tend to push everyone away when you're feeling vulnerable."

"Then maybe you should take a hint."

He sat down with a smile. "I'm family. You can't get rid of me."

She joined him at the table. "I've avoided contact with everyone to keep them away from the FBI. If I'm being followed or wiretapped, it could expose the team. Right now, as far as the FBI is concerned, I'm helping them get at our fathers."

"And Logan?"

"Knows the truth even though he can't prove it. He keeps asking about my crew, and although I've told him I work alone, he doesn't believe me. I told him if he pushes it, he can arrest me and forget our deal."

"I'm sure Nikki and Audrey would appreciate that, but you're the team captain."

Mia scooped up a tuna roll and placed it on her plate. "They can function just fine without direction. They don't really need me now. They have my notes and plans. They're capable of executing it."

"Doesn't mean they're not worried about you. We all are."

"Logan was supposed to be a means to an end and I failed. Nikki and Wade warned me not to fall for the mark, and I did."

"Do you trust him not to continue investigating?"

"I do." Logan was honorable and honest. He would keep his word, even if he was unhappy about it. Mia ate some sushi, but she didn't taste anything.

"Maybe it's time to stop," Jared said. "Like Nikki said, it's been a good run. You're at the point that our fathers will be caught. That's what you wanted, right?"

That wasn't all she'd wanted, though. She wanted to hurt them. She wanted to ruin the men who wouldn't be punished for participating in their fathers' crimes. "That was the ultimate goal, but now that I've seen the list, Jared…" She shook her head. "It's so much bigger than I thought. If they have access to all those pieces of art, they'll escape again."

They ate in silence for a while. Mia wished she could turn back the clock and never get involved with Logan. Her life would be so much simpler if she'd stayed the course and only focused on the mission.

"Audrey mentioned the little side project you have them working on."

"And?"

"Why didn't you say anything to me about it?"

"I didn't think I needed to run everything past you. I don't need it sold. The Hurley painting is my apology to Logan."

Jared chuckled. "You think giving an FBI agent a stolen painting is a good apology?"

"The painting is rightfully his family's. I'm simply doing more of what I have been. Righting the wrongs of others." She should feel prouder, more accomplished... more something. But since the day Logan had followed her, her victory had felt empty.

Her phone rang, and her heart stuttered, hoping to see a gif from Logan. It was a call from a blocked number. She figured it was her father. "Hello."

"Honey. How are you? Is the connection good on your end this time? Can you hear me okay?"

"Yes, Daddy. I can hear you fine. I have a plan."

"A plan for what?"

"I have a way for us to meet. Jared has a connection." She flicked her eyes to her cousin who was staring intently at her. "He can forge documents. We can get you and Uncle Cesar new passports and IDs."

"I have ID, sweetie. I need money."

"I know. I can bring you money. I haven't seen you in five years, when you snuck off in the night. I think I deserve a proper farewell."

"It's risky."

"The FBI aren't even really looking for you. Every six months or so, they stop by to ask if I've heard from you. That's all." Up until recently, that was true.

"What do you tell them?"

"That I haven't heard from you." She clenched her teeth and took a cleansing breath. "Please, Daddy. I'll come to you with the new IDs and cash. At least enough to get you started. Then we can come up with a plan to get you the rest." She lowered her voice as if someone else might be listening. "Caleb Small's painting was just declared a forgery, too. Someone's out to get you."

"What? I haven't heard from Caleb."

"Everyone here is talking about it."

"How soon can you get away?"

"I can probably have a flight booked for this weekend, assuming we can get the documents in time."

"Can you bring the artwork? If I reach out to my friends, can you pack and bring at least a few pieces that I can sell here?"

"I think so? I'll have to look into how I can do that without checking them. Could you imagine a priceless painting being banged around like Samsonite luggage?"

"Buy an extra seat in first class and carry them on. Cesar and I brought two when we left the country."

Son of a bitch. At least she knew he trusted her because he was revealing more now than he had five years ago. "Let me see what I can do. Where do you want to meet?"

"How about Greece? We haven't been there for years."

"All right. Text me a number I can reach you at, and I'll let you know when I have the art and my flight booked."

"Thank you, kitten. I knew I could count on you."

"Of course, Daddy." It took a lot to not gag on the words. They disconnected and she turned to Jared. "We've got them."

TWENTY-EIGHT

IT TOOK MORE than a few days to coordinate all the moving pieces, but by the time they did, Mia had a plan of her own. A full week later, she was ready to go. She'd arranged to pick up the paintings from her father's friends, which London had rushed the forgeries for. Those paintings would be sold just like the others. She had plans all around to make sure Dwayne Benson didn't escape justice this time.

Her nerves were rocky because while she'd been working with the FBI over the course of the week to ensure everything was running right, she hadn't had any interaction with Logan. Only a week and she missed him. Her phone sat mostly silent instead of pinging with random gifs to make her smile. Today, she would have to face him. He was accompanying her on the flight.

As if she couldn't be trusted to complete her mission.

At eight a.m., her house was swarming with FBI agents. Her gut churned with memories of the last time she'd experienced this, when they came to arrest her father. This time, however, they were there for her. Stokes showed her the new passport and ID they'd created for her father and uncle.

Lewis ran down how they expected things to happen. When they landed in Athens, Logan would step back and follow Mia in case her father didn't show at the airport like he was supposed to.

"I know you think he trusts you," Lewis said, "but he's cautious. There's a possibility he'll call to give you directions to meet him somewhere."

"What if he does come to pick me up?"

"Local police and Interpol will arrest him on the spot."

"And if I have to meet him?"

"Logan will follow at a discreet distance. Depending on where he wants to meet, we'll grab him when it's safe to do so."

"So I might have to keep playing this game to convince him I'm on his side." She breathed that idea in. It was one thing to do it over the phone, but something different having to face him.

"I have no doubt you can play the man. I've never met anyone with a poker face as good as yours," Logan said.

Figures. The first words he spoke to her and they were an insult. At least she thought they were an insult.

Logan had picked up the two portfolio cases that held the paintings. Each case was plywood with a waterproof coating and reinforced hinges. She could carry them by their handles or wheel them behind her. As her father directed, they would stay with her instead of being checked as luggage.

Logan and Halloran opened each case and inspected the paintings.

"You have any idea if these are real or fake?" Halloran asked.

Logan looked over at her. "I have no idea, but probably fake. Everything that Dwayne Benson has wanted has gone to shit."

"But if they are real, and he gets away with these..."

"He won't," Mia said. She'd make sure of it.

"Why are we actually bringing these instead of carrying empty cases?" Halloran asked.

Even though she was sure the question was meant for Logan, she answered. "As you said, my father is cautious. If he asks to see the paintings, and the cases are empty, he'll immediately know I betrayed him."

"We don't want to risk that given that he might open them in a public space. Although he's never been violent, it's a risk," Logan added.

"He also hasn't said if my uncle will be at the airport. I don't want him to get away either."

Halloran nodded. "Athens authorities will be there standing back in case you need help. Anything else we need to know before you head out?"

Logan and Mia both shook their heads. Agent Stokes drove them to the airport. They were all silent for most of the trip. When she pulled up to Departures, Stokes finally shifted in her seat to face Mia. "I know Logan made a deal with you, but if you play games or put anyone in danger, I will lock you up."

"There is no need to worry about me. I've been working toward this plan for the past five years. Let me remind you that it was my actions, not the FBI's, that got us here. I may not be proud of what I've done to make it happen, but in this case, the ends absolutely justify the means." She opened the car door, stepped out, and moved to the back to retrieve her bag and the paintings.

Logan reached in for one of the cases.

Mia cut him off. "I have it."

"Fine." He grabbed his own small backpack and followed her into the airport.

Once they were through security, Mia said she

needed the restroom. Logan offered to keep her things, but that would negate her plan, so again, she told him she could handle it. She hustled to the restroom where she stood in front of the mirror and waited for Nikki to arrive.

If she hadn't been looking for her, Mia would've missed Nikki. Today, she was a redhead who wore the image-altering glasses again. She set the new case down and grabbed Mia's. Mia touched up her lipstick, taking a few extra moments to allow Nikki to clear the area, and then she returned to where Logan was waiting for them to board.

They called passengers for first class, and Mia stood. "Let's go."

Logan remained sitting. "The FBI doesn't fly first class. We're coach all the way."

"Lucky for you I had you upgraded. I don't want you accusing me of anything shady."

"I don't want your money."

"And I don't want you to look at me like I'm a criminal," she whispered harshly.

"But you are a criminal," he whispered back.

"Whatever. Sit in the cramped seats. Enjoy your tiny bag of peanuts. I'll see you when we land." She turned and stalked off. In all honesty, she'd upgraded him so they would have a chance to talk and clear the air.

Behind her, he heaved a heavy sigh that bordered on a grunt. "I've already broken so many rules with you, what's one more?"

"It's a rule that you have to suffer in coach?"

"This skates the line of a bribe."

She rolled her eyes. "Well, considering we have been seeing each other socially, and we've been intimate, I think the powers that be could assume I just wanted to sit with my boyfriend."

As soon as she said the words, she wanted to reel them back in. Luckily, the line was moving and they were through the gate and on the plane without her having to look at him. In first class, she debated where to set the paintings. She had two seats together and one across the aisle. She could sit beside the paintings or she could sit beside Logan. Without too much more thought, she set the cases across the aisle and buckled them in. Then she scooted over to the window seat. Logan would take the seat beside her, but she was immediately reconsidering the seating arrangement. He was still contentious, and spending the next twelve-plus hours trapped in close proximity might not have been her best idea.

Once settled, she pulled her notebook and laptop from her bag. She had plenty to do for her exhibit, and since she was going to miss a few days of work, she planned to accomplish some things remotely. Takeoff was smooth and Mia began sketching out her ideas for the layout of the exhibit. Ultimately it would be the team's design, but she'd been envisioning this exhibit since she first pitched it.

Logan sat beside her with an open paperback. However, she couldn't help but notice that he hadn't turned the page once. "Is the book that bad?"

"Huh?" He turned and looked at her.

"You've been staring at the same page since you sat down. If the book isn't holding your interest, maybe you should try another one."

He closed the book and she saw it was a spy thriller. Figured.

"I've got a lot on my mind." He shook his head. "No. Mostly it's you."

"Me?" She closed her sketchpad and twisted in her seat. "I thought I'd be the last thing on your mind."

"You should be and that's part of the problem. I genuinely like you, Mia, and it's bugging the heck out of me."

Heat rose in her cheeks and she smiled. "I like you, too. That wasn't part of the plan."

"What was the plan? String me along until you could blow up my case?" He kept his voice low, even though the cabin wasn't full.

"No. At first, I just wanted to have an idea of how close you were to figuring out what I was doing. I didn't have a plan to change your course. It was just about protecting myself."

"And your team."

"Hypothetically."

"How long has this been going on?"

She considered his question. It might not be wise to be honest with him, but they needed to air things out. "The beginning of the summer."

"Why?"

"I told you why. While I might have omitted certain things from our conversations, I didn't lie to you. I hate what my father did. My anger worsened when it became obvious that the FBI couldn't do anything to bring him to justice. I want justice for his victims. I want to feel good about my name." She probably wasn't explaining it as well as she could, but she didn't know how to make him understand the need to overcome the looks and whispers and *know* she'd done the right thing.

"Your father disappeared five years ago. Why now?"

"Because I turned thirty in December. That gave me access to the trust fund my mother had set up for me. I've been using that money to fund my project. The profits have all gone to the victims."

"If you're spending your money anyway, why not just cut them checks?"

She was really getting tired of that question. Maybe that would've been the quick solution, but it wasn't the best. "Partially because my inheritance isn't that big. Mostly, it's because I wanted those men to suffer the same humiliation I've lived with for years. They are as guilty as my father and uncle, but no one is going after them. They shouldn't get away with profiting from his activities. They're still *thriving*."

The thought made her angry all over. She and her mother had paid a bigger price than any of her father's friends. "My mother had to take an early retirement because no one would trust her as their lawyer. For months, any time we showed our faces in public we received ridicule. As if we had no right to live our lives. And so much of that came from the very people we once considered friends."

"So it's about revenge."

She'd danced around the topic plenty, but she was at the point that she was fine owning it. "Yes. Sometimes an eye for an eye is justice."

"But not legal."

"The law isn't always right." It seemed as though they would always be at this impasse. "I'm sorry I hurt you. I truly am. But I don't regret what I've done. It's gotten us here, and so many people who were struggling because of my family are now breathing a little easier. I can't be sorry for that."

Heaviness pressed on her chest. She wanted to reach out and touch him, hold him close, feel the safety in his arms. She swallowed past the tightness of her throat. "Please know that if we met at any other time in our lives, I would've fallen head over heels in love with you. In a very short time, you made me happy. You enabled me—for a while—to be myself, let my guard down and enjoy life. For that, I thank you. For the first time in years, I feel like I can have happiness in my future. That's a gift I can never repay."

She didn't think her words would have much impact on him, but she needed him to know that their relationship meant something to her.

"Another time or place, Mia, and I'd be all over that." His voice held the same sorrow she felt.

She cleared her throat and reopened her notebook. Her heart had been broken numerous times, and she knew she'd survive. But she couldn't help but wish she would've met Logan somewhere down the road, when her father was behind bars and she was free from his shadow.

Maybe someday.

LOGAN WAS MISERABLE. He had been for more than a week now. He'd missed Mia and sitting beside her, within reach without having the right to touch her, was torture. He kept thinking about what Mae had said. Could he forgive what Mia had done? Might still be doing? She wasn't looking for forgiveness. She admitted to having no regrets.

He turned on the TV screen in front of him to choose a movie. The first one advertised was *Ocean's 8*. Seriously? Was this the universe sending him a message?

He got it. Mia wasn't a criminal in order to line her own pockets. To a certain degree what she was doing was noble.

But it was still illegal and he was an officer of the law. There was no way for them to be together, existing on opposite sides. He wasn't willing to walk away from his career.

What if she did? If she stopped stealing now, could they have a future?

Logan would like to think so. He flipped through other movie titles. After he had Benson and Towers in cuffs, he and Mia could talk about the future and where they fit.

The flight was long and boring, but Logan had to admit that flying across the Atlantic in first class was definitely the way to go. He was able to stretch out and actually sleep horizontally. They fed him real food. He might never fly coach again.

When breakfast was being served, Mia was still sleeping, her breaths quiet and even. Logan watched her for a few minutes. She was so beautiful. Her eyes slit open.

"Are you being a creeper, Agent Ford?" Her voice was husky, and the sound wrapped around him and squeezed.

"I was about to wake you for breakfast."

She stretched and sat up, looking completely unwrinkled for having spent the night on a plane. "Waking me does not involve staring."

"I wasn't staring."

"Yes, you were," she said with a raised brow.

The man sitting diagonally across from them said,

"She's got you, man. Can't say I blame him, though, miss."

She just smirked at him with her crooked, knowing smile. Yeah, he'd definitely missed that. The flight attendant came around and handed out breakfast.

As they ate, Mia asked, "Any word on your transfer? Are they going to let you stay in Chicago?"

"If I make this bust, I can pretty much have my pick of cities."

"But you want Chicago, right? It's where your family is."

"Yeah." *It's also where you are.* But he couldn't say the words. Eye on the prize. Dwayne Benson and Cesar Towers first. Getting Mia to give up her life of crime, second.

"What's the plan once we land?" she asked.

"Before we deboard, text your father and see if he responds. Local police are meeting us at the gate. I'll stick with them. If your father is there, we'll wait for you to hand off the art, then we'll arrest him. If he's not there, the police have a cab that an officer will be driving. He'll take you to your father, while I follow with the cops."

She bit her lip, suddenly looking concerned.

"You'll be safe. I won't let anything happen to you."

"It's not that. I know my father won't hurt me. But…"

"What?"

"I'm wondering if there's any way I can meet with him and not have him know I handed him over to you."

"Why? I thought you'd want to look him in the eye and make sure he knew you were the one who took him down."

The corner of her mouth tilted up a fraction. "While

I absolutely would enjoy that, part of me is afraid he'll escape again. I would lose the edge I have now."

"At what cost to you, though?"

"What do you mean?"

"I saw it on your face when he called. It chips away at you. If you keep trying to play him, stay one step ahead, he'll keep taking little pieces of you."

She sat back, her eyes wide. "That's…something to think about."

Over the last few hours of their trip, they chatted about work and family the same way friends would. He loved the ease of their companionship. When it was time to fasten their seat belts for landing, he didn't think he imagined the sadness reappearing in her eyes. The morning had been a nice reprieve for both of them.

He was hoping for many more such mornings.

TWENTY-NINE

It TURNED OUT that having a relaxing flight was a good thing because from the moment the wheels touched ground, he was on high alert. He'd known going in that this case would make a difference in his career; but now it was about making things right in his personal life, too. No way was he going to let Dwayne Benson slip away.

He waited while others deplaned and Mia texted her father. He leaned over to see what she was typing and she shot him a glare. Then she turned the screen to face him.

"See? Not trying to double-cross you."

Daddy, I'm here. Are you at the airport?

"I didn't think you were doing anything wrong. I'm just amped up and want to move."

A moment later, she had a response. "He's here. He has a car pulling around to get me. Let's go."

Logan helped her carry the art cases off the plane, and at the gate he introduced her to the police who were waiting for them. He handed her the cases. "We'll be right behind you."

"Okay." She smiled up at him and then turned away. "Mia."

She stopped and looked over her shoulder.

He stepped closer. "If something doesn't feel right,

get out of the way. If he's lying right now and you have to get in a car, know that I will be right behind you."

"Thank you for the reassurance."

"One more thing."

"Yes?"

"When this is over, we need to talk. Really talk about us."

"Is there still a chance for an us?" Her face brightened and he could've kicked himself for playing a role in her sadness.

"I think there can be. I'll see you soon." He kissed her temple. "Be careful."

He watched her weave deftly through the crowd, never losing her stride. He hitched his backpack on his shoulder as the cops came up to him.

He spoke to the man in charge, Lieutenant Baros, who headed the International Police Cooperation Division. "Thanks again for your help on this."

"We're happy to do our part. I've got two plainclothesmen stationed outside." He looked to where Mia was heading to the doors to exit. "I think we can move now and wait for your man to show. If you want to give me your bag, I'll have one of my men put it in our car."

"Thanks. I appreciate it." Logan handed off his bag, and as they moved through the throngs of people, his focus remained on Mia.

She stood on the other side of the glass door, bag at her feet, art cases in one hand and her phone in the other. As she spoke, she looked up and down the curb.

Logan followed her movements. He prayed Dwayne showed because he didn't like the idea of Mia getting in a car with an unknown.

"She is brave to do this, no?" Baros asked.

"Yes, she is. It's been her mission for years to bring him to justice."

"Then let's make sure the pretty woman completes her mission."

MIA WAS BEGINNING TO doubt the plan. Her father had said he was pulling up, but it felt like it was taking forever. Than a black town car pulled up at the curb and a moment later, her father stepped out. He wore a gauzy white shirt, Dockers, and a fedora. He'd put on some weight, but she'd recognize him anywhere.

"Kitten! I'm so glad you made it! How was the flight?" He stepped closer and reached for the paintings.

Mia stood in shock. He was really here right in front of her, greeting her as if she was home from college for the weekend. In a blink, she was twenty again and her life was perfect. She swallowed hard. Looking her father in the eye was so much more difficult than she'd anticipated. Her anger and bitterness warred with the love and devotion she'd had for him when she was a child. He had been a good father.

He paused mid-stride and looked around. "Is something wrong?"

The paintings. He needed to have them in his possession. She shook her head and handed the cases to him, which he immediately shoved into the car.

Then he closed in on her with open arms and she wanted to let him hold her. She jolted and stumbled back, almost tripping over her bag, but strong arms caught her.

"Dwayne Benson, you're under arrest," Logan's voice said clearly as he steadied her.

"What? Who are you?"

"Agent Logan Ford, FBI."

"You have no jurisdiction here."

"But I do, sir," the local cop said.

Mia was in a daze. Her heart thundered in her ears. Logan's hand was still on her arm, as if she couldn't stand on her own. Could she?

"I haven't broken any laws in your country," her father said.

"This is an interdepartmental arrangement. Interpol will be meeting us at the station."

A moment later her father was in handcuffs, calling her name. He didn't sound angry, just confused. Suddenly she could take a deep breath. She filled her lungs and calmed her heart. She felt like a boulder had been lifted from her, and she smiled.

Logan stood in front of her, lowering himself to look directly into her eyes. "Are you okay?"

She nodded, unsure of the words to say. "Better than okay. I feel free."

"Good." His fingers grazed hers. "Where are the paintings? I need to take them in as evidence."

"In the car."

"Do you want to come with us?"

She shook her head. "No. I've done my part. It was much harder than I thought it would be. I don't need to be involved more. I'm going to go to the hotel and sit by the pool and drink champagne to celebrate."

"I don't know how long I'll be."

"You know where to find me. I'll be waiting." She stretched up and kissed his cheek. "Thank you for your trust and being there to steady me."

This wasn't just a light at the end of the tunnel for

her life—this was a glorious sunrise, and she was finally going to seek out happiness.

LOGAN RODE WITH LIEUTENANT Baros while Benson was in the back seat of a squad car. When they got to the station, he carried the artwork in to log as evidence. He didn't need to interrogate Benson because he'd already been indicted. Logan was banking on him rolling over on his brother-in-law. With any luck Cesar Towers was in town and they'd be able to pick him up by dinner.

As he opened the first case, his phone rang with a call from Stokes, and he answered with, "Hey, we got him."

"Any issues?"

"None. Interpol is talking to Benson now to see where Towers is."

He clicked open the second case. His lungs locked and his mouth went dry. It couldn't be. "What. The. Fuck."

"What?" Stokes said.

"The second painting has been replaced."

"With what? How?"

"With a painting that was stolen from my family decades ago." He couldn't believe it. He started to laugh.

"What is so funny?"

"She made sure her father was picked up with stolen goods. It must've been her contingency."

"Watch yourself with that woman. She's tricky. Willing to get caught up in the arrest for handling stolen property? She's tough."

"Determined. I'll check back once I have more info."

They disconnected and he stared at the Hurley painting. It was more than he could've imagined. He snapped a picture of it and texted it to Joe with a message to start looking for the provenance. The family's prized possession would be coming home.

He checked in with Interpol and Baros. It hadn't taken long for Benson to give up his brother-in-law. Cops were on the way to his hotel to pick him up now. Logan couldn't figure out why they'd traveled together. They really had no clue it was a setup.

A few hours later, he left the police department, knowing that Benson and Towers were safely locked up and would remain so until their flight tomorrow. He didn't know what Mia's plans were, but they had tonight.

He went to the hotel where they had booked separate rooms. After checking in, he dropped his bag in his room and went down to the pool.

Mia was stretched out on a lounge chair wearing a skimpy red bikini. Even though she wore sunglasses, he knew her eyes were closed. She was probably exhausted. He sat on the chair beside her.

She jolted up. "What happened?"

"Your father was in possession of the Hurley painting that belongs to my family."

The corner of her mouth tilted up. "Really? He's a sneaky son of a bitch." She shrugged as if to say *you never know*.

He leaned forward, forearms on his knees, and removed his sunglasses. "I get the when of this. You took off unaccompanied to the bathroom at the airport. What I don't get is why."

She sighed and slid her sunglasses down her nose. "Regardless of what you think of me now, I feel bad about using you."

"And you thought the way to make that up to me was to steal a painting."

"I did what I always try to do—make thing right." Her eyes were bright and clear, a hint of humor glinting. "The Hurley belongs to your family. Someone took it. Imagine how much different your life—Joe and Mae's life—might have been if they'd had this painting."

He couldn't argue that, but it still felt wrong. "I have one more question for you."

She pushed her glasses up on her head, stared straight into his eyes, and waited.

"What happens now?"

"In regards to?"

"Your criminal activity. Forgeries. Us." The last word came out softly, as if he shouldn't have said it. Hell, he probably shouldn't have.

"Off the record? Between the two of us?"

That didn't sound good, but he nodded. He needed to know.

"My father sent me a list of his holdings. At least thirty pieces of art." She sat all the way up and set her feet on the ground. Her knees nearly touched his. "My original plan involved twelve. They were pieces that I knew could bring in enough money to make a difference to his victims and hurt him. It's barely a dent."

"So you're going to keep going? Even though we have him?"

"I don't know."

His heart thumped harder. He'd really believed that her father's arrest would be enough.

She reached over and touched his hand. "Part of me is afraid that he has enough contingencies to escape again. I can't let that happen."

He took her hand in his. "It won't. We have him and your uncle. We fly back to Chicago tomorrow." He ran his thumb over her knuckles and asked her the hardest question. "Would you stop if it meant we could be together?"

Her eyes went glassy and she swallowed hard. "Yes. As long as my father is brought to justice."

He looked for signs of a lie but saw none.

"I can walk away from this mission of mine, and I am willing to do that to have a chance for us."

His heart raced now in happiness.

"But." She took in a sharp breath. "I want you to understand that if he escapes, if he gets off, I will go after him again."

Logan had no worries there. He'd personally make sure the man faced trial. "You can make that commitment to me without checking in with your partners?"

"I work alone," she said, smirking.

"Thought we were being honest."

"You're still FBI and my hypothetical team isn't safe from you."

"You think you're safe from me?"

"I've never felt safer than when I'm with you, so I have no worries. And you should know by now that I call the shots, so walking away doesn't require anyone's approval."

She was still cautious with her words, but he wanted to believe her.

"You said you're flying home tomorrow?" she asked.

"Yeah. Aren't you?"

"I think I'll stay another day. I don't think I could handle being on the same plane as my father for twelve hours." She stood, still holding his hand. "We have to-night, though, right?"

"Yes." He couldn't say no to her.

TWO DAYS LATER, Mia walked into the apartment, where she'd called the team to meet. The last meeting with her in charge. It was bittersweet, but right. She'd done what she'd set out to do, and her role was over.

She set the meal she'd brought on the table and spread out the food before getting plates and utensils from the kitchen. As she carried wine and beer to the table, the front door opened and Jared and Audrey walked in. She greeted them.

Jared already knew her plan, but she wanted to be the one to tell the women. Nikki and London came in next, chattering about going dancing at a club. Nikki was saying they wouldn't have to go out if they got a shot machine for the living room.

Mia smiled and shook her head. She had no idea what a shot machine even was, but knowing Nikki, it had to do with getting drunk.

"Ooh…this is an amazing spread, Mia. Better watch it or we'll get used to the fancy meals," Nikki joked as she took a seat. Audrey and Jared sat next to each other and London sat on the other side of Nikki.

Mia remained standing. "As you know, everything in Greece went off without a hitch. My father and uncle are sitting in jail waiting for trial." Her throat tightened. "None of this would've been possible without all of you. What started like a fever dream five years ago, you helped turn into reality. Thank you." She raised a glass to toast.

Audrey sipped. "Why doesn't this feel like a celebratory drink? It sounds like you're cushioning bad news."

Mia shook her head with a smile. "Not bad. I don't know how much Jared told you, but everything that happened between Logan and me exposed my plan." She held up a hand. "You're all safe. While he knows I wasn't working alone, I never admitted that, and he has no idea who you are."

"But he could find out if he wanted," Nikki said.

"Probably," Mia agreed. "While in Greece, I agreed to stop stealing as long as my father paid for his crimes."

"What?" Nikki said. "You're just quitting?"

Mia offered a slow nod. "Logan and I have agreed to give a relationship a try. It might not work out, but I've lived the past five years doing nothing but thinking about how to take my father down. It's time for me to take a shot at happiness. That can't happen as long as he's FBI and I'm running a criminal enterprise."

"Good for you," London said.

"So you're walking away? Does that mean we're done?" Audrey looked between Jared and Mia.

Mia pressed her lips together. "That's entirely up to you. You have the lists of my father's properties and his victims. I've already given Jared my inheritance to use how he sees fit. I believe that what we've done here has made a real difference in the lives of the people we've helped. I'm all for doing more of that." She swallowed, took a deep breath, and added, "I just can't be a part of it."

"What about you?" Audrey asked Jared.

"If you ladies want to finish what Mia started, I'm here. I already play in the shadows. That's never really been who Mia is."

"But if you're with Logan, and you're paying for our work, he'll find out," Nikki said. "He could come after us."

"I promised him that I could walk away. I didn't say no one else would continue with the forgeries."

Nikki lifted a shoulder. "That doesn't seem completely honest. I'm pretty sure that would be a deal breaker for an FBI agent."

"He has no reason to keep looking. But if he does, Jared will know and you can plan accordingly." Mia made eye contact with each woman. "If you decide we go out like this and end the project, I'm okay with that, too. I may have started this venture, but we've become a team, so I feel safe in leaving it in your hands."

Jared clapped his hands together. "No decisions have to be made now. Tonight is for celebrating. Dwayne Benson and Cesar Towers are behind bars." He lifted a glass. "To revenge."

"No," Mia said. "To justice."

EPILOGUE

Two months later

TWO HOURS INTO her big night, Mia was exhausted. She'd been working nonstop to make this exhibit everything she'd envisioned. She was proud of it. It was that pride that had her irritation growing because the hors d'oeuvres were not quite what they had discussed. She had to remind herself that she was not in charge of the catering. The exhibit was her baby, and people came out to support her. More importantly, they were enjoying the exhibit.

"Mia."

At the sound of her mother's voice, Mia turned from the rail where she had been watching the crowd, making sure the flow of traffic was working as she'd designed. Her mother was crossing the hall with her hand wrapped around Logan's arm.

Mia took a deep breath and smiled. "You made it."

"I wouldn't miss this for anything." Beverly stepped closer and pulled her in for a hug. "I'm so proud of you."

"Thank you." She basked in her mother's words and warm arms for a few minutes.

Beverly stepped back. "Excuse me now while I go get a glass of champagne and take another walk through the exhibit."

"Would you like me to take you around?" she offered.

"No," her mother said with a knowing smile. "I think Logan would like some of your time."

Mia waited until her mother reached the stairs and then she turned back to Logan, whose eyes never left her. She looked him up and down. "You look pretty good in a tuxedo."

"Nowhere near as amazing as you look in that dress." He reached for her hand and pulled her close, leading her behind a pillar. "I know you have a million things to worry about tonight, but give me three minutes."

"Only three?"

"I'd love more, but I'm a realist." He lowered his mouth to hers and kissed her deeply, keeping his hands on her hips. When he pulled away again, his eyes were dark and his smile dangerous. "You have no idea how badly I want to mess you up right now. Run my hands through your hair. Kiss my way down your body."

"As lovely as that sounds, I'll have to take a rain check. If you come to my place tonight, you can do whatever you'd like."

"Sure you won't be too tired after all this partying?" he whispered before tugging her earlobe with his teeth.

She shivered. "I'll be fine." Pressing a hand to his chest to move him back before things could go further, she inhaled deeply. His scent surrounded and calmed her. "You're quite the distraction, Mr. Ford."

"You looked like you could use one."

They turned together, holding hands and headed toward the stairs.

"Speaking of distractions," he said. "I just got word that two more paintings belonging to your father's friends were found to be forgeries."

"Really?" At the bottom of the steps, she picked up

two glasses of champagne from a waiter, handed one to Logan, and took a sip from hers.

"I don't suppose you would know anything about that?"

"Probably not," she answered.

"You agreed to stop."

"I promised I would no longer steal as long as my father was brought to justice." Letting go of that driving force had been freeing. She was no longer weighed down by constant plans for revenge. Instead, she spent her evenings with a man she loved. She didn't want to go back to the plotting and planning.

He took a sharp inhale. "He's in custody. It's no one's fault that the wheels of justice move slowly. He will go to trial."

She patted his arm. "Relax. I had nothing to do with the forgeries you're talking about." Then she had a thought. "Unless...whose art?" If it was Darren Turner's statue, technically she would know something about it. He hadn't tried to sell yet. At least not that Mia was aware of.

"Does it matter?"

"There might be a few things that were handled before you began your investigation, and if one of those came to light, I'd be lying if I said I knew nothing about it. I promised not to lie to you."

He laughed, leaned forward, and kissed the top of her head. "I need to learn to stop asking you such questions."

"That would probably be for the best."

In the last two months, their relationship had solidified. Logan didn't pretend she hadn't been a criminal, but he mostly trusted that she'd quit. And she felt freer for it. For the first time in years, she was happy. She was actually looking forward to the future. Her life was full of good things. She and Logan were trying to take things slow, rebuild the parts of their relationship that had been shaky. The fact that he was willing to give her the benefit of the doubt and trust her word was enough to make her really okay with walking away from being a criminal mastermind.

She still occasionally saw Nikki, Audrey, and London, as friends. They got together for dinner and a movie like normal women. They talked about relationships and non-theft work—which meant that Nikki was typically quiet, although she had started doing some security work for Wade. And she didn't totally hate it.

Mia looked up at Logan and her heart swelled.

"What?" he asked.

"I'm just really happy right now."

"I'm glad. I'm happy, too." He pressed another kiss to her temple. "There's your cousin." Logan pointed toward the middle of the room. "I bet he can show me the way to a good whiskey."

"I'm sure he can." Mia took his glass of champagne. "I'll see you late tonight?"

"Absolutely."

LOGAN QUICKLY CROSSED THE room and approached Jared. "Let's get a drink."

"Good to see you, too, Logan."

They walked together to the bar that was set up in the corner. Jared ordered two glasses of whiskey and left a generous tip for the bartender. After handing one to Logan, he asked, "Enjoying the exhibit?"

"It's interesting."

"I haven't had much of a chance to see it. Let's walk."

Logan followed Jared toward the beginning of the exhibit. He'd already been through twice, once on his own and once with Mia's mother. "I've heard a few more forgeries hit the market."

"Hmm."

The noncommittal sound irked Logan. "Look," Logan said, putting a hand on Jared's arm.

Jared simply stared at Logan's hand until he removed it. "Mia told me you were no longer investigating the forgeries."

"It doesn't mean I don't hear things."

Jared nodded. "What have you heard?"

Logan released a deep breath. He would probably never be friends with Jared, but Mia cared about him, so by default, Logan felt the need to help. "Can we drop the pretense?"

Jared moved toward the wall, tucked a hand in his pocket, and sipped his whiskey. "There's no pretense here, just self-preservation."

"Then let me start. Although Mia's always said she worked alone, I know that's not true. And since you're the only person who matters to her, and given your less-than-aboveboard line of work, it doesn't take a genius to figure out you're heading up her mission of revenge."

Jared made no response. Not even a twitch of his eye.

"And I'd lay money on your girlfriend being behind getting someone through security systems."

That one hit the mark. It was a small shift, just a tightening of his hand on his glass, but Logan saw it.

"I get that you and Mia have had a tough time. Your fathers are jerks. I also know she doesn't have too many people in her corner." He shifted to mimic Jared's stance. "I'm one of those people, so I'll protect her and those she cares about."

"What are you getting at?"

"First, hypothetically, if you were involved in anything less than legal, no one should ever know. Mia would be devastated if anything were to happen to you. Second, make sure nothing ever blows back on her."

"First, I take care of my own. Second, that goes without saying. Like you, I protect those who matter."

Logan understood that. Family mattered above all else. He had no doubt Jared and Mia's old team were continuing to replace art with forgeries. Given who they were stealing from and where the profits were going, he had a hard time mustering any outrage. Sometimes the scales of justice needed a little help finding balance.

"Is there anything else?" Jared asked.

"Yeah." He drained his glass as he considered how to phrase the information in a way that wouldn't compromise his ethics any more than they already had been. "With the trial coming up soon, there's a lot of scrutiny on properties insured by Atlas."

"Interesting." Jared, too, finished his drink and stepped away from the wall. "Why?"

Logan knew the man wasn't asking why he issued the warning, but why he was helping. "Because I love your cousin and I plan to spend the rest of my life with her. That means I have to accept all of her."

"Good answer."

Then Jared walked away and Logan returned to Mia's side.

"What were you talking to Jared about?" she asked.

"He was doing the big brother thing. You know, the 'you better not hurt her or else' bit. I've done it a number of times. It's kind of expected." It was close enough to the truth, and the only way to truly protect her was to make sure she kept her distance from the crimes her cousin might commit.

"I'm six months older than he is."

"It's not about age. It's his duty."

She rolled her eyes. "Men." But then she smiled crookedly in the way he loved so much. "What did you say to his threat?"

"I told him he had nothing to worry about because I love you and I plan to spend my life with you." He spoke the words casually, as if they were a given. For him, they were. The last two months had cemented his feelings for Mia and he loved everything about her. Getting past her criminal activity hadn't been as difficult as he'd thought. After watching some of the tactics her father had tried using, he understood her need to stop him. Her resilience only made him want her more.

Of course, getting her to understand that he was all in and not going anywhere was sometimes an uphill battle, as if she expected him to disappear, so he wanted her to be clear.

Her mouth dropped open and she took a sharp intake of air, but she recovered quickly. She narrowed her eyes. "Are you seriously proposing to me now? Tonight? When I'm swamped with work?"

He smiled, happy that she didn't blow past his message as if it wasn't real. "Relax, babe. This is not an official proposal. I'm just stating my intentions. I've already wooed you. You'll know when I'm proposing."

"You're awfully full of yourself." Her snarky comment was followed by her crooked smile, the one meant for just him. And she stared straight into his eyes, no lies, no games, just open and honest.

"And yet you love me."

"Yes, yes, I do," she said as she took his hand and held tight.

With those words, Logan felt the puzzle pieces of his life snap together perfectly.

* * * * *

ABOUT THE AUTHOR

SLOANE STEELE IS the pen name for Shannyn Schroeder. Shannyn is a part-time English teacher, part-time curriculum editor, and full-time mom, even though her kids are pretty self-sufficient teens. In her downtime, she bakes cookies, reads romance, and watches far too much TV.

Sloane is planning a Counterfeit Capers novella for late 2021: *The Thief Who Stole Christmas* (London's story). To find out about other books by Sloane Steele or to be alerted to new releases, sign up for her newsletter at www.subscribepage.com/sloanesteele.

If you want to connect with Sloane (and Shannyn):

www.SloaneSteele.com

www.Instagram.com/sloanesteeleauthor/

www.Twitter.com/SSchroeder_

www.Facebook.com/shannyn.schroeder/

Get 4 FREE REWARDS!

We'll send you 2 FREE Books plus 2 FREE Mystery Gifts.

FREE Value Over **$20**

Both the **Love Inspired®** and **Love Inspired® Suspense** series feature compelling novels filled with inspirational romance, faith, forgiveness, and hope.

Visit
ReaderService.com
Today!

As a valued member of the Harlequin Reader Service, you'll find these benefits and more at ReaderService.com:

- Try 2 free books from any series
- Access risk-free special offers
- View your account history & manage payments
- Browse the latest Bonus Bucks catalog